Dark Corners
A Roman Cantrell-Nikki Holden Mystery
Book Two

Elaine Raco Chase

eBook Edition
Copyright and License Notes

Trademark, Brand and Product Acknowledgements are used with the utmost respect and admiration.

This book has been line-edited for grammar and typos by a wonderful group of readers and editors – but it was written by a human and not a computer and nothing is perfect.

Authors Note: This eBook does **NOT** match with the original paperback Bantam Book from 1988. It has been completely updated, with new characters, expanded and has many new scenes.

Dedication

Special thanks to **Linda Seib Guiton** for her invaluable editing help.

Diane McCart – my bestie for too many years and Florida expert!

For my late Dad, **Ernie Raco**, who fed my interest in writing mysteries & thrillers.

Always to my husband, Gary & children Marlayna and Marc

Praise for International Bestselling Author Elaine Raco Chase's Books

Dangerous Places (Roman Cantrell-Nikki Holden Mystery I)

"Roman and Nikki – a star-crossed duo we are rooting for" – BookList

"On the most wanted list! A fast-paced and entertaining story" – Orlando Sentinel

"An intricate plot leavened with humor and romance" – Rave Reviews

"A mystery guaranteed to whet the appetite for more." – Hearst Cablevision

"A well-done murder mystery. Winner: Silver Certificate for quality of writing, excellence and entertainment." – Affaire de Coeur

Romantic Times Top Hot Pick – March, 2016: *Romantic suspense aficionados are in for a real treat as pioneering romance writer Chase returns with an exceptional tale.*

"Elaine Raco Chase has mastered dialogue, with timing, humor, and the play of give and take so necessary to a conversation. In Dangerous Places, all of these pieces fall into place with a wonderful mystery, a cast of secondary characters that range from distasteful to delightful and two star players that show influence (noted by the author) of Dashiell Hammett." I am Indeed

"The suspense builds as events unfold, each hard-hitting twist and turn driving the plot to a surprising and heart-stopping conclusion. The dialog is intelligent, witty, and at times laugh-out-loud funny—it will remind you of the glory days of Hepburn and Tracey. Nikki and Roman became my instant favorite dueling characters,

and I can't wait to see where their budding partnership takes them next." Dangerous Places is a clear winner, a Five Star read all the way! – Beach Bum Books

Writer's Digest Books - Amateur Detectives:

a writer's guide to how private citizens solve criminal cases
(1996)
Elaine Raco Chase and Anne Wingate
Nominated for Agatha Christie Award for best non-fiction book
Part of the FBI Forensic Library in Quantico

Dark Corners (Roman Cantrell-Nikki Holden Mystery II)

**All over south Florida people are seeing things – things that can't be real –
or can they?**

Nikki's boss gives her the most bizarre assignment of her career. More than 200 solid citizens have reported sightings and contacts with UFO's! Soon she's on the trail with help from the University of Tennessee Space Institute & the Air Force!

Roman comes to the aide of an old Army buddy and finds himself with the most baffling case of his career. Did the US Army actually hijack an armored car? Or is his buddy feeding Roman a pack of lies?

When their cases converge – Roman and Nikki become trapped in a plot that's stranger than science fiction but as real as death in Dark Corners

Romantic Times' Top Hot Pick for Romantic Suspense – October 2016!

DARK CORNERS
Elaine Raco Chase

Chapter 1

Nikki Holden?" A neatly chignoned head leaned farther out the window of the Mini Cooper to speak more clearly into the security intercom at the gate. "Teresa Hutton, here."

Nikki puzzled over the name and the strong British accent. Neither was familiar. "Yes?"

"About an assignment, Ms. Holden." When there was no immediate response, Teresa decided to play her trump card. "Mathew Cortlund suggested I pop 'round."

The black wrought-iron gate relinquished its security stance. With a satisfied smile, Teresa shifted gears and piloted the red and black hardtop along a drive that shadowed Fort Lauderdale's Intercoastal Waterway.

A Spanish hacienda appeared, centered in her windshield. The white house sprawled pristine and tranquil. A distinct contrast to the tall well-built redhead bounding barefoot down the flower-bordered front steps wearing worn denim cut-offs and a white camisole.

Teresa had known of Nikki Holden's reputation as a journalist and had taken the time to scrutinize and assess her impressive body of work. She had read Nikki's articles and reacted to them.

Reacted? Yes. You had to. Nikki constructed words into sentences that created images. Strong, harsh, incisive images that aroused the mind and vexed the conscience. It was an enviable talent, a talent used to discover the unusual. A talent that dug, sifted and, when the occasion called for it, bullied out the facts.

Teresa was counting on all of that, plus Mathew Cortlund's assurance that Nikki was kindled for a challenge. He'd been right. Her excitement was visible.

"Sorry, I really should have telephoned first." Teresa extended her hand, liking the firm response. "Rather rude of me just to pop in." She studied the redhead. "You're looking quite fit. Had a bloody bad time of it. I read the local papers and Matt filled me in."

"A suntan helps. Cuts and fractures heal. Bruises fade." Nikki massaged her cheek. "The jaw was more fractured than broken so bands quickly replaced wires. I graduated from liquids to baby and soft food faster than expected. And I've been able to talk coherently for nearly three days. No more texting, writing with dry markers on white boards or burning through packs of Post-it notes." She winked. "More importantly all the get-well flowers are gone. The house was like a funeral parlor. I swear on a few wreathes deepest sympathy was under the get-well banners."

Nikki had been busy with her own evaluation. Teresa Hutton was in her early forties. Her designer two-piece summer business suit complimented her petite compact figure and matched her perfect English rose complexion. While Teresa Hutton appeared soft and comfortable, her brown eyes were sharp. A disarming hominess instead of the expected English reserve. Nikki's smile came easily. "So...you said Mathew Cortlund sent you?"

"He didn't call you then?"

"No."

Teresa relaxed.

Nikki's titian brow arched. "Matt loves surprises."

"But you don't." Teresa's ears and eyes registered the woman's impatience. "Neither do I, Ms. Holden."

"Make it Nikki."

She nodded her thanks. "Mathew said as managing editor, it was up to me. And I've had the devil's own time making up my bloody mind about inviting you in on this story. I do have a regular staff." Teresa's lips puckered briefly. "However, your byline symbolizes unequivocal credibility."

"Sounds big..."

"Could be." Teresa Hutton squared her shoulders. "Yes, this could be big. Very big indeed. I've checked you out and read many of your articles. Quite thoroughly, to be frank. And I feel you're the perfect journalist to handle—"

A car horn interrupted as a silver Jaguar pulled up, blocking the Mini Cooper.

"Roman Cantrell." Teresa stated, staring intently at the tall, broad-shouldered man whose quick, purposeful stride ate up the distance between them. She'd also read about him in the papers. Here was a man who exuded power both physically and professionally. His black hair and dark stubble accentuated features that looked as harsh in person as they had in print.

"You're early tonight," Nikki smiled at him.

He folded his sunglasses into the pocket of his taupe blazer. "I brought you a surprise."

"You brought. Matt sent. Your reputation preceded you, Cantrell. Teresa Hutton recognized you the instant the car door opened."

He accepted the woman's proffered hand. "What gift is Matt sending this time?"

"An assignment," Nikki announced.

Teresa noted the immediate change in Roman's expression and posture. The man had gone on alert. The rawness in his dark eyes echoed in his deep voice. "Where?"

"Why...I don't know," Nikki frowned. "We were just getting to the details. Teresa?"

"Here, actually, in the Fort Lauderdale-Miami area." She was still conscious of Roman's guarded, exclusive attitude. "It's a piece on aliens."

"Well, Florida's the perfect place," Nikki nodded. "What are you after? A story on the effects of the new residency path for some illegal aliens?"

"Well...no..."

"The legal aid clinics that highlight the dilemmas faced by thousands of immigrant families?"

"Not exactly."

"Growing pockets of subcultures that are putting a different set of problems on communities like housing, schools, the wide-spread employment of illegals on construction jobs?" Nikki frowned when Teresa again shook her head. "The approximately ten thousand child migrants who are unaccounted for...no? Well...how about the coyotes who smuggle in...no? Ummm...human trafficking?"

Teresa shook her head. "All are jolly good ideas, Nikki, but that's not our type of alien."

Chapter 2

Roman's brow furrowed. "Not *your* type of alien? What the hell does that mean?"

"Well...our alien is..." Four eyes followed the direction of Teresa's forefinger.

It pointed up.

Nikki's laugh was airy but forced. "Are we talking extraterrestrials? From a galaxy far, far away? A close encounter of a third kind?"

"Exactly."

Gripping her arm, Roman pulled Nikki back and up a step. "Didn't I tell you to check carefully before letting anyone pass the security gate?"

"She looks perfectly harmless."

"I once collared a child sex offender who had the most angelic demeanor."

"But *Matt* sent her." Nikki forced another smile, her voice a kindergarten singsong. "Teresa, you did say Mathew sent you? Mathew Cortlund? Cortlund Publishing? In Chicago?"

"Right-o." Teresa was wholly patient and amused by their stage whispers. "Mathew Cortlund, the man with the gravel voice, bald head, bulldog build and an endless supply of the most fragrant Cuban cigars."

Roman exhaled noisily, his fingers massaged his stubbled jaw line. "That's Matt. You didn't tell me he was a member of a cult—"

"Will you please shut up," Nikki muttered. "I'm sure there's a perfectly logical explanation. There is, isn't there, Miss Hutton?"

Teresa sighed. "Yes, quite logical." She reached into her colorful paisley Vera Bradley tote. "I should have fully introduced myself right from the start. This will undoubtedly answer all your questions." She handed them a newspaper.

Roman snapped it open, stared at the masthead and snorted. *"Scuttlebutt.* What's Matt Cortlund got to do with you and this...this supermarket trash?"

"Tabs. Tabloids," Teresa corrected him. "Much prefer that to trash. Mathew Cortlund bought it. Last Monday. And I'm the managing editor here in the states."

Nikki winced at the color photos and balloon headlines. *"MOVIE SET SHUT DOWN AFTER STARS ARE EATEN?"* she read aloud.

"They were making a live-action *Bambi* when poachers..." Teresa explained.

"ELVIS SINGS ME TO SLEEP AND THE SONGS ARE HITS!"

"This woman has had Elvis come to her in visions and written down..."

"YOUR PET COULD BE A SPACE ALIENS

"According to some reputable scientists, they are finding odd DNA..."

"THE AMAZING SEXUAL POWER OF KETCHUP"

"Say, let me take a look at that one," Roman made a grab for the paper.

Eluding his hands, Nikki crunched the tabloid into a ball and tossed it at Teresa. "'Reputable scientists, I think you said? Are those the same scientists who deny climate change and still insist the world is flat? What reputable human would contribute to such bizarre articles, zany UFO stories, psychics, celebrity gossip and – excuse me for almost forgetting – blood and gore!"

Nikki's upraised palm forestalled any interruption. "Oh, but I'm sure you can come up with just about any incredible story, find somebody who's had that experience or believes they've had that experience and for twenty bucks get them a Ph.D. through the internet.

"I will admit I've read your exotic headlines at the checkout counter. They scream: werewolf babies, miracle diets, miracle cures, murder, reincarnation and the inevitable ghosts of famous people. Death is your main event and the safest. After all, the dead can't challenge or sue.

"When living people become fodder for one of your blazing headlines and try to sue...I remember one lawyer telling me you use the 'Scorpion Defense.' Tabloids spend a lot of money to employ powerful law firms that fight back and know how to deter lawsuits with harsh, well-practiced scare tactics. People know they are going to get stung, know they will spend a fortune and know it will take years to litigate. So they just don't bother to sue.

"You publish sixty full-color pages of blatantly sensational tawdry, nonessential, pun-tuated hallucinations. You work on the fuzzy periphery of news. You exploit and capitalize on whatever weirdness is bubbling at the bottom of someone's brain. You get hit by a lawsuit and claim you were victim of..." Nikki made air quotes..."unfortunate inaccuracies. You use weasel words like 'informed sources' 'alleged' 'un-named sources' or 'according to some reports.'

"My favorite has always been the alien couple who tried to sue the Earth for custody of their child Michael Jackson." Nikki shook her head and shivered. "That, lady, is your entire paper.

"Yes, Teresa Hutton, I can see why you'd want a credible byline for your weekly scandal sheet. Your type of journalist engages in nothing more than a frenzied competition of hysterical headlines. Yes, I'm well aware that assorted tabloids have brought down politicians, criminals, drug lords, actors and pseudo-philanthropists. Those accolades are damn few and far between."

Nikki looked skyward and shook her head, "Just for the hell-of-it, where are these aliens from? Venus? Mars? Have you found someone who's discovered yet another planet? Another galaxy? Or perhaps they've just returned from where no man has gone before and are bringing the aliens with them? I realize there's been a plethora of when aliens attack and lost-in-space movies and TV shows...but it is all fiction."

Teresa found herself blinking rapidly, not only from the stinging verbal assault but from the intimidating weapons that were Nikki Holden's ice blue eyes.

She inhaled a deep calming breath while her tongue moistened dry lips. "You certainly can throw some sharp sarcastic knives." Squaring her shoulders and stiffening her spine, Teresa stared Nikki straight on. "But if you don't mind, now I'll have my say.

"Our weekly scandal sheet will be celebrating one hundred years in print this coming December. We play hardball just like every newspaper and we seldom receive any praise from our journalistic colleagues. However as to that, we really don't mind. You see, our weekly readership is in excess of six million; our gross revenues last year were over half a billion dollars.

"We give people what they want, especially that full color format. Believe it or not, Nikki, surveys declare the credibility of tabloids equal to publications like your *Reader's Digest*. We're a lot like poetry. We suggest more than what we say. Some have called it a radiance of meaning."

Teresa's lips twitched at hearing Roman's strangled cough. "I've heard it all. During the last ten years, I've suffered through more slings and arrows than bonny Will Shakespeare ever imagined. However, in your case, Roman Cantrell, a thank you might be in order. Why? Well, *you've* tracked and found missing children and each week *we* run twenty-five photos and stories to aid in that hunt."

She refocused on Nikki. "We have some very talented reporters at *Scuttlebutt*. Each of them is just like any good reporter or investigator. He or she talks to the right people and always gets the right answers. I know. I worked my way up from reporter to senior editor and now, Matt Cortlund has made me managing editor."

Teresa tucked a stray brunette curl behind her ear. "I can proudly say that many university law professors, including those at Syracuse, Berkeley, Columbia and Hofstra to name-drop a few, are using our celebrity stories instead of casebook examples of people the students have never heard of.

"The world is changing and today's students know so much more with the internet and web blogs. Law professors have personally told me that they are finding teaching value in the tabloid culture. There's more interaction and less glazed eyes when they use *Scuttlebutt's* stories on what celebrity died intestate, or child custody issues of movie stars, or even real estate sales.

"Now, as for this story on aliens..." Teresa paused, took a deep breath and continued. "We did not go looking for them. This is not a hoax or a setup. They have found us. Florida, I mean. Two hundred sightings in the last three weeks.

"I'm not talking crackpots, Nikki. There have been reports from doctors, lawyers, police officers, housewives, construction workers. A few recorded the UFO's on cellphone videos to show off. Mass hallucination? Mass hysteria? Mass invasion? That's the assignment. That's what a reporter, a *credible* reporter, an open-minded reporter will need to investigate.

Teresa cleared her throat and continued. "Stephen Hawking, with a few others, is getting ready to launch a nanocraft to explore Alpha Centauri, our nearest star system.

"NASA using the Kepler Space Telescope just discovered more than twelve hundred new planets, more than double the number of alien worlds. Nine of the planets are potentially habitable as they contain water. One astrophysicist stated that there are over ten billion habitable planets in our galaxy. Just maybe one has decided to pop in for a visit"

Nikki's concentrated study of Teresa Hutton's set mouth didn't waver, even though her next question was directed at Roman. "So, Cantrell what's *your* surprise?"

"Pizza. Three large ones. Loaded with everything including anchovies. Rudy created a New York, Chicago and Sicilian mix with a soft crunchy stuffed crust." He tugged the copper braid that curved against her shoulder; his deep voice vibrated against her ear. "This is it, kid. No more jello, no more soup, no more pudding. I thought a celebration was in order."

Roman watched her smile but noted her eyes were still focused on Teresa. Who, like himself, waited for her decision.

Nikki shoved her hands in the pockets of her shorts. "Tell me, Teresa, do you suppose pizza is part of an alien's diet?" Her smile broadened at the responding shrug. "How about yours? We could call this our first editor/reporter business dinner."

"You...you're accepting this assignment?"

"Surprised?"

"Frankly, yes."

"Shouldn't be. Your speech hired me." Nikki noted her confused expression and explained. "We're a lot alike. I stand by each and every word I write. You championed your publication. We both have dodged our share of slings and arrows. And, to misquote Voltaire, while I may disapprove of your publication, I will defend to the death your right to publish it."

A grin sliced across Nikki's face. "Besides, you've piqued my interest. Two hundred sightings? You're right, they can't all be hallucinations. Unless, of course, it turns out to be from starvation."

Roman laughed. "Subtle, isn't she?" He shucked off his raw silk jacket, pulled apart his tie and tossed them both at Nikki. "Take these and lead the parade into the air conditioned indoors while I retrieve dinner."

Chapter 3

Teresa Hutton didn't try to mute her audible gasp at the expansive view from the wide foyer. She could see straight through to the back of the house where a wall of windows blurred the lines between indoors and outdoors. The late afternoon sun and low clouds cast a silver glow on an infinity pool that seemed to merge with the ocean that melded into the sky. Teresa reluctantly blinked free of the dynamic vision to further examine the house and furnishings.

Clean. Classic. Modern. Open concept. Skylights allowed natural light to stream into the open room, highlighting the light gray walls and matching slate tiles as it slanted across the massive white leather sectional that held court in the living room. Black lacquered Oriental accent pieces amid glass accessories made definitive statements against the modern décor.

"I see someone collects seashells and plants," her fingers filtered through a robust Boston fern.

"Nikki actually made those matching shell-filled lamps," Roman bypassed the dining room and led the way to the kitchen. "She turned into a real collector when I took her on a tour of Captiva and Sanibel Islands a few weeks ago."

"The housekeeper's the florist," Nikki continued. "Every week there's another occupant to this green menagerie. Thankfully she knows what each plant requires. I have a brown thumb." She gestured to one of the bar stools that flanked the massive L-shaped island. "Make yourself comfortable. What can I get you to drink? There's lemonade, tea, coffee, beer, wine?"

"Tea."

"Hot or iced?"

"Iced would be quite wonderful." Teresa settled comfortably on the black padded leather seat and quickly became absorbed by more than the crisp black and white kitchen decor. The couple went about their respective tasks with orchestrated ease. Yet, she knew from Matt Cortlund that the Cantrell-Holden liaison was only ten weeks old. With all that time being recuperative for Nikki and nursing duties for Roman.

Teresa accepted a tall ice and tea filled glass with a silent nod and a grateful expression while she listened to Roman's teasing about how Nikki's pizza should be served. Roman Cantrell, she decided, was a man noticeably in love.

Granted, she had witnessed no exchange of verbal intimacies, no passionate kisses, no suggestive clinches, nothing overt. But little things caught Teresa's trained reporter's eye.

A look that was more sensual than a touch. A tone that held more meaning than words. An attitude that was wholly exclusive. And a posture that exhibited protective tenderness.

Roman Cantrell. Army ranger. Sniper. Mercenary. Tracker. Private investigator. Recently a one-man jury. An avenger.

Yet this man whose skilled, calloused hands had dealt many a deathblow was carefully centering white china plates on black linen placemats. His hawkish features were effortlessly transformed by a grin when replying to one of Nikki's acerbic witticisms. Roman Cantrell was a man happily held captive.

Teresa let a mouthful of iced tea consume her smile while her thoughts shifted to Nikki Holden. The woman was, on first impression, more masculine than feminine. Despite the curvaceous body and fiery coloring, Nikki projected a tough, resolute and, at times, emotionless image. It showed in her walk, her firm handshake, her attitude and speech. No finishing school manners here.

Streetwise. Street-raised. Police record. Paroled in Mathew Cortlund's custody. A real ball-buster professionally. Teresa realized most of her information on Nikki was grist from the vast journalistic rumor mill.

Facts, however, couldn't be denied. Nikki Holden created odds. She was known for taking a tip and turning it into headlines. Her printed words birthed more enemies than friends. But the woman had a stable of powerful friends - on both sides of the law.

She was a journalistic nomad. No two stories were ever filed from the same city. Teresa wondered if Roman Cantrell had a prayer of changing or confining Nikki Holden for more than a few months.

"I still think you should cut the pizza into tiny bites and use a fork to-"

"Seriously? Cantrell that's sacrilege. Especially coming from an Italian. Even in Naples, the birthplace of pizza, when the pie comes out, you cut it in quarters and fold it...just like New York." Nikki settled onto the matching stool next to Teresa and eyed dinner with an obvious appetite.

"I wish she'd look at me like that," Roman quipped to Teresa.

"Cover yourself with mozzarella and anchovies and I will."

"The gospel according to *Scuttlebutt* says ketchup," Roman offered. "How 'bout it, Teresa, does it work?"

She returned his grin. "As I recall, one of the blokes in our mailroom recommends ketchup quite highly."

"There ya' go." His elbow nudged Nikki's.

"You two can discuss the sexual merits of tomato products all night. I am going to eat." With that declaration, Nikki took a deep breath, cleared her throat and for the first time in eight weeks sank her teeth into solid, crunchy food. "Mmm..."

"That's a groan of ecstasy if I've ever heard one." Roman pronounced happily. "Everything working all right?"

"Mmm...fine...heaven actually..." She laughed, pulling on a string of cheese. "You'll have to excuse me, Teresa, while I wallow in delight. Cantrell, I'll leave you to play the perfect host."

Four slices later, Nikki came up for air and took over the conversation. "Okay, Teresa, talk to me about your type of alien."

Reaching for the ice tea pitcher, she refilled both their glasses and moved a spare napkin to blot the moisture on the black quartz countertop.

"'You're right, Roman, she's not very subtle." Teresa wiped her hands on a napkin before reaching into her tote for a leather-bound notebook. "Our aliens have been sighted from various points around the globe for hundreds of years. Mysterious objects in the sky. Granted, quite a few have logical explanations."

"More than a few have logical explanations, Teresa," Nikki corrected. "I just spent eight weeks binge-watching enough TV programs including the Weather Channel to know you're talking meteors, planets, rockets, stars, artificial satellites, Saint Elmo's fire, space garbage and assorted weather balloons. Right?"

Teresa nodded. "Excellent, Nikki. There have also been a few attributed to some very interesting experimental aircraft as well as their exhaust or contrails. Atmospheric conditions can produce some bloody incredible optical illusions."

"So can Mother Nature both with artistry and horror." Nikki pulled another slice of pizza out of the box. "I saw *The Weather Channel's* program on shelf clouds and damn they looked exactly like the UFO's Hollywood created for more than a couple blockbusters. Then those massive supercells that plowed the Midwest earlier this year...well watching a half-mile wide tornado spawning underneath a wall cloud looked more like Hollywood special effects than Mother Nature...hell even I did a double-take."

"Yes, but Florida has had none of that type of weather phenomena, especially in the past three weeks." Teresa sifted through the pages of her notebook. "People reported a host of flying objects and more than a dozen also claimed to have seen glowing objects on the ground and in the air."

Nikki groaned while relocating the anchovies Roman had pushed onto his plate to her pizza. "Not the old glowing objects again. There are private launches daily off Cape Canaveral. I read in the paper that over ten thousand people got together to launch Chinese lanterns for some charity event in Jacksonville three weeks ago. That's right in your timetable.

"Combine that with all the leftover fireworks that are buy-one-get-ten-free, sprinkle in the LED-lit kites and drones, the idiots who are assaulting pilots using lasers – *voilà* there are your glowing night objects. Hell on-the-ground glowing objects are probably caused by pollution." Nikki continued.

"Blue microbes have been making some parts of the Atlantic glow. Right up the road in Cocoa Beach, their bioluminescent kayaking tours started in July. The Banana River glows in the dark with assorted plankton and algae."

Nikki's mouth twisted. "I remember watching one documentary where people actually thought they'd found an alien spaceship in the Banana River and it was nothing more than a manatee covered with luminescent algae. Then a group of night fishermen claimed an alien shot up from the river. That turned out to be a jumping fish that glowed green. The ecosystem is way off kilter but it doesn't mean there are aliens.

"Florida has enough swampy areas in the fifty-mile radius of those sightings to make a convention of botanists happy." At Teresa's puzzled expression, Nikki explained. "There are hundreds of plants that are bioluminescent. Roman's gardener/handyman just ordered four flats of *Arabidopsis* plants for the front walk and around the lanai. He'll add those to the solar lights and no outdoor electricity will be needed.

"Foxfire is a bioluminescence emitted by some fungi that can glow green or red. Florida has a lot of radon gas pockets and at different temperatures it becomes chemiluminescent and glows red. There is lot of poorly understood natural phenomena.

"So many things in nature glow besides plants and fish. It could have been a swarm of fireflies, glow worms, lightening bugs, butterflies, moths or kids playing around with assorted glow-in-the-dark balloons, bracelets and sticks.

"Hell with all the X-rays, MRI's and CT scans I've had over the past ten weeks, I bet if you grab my ass and shake me up and down I probably glow. Don't even think about that Cantrell." She warned noting his rather wicked grin. "I have a feeling most of those glowing optical illusions came from an eighty-proof bottle."

"But not foo-fighters," Roman thumbed the lime wedge into the bottle of Corona.

"Foo-fighters?"

"From...ummm...1939 into the fifties, many military and civilian pilots reported seeing strange moving lights. The Air Force thought it important enough to set up Project Sign. Granted, the scientists they hired came to the conclusion that only eighty percent of the sightings had astronomical explanations. Why are you staring, Miss Holden?"

"I hadn't realized I was living with an ufologist."

"Hey...watch your language," he winked, "I read a lot of science fiction articles and—

"Byword is fiction, Cantrell."

"What happened to Ms. Open-mind? Let me refresh your memory about the well-publicized Project Blue Book that hit the internet a few years ago along with Project Sign and Project Grudge. Over twelve thousand sightings and the only conclusion drawn was the UFOs were no threat to our national security."

Teresa snickered. "I believe that was done to stop public panic because seven hundred of those sightings still remain unidentified. France also added to the internet three decades of information on its UFO sightings. Of which only nine percent were ever explained." Her finger tapped against the counter. "What I found most fascinating from their files was the 1994 Air France flight over Paris that saw a large brown-red disk hovering and changing shape on the horizon. That has never been explained."

"Sadly even the Queen's own RAF Air Command shut down their UFO task force after fifty years for bloody budget reasons," Teresa groused. "Just recently glowing orbs were actually tracked by the RAF when they flew out of a lake in Northern Wales. Then in the same week, multiple glowing orbs were sighted over Alaska, Arizona, Austria, Holland and Australia. As well as one hundred twenty seven miles from here in LaBelle."

Nikki frowned. "Teresa, are you telling me those glowing orb sightings were all within the same week of each other and within the timeframe of the last three weeks here?"

"I am and I don't believe in coincidences." Teresa slid another brimming file folder toward her, her finger pushing through color photographs. "Not only did all those areas have the glowing orbs in common but now they all have this exact same crop circle designs appearing within five miles of the sightings."

Nikki's blue eyes narrowed at the intricate designs the digital photos exposed. "Well you're right, they are all the same. Sort of a mix of Celtic symbols...the triskele and the shield knot. Cantrell, what do you think?"

"I've seen a lot of tats displaying the shield knot; it's a symbol of protection." He tapped the square shaped emblem within a circle. "What's the triskele symbol stand for?"

Teresa jumped in. "The three interlocking spirals stand for the 'three realms' land, sea and sky."

"Or for the goddess Brigid, an Irish saint who is celebrated for healing and unity. However her feast day is at the start of February and we're at the end of July so..." Nikki added then grinned at them both. "I did an article years ago about Druid mythology."

"So the duplication of the crop symbols being found exactly in the same area as the glowing orbs is not sparking your interest?" Teresa countered.

"I didn't say that," Nikki amended. "Personally, I find crop symbols oddly interesting. Most have logical explanations and are not alien calling cards. Scientists have said vortices like dust devils get caught up and the charged spinning air can appear to glow and create circles. Then there's electromagnetic radiation but most probably they're hoaxes. I mean they have been humanly duplicated using stalk stompers and garden rollers and a pattern."

"Duplicate hoaxes across four continents?" Teresa looked at her over the rim of her ice tea glass.

Nikki threw up her hands in defeat and reached for the ice tea pitcher. "You have me there."

"Since the internet, there's been an explosion of photos and information from around the world linking the visits of space travelers with ancient civilizations." Teresa added another thick file to the countertop. "Recently a team of archeologists discovered a near duplicate to Stonehenge with ancient carvings in your Lake Michigan including the Mastodon rock which appears to be over ten thousand years old. Here's a picture of the stunning Mogao Caves in Dunhuang, China that are over fifteen thousand years old."

Her pink tipped fingernail flipped through more photos. "Look at this Neanderthal cave, the Bruniquel in France, that's over one hundred eighty thousand years old and shows how they used stalagmites as building material. I love these shots by Greek archaeologists of the underwater ruins that were created over three million years before mankind existed. Look at the paved floors and colonnades. Just more evidence that visitors from outer space...Now, Nikki, why the raised eyebrow?"

"Evidence? Give me a break, Teresa! Giving credit for cave drawings, rock carvings, the pyramids, Aztec and Mayan temples and just about anything over ten feet high to..." Nikki made air quotes..."'gods from outer space' is ridiculous. Hell, ants, one of the lowest and tiniest forms of life, create huge underground nests that can run to forty feet. Why deny that humans could dream up and build such structures? Why deny early man was imaginative and artistic?

"I just saw the aerial photo of the Tianfu International Airport in China and it looks just like the face of the alien character in that movie *Independence Day*. So to deny the fact that man can design and construct what appears to be alien in origin is ridiculous."

"A Frank Lloyd Wright or Andy Warhol with Aztec plumes?" Roman grinned, then cautioned. "Better watch out, Nik. I think that constitutes a belief in reincarnation." He glanced at Teresa.

"I'll leave that discussion for perhaps...another assignment?" Teresa arched a dark brow.

Nikki made a face at the two of them. "Christ, we could round-robin this for centuries."

"Or," Teresa flipped more pages in her notebook, "we could believe in the star-like configuration that left a green cloud in its wake that was sighted by two commercial airline pilots and their one hundred passengers. Then there was the British Airways jetliner that had to divert over the Soviet Union to avoid what all five crew members reported as an object with twinkling lights flying directly toward them before vanishing. And I'm sure you remember the FAA investigation when the Japan Air Lines cargo jet crew sighted three UFO's in the clear night sky over Alaska, one as big as two aircraft carriers. Those three showed up on the cockpit weather radar."

Nikki wrinkled her nose. "Didn't the FAA dismiss the radar notations as clutter and split images."

Teresa shrugged and reached for another slice of pizza. "Their denials don't surprise me. They always log UFO sightings as burning space debris, but these last two reports had no scientific explanation attached. We've also learned that the US Navy might be concealing a UFO they hauled out of the Puget Sound in Washington State." She pulled more folders out of her tote bag, adding them to the growing stack on the quartz countertop in front of Nikki.

"Here's a radar man who reported a blip giving a doppler effect on his system. That UFO was going a mere fifteen thousand miles an hour and four beeps later had disappeared. Next is a statement from a United Airlines pilot who says a UFO whizzed by him and he was at seventy-five thousand feet. Plus, there are a staggering ninety thousand UFO cases currently being investigated by the Center for UFO Studies in Illinois, which is staffed by some of the top scientists in the US and Canada."

Teresa took a deep breath. "If that's not enough, explain to me what's been happening in Ohio which is becoming an alien-sighting hot spot. In the past two months, there have been almost daily sightings of UFO's over a variety of cities in Ohio but mostly over Wright-Patterson Air Force Base. Wright-Patterson is believed to house evidence of UFO and extra-terrestrial sightings from 1947 to 1969. Even more than the fabled Area 51 in Nevada."

Nikki stared at Teresa for a long moment. "You're making this sound like...oh, I don't know a galactic Watergate."

"GalactiGate. What a wonderful headline buzzword!" She hastily scribbled a note. "And bloody accurate. By using the Freedom of Information Act plus the newest files the CIA just put on the web, we've been able to ascertain that for the last nearly eighty years American scientists have been trying to find out how UFO's work."

"How?" Roman echoed, "Not if?

"Right-o. I've a report from an aeronautical engineering professor who says that the US Air Force built and flew a saucer-shaped craft in the late forties."

"I've heard of it," Roman nodded. "It was nicknamed the 'Flying Flapjack' because of its shape. It had a little bubble where the cockpit was and if you were directly below it, it appeared circular. Some say that experiments are still being carried out."

"Real flying saucers." Nikki mused.

"They are quite able to fly." Teresa said. "Just like a Frisbee, the spinning motion..." she shuffled through her notes, "...gyroscopically stabilizes it."

"Spinning. Bullets and bombs are stabilized in the same way," Roman added.

"Truthfully, Nikki, I personally can't decide what to believe about aliens, UFOs and previous space visitations." Teresa rubbed her forehead. "I do know that other countries take what we view as a UFO hoax more seriously. For over ten years, France's equivalent of NASA has logged over sixteen hundred UFO sightings that include military observations. Thirty-eight percent are still unsolved. Even Russia has a similar UFO fact-finding program.

"I must say, though, I think it's bloody egotistical of us to think we're the only creatures inhabiting the universe. Just last month, it was discovered that King Tut's dagger along with its highly ornamental blade was made from an iron meteorite. It even mirrors the time hieroglyphics began or were original hieroglyphics just appropriated from the dagger?"

"Are you trying to say the Boy King was actually an alien?" Nikki shook her head at Teresa's smiling face.

"Will it help you to know I've got a ream of NASA photos that show a humanoid monument on Mars."

Nikki sighed. "A humanoid monument? It's probably a pile of rocks or the results of nature or—"

"No. Computer enhancement shows a definite geometric pattern that a noted astronomer says represents the sun rising on the summer solstice, exactly half a million years ago. I know what you're thinking, Nikki, but remember that the earth is four point six million years old and some savvy aliens could have already visited, witnessed our Ice Age, then left this...this 'cosmic greeting card.' We sent off a greeting capsule ourselves in 1972, containing a stick drawing of a man and a woman, an outline of our solar system and other scientific information that says we're here."

Teresa leaned forward, her face animated. "SETI researchers know that travel between stars would be prohibitively expensive and time consuming. Other civilizations could send messages across one thousand light-years of space easily. Earlier projects have involved the detection of radio signals from intelligent life in outer space and—"

"Have any been found?"

"Not yet, Nikki, but you must realize that the search has been limited. Now, over eight million channels can be listened to simultaneously and compared by computer. The natural radio noises are eliminated, and when a stronger-than-average signal occurs the computer notes a possible extraterrestrial signal. They're using..." Teresa again consulted her notes, "...1420.4 megahertz frequency emitted naturally by hydrogen atoms, the most abundant element in the universe and a frequency that would be known by radio astronomers everywhere.

"SETI also embraces the Fermi Paradox," at Nikki's bewildered expression, Teresa flipped back a few pages in her notebook. "In 1950, Enrico Fermi, the Italian physicist, realized...and I'm quoting: 'that any civilization with a modest amount of rocket technology and an immodest amount of imperial incentive could readily colonize the entire galaxy.' I realize they were talking ten million years but that's quite a short period considering that the age of our galaxy is roughly ten thousand million years old."

Teresa looked up and smiled. "In 2003, the Kepler Space Telescope scientists found that one in five sun-like stars have an Earth-size planet orbiting around a habitable region where water would be possible. I know that could just mean bacteria or it could mean starship flying extraterrestrials." She tapped her notebook page.

"I love that SETI sites the *Drake Equation* which estimates the odds of intelligent life as: N equals the number of civilizations in the Milky Way galaxy whose electromagnetic emissions are detectable. R*equals the rate of formation of stars suitable for the development of intelligent life. Fp equals the fraction of those stars with planetary systems. Ne equals the number of planets, per solar system, with an environment suitable for life. Fl equals the fraction of suitable planets on which life actually appears. Fi equals the fraction of life bearing planets on which intelligent life emerges. Fc equals the fraction of civilizations that develop a technology that releases detectable signs of their existence into space. L equals the length of time such civilizations release detectable signals into space." Teresa looked up. "I realize none of these values are known right now but...and of course there's the latest testing of Einstein's Theory of Relativity and dark matter that says...

Leaning back, Nikki closed her eyes and ears against Teresa's continuing discourse. She didn't understand this guy Drake's equation or Albert Einstein's theory any more than she understood one of Rudy Borgianno's elaborate French recipes.

Teresa Hutton had bombarded her with facts, figures, hypotheses and speculations. Total effect: mental confusion. While the self-imposed darkness and silence calmed Nikki's brain and tranquilized her nerves, it ultimately provided no answers. Well, there was one bright spot – it was an assignment. It certainly was different. And the different had always been her forte.

When she reopened her eyes, she discovered both Roman and Teresa staring intently at her. Roman's expression was one of concern. "Don't worry, Cantrell, the jaw is just fine. Only a minor ache and a couple of twinges. I'll even eat more of Rudy's outstanding pizza just to watch you grin. Now, Teresa, let's hear about the two hundred sightings in Florida."

"What's exciting about them is that there have been dozens of highly credible witnesses along with a number of independent sightings as opposed to multiple sightings."

"That makes a difference?"

"Decidedly. When you have a group of people or even two or three, a psychologist can always argue that each was affected by the others. These sightings, however, were separated by both time and area."

Nikki exhaled a musical sigh. "I hesitate to ask, what was it everyone sighted?"

"Well..." Teresa again flipped through the pages of her notebook. "Two objects glowing red, rotating and hovering then disappearing. Both a computer programmer and a dental technician said it reminded them of the planet Saturn. We've also received reports on a boomerang-shaped object."

Teresa glanced up at them, noting that Roman had slid a protective arm around Nikki's waist. "That I found terribly intriguing because a similar object was sighted two years ago over Westchester County in New York and by an Air France pilot over Paris just last month. Both described the exact same thing: large brown-red curved space craft that hovered and changed shape. We also have fifty reports from people who've seen landed crafts that disappeared when approached. Now, I know you're not going to like this, but quite a few suggested that the ships have an invisible cloaking device."

Nikki drummed her fingers thoughtfully against the counter top. "Why Florida? Was the weather over Ohio not welcoming?"

Teresa wagged her finger. "One reputable scientist feels that highly evolved alien beings use Florida as an energy spot where they can influence the earth. That these are warnings from extra-terrestrial intelligence to stop earth's own annihilation."

Nikki groaned. "More than likely it was the Star Trek-Star Wars festival playing on TV this past month"

"You think it's nothing more than wishful thinking by two hundred avid Trekkies and Han Solo wanna-be's?" Teresa reached for her notebook. "How about if I add this? Just a year ago, former Canadian Defense Minister Paul Hellyer came out against scientists for dismissing the evidence of 'authenticated' alien contacts. I'm quoting here: Hellyer did say that while eight out of ten UFO reports are false or mistaken, the reminder are so interesting and amount to overwhelming evidence.

"Hellyer has had his own encounter with a UFO over Lake Muskoka just north of Toronto. Hellyer went on to say that some of them look just like us. They could walk by on the street and you wouldn't know it. Those are what he's investigating right now."

Nikki ignored Teresa's beaming smile. "Those Florida landings? Where were they?"

"In a fifty-mile radius of here." Teresa bit her lower lip before adding, "I thought, perhaps, if you're free tomorrow we could talk to a few people, check out the alleged landing sites and ..." she shifted uncomfortably, "hunt for aliens. What do you say?"

Pizza an inch from her mouth, Nikki sighed. "What else is there to say but fire up the dilithium crystals and 'beam me aboard, Scotty'?"

Chapter 4

"Cantrell, I really think we're taking a big chance doing this."

"Swimming?"

"Swimming *au naturel* by the light of the full July moon."

Roman's voice was a conspiratorial whisper. "It is midnight. It is our pool. There's black screening, a privacy fence, a tall hedge and you are sitting on the underwater light." His fingers sent a warm ripple in Nikki's direction. "So, who's to see?"

"If you believe Teresa Hutton's evidence, the night has a thousand eyes. I just hope all one thousand of those eyes aren't confined to a single alien!" Nikki listened as a masculine laugh was converted into bubbles.

Settling herself farther into the end of the large, frothing Jacuzzi, she watched his sinewy physique fracture the water's surface with smooth, graceful butterfly strokes. It seemed only seconds before he was once again at her side. "Very nice, Cantrell, a perfect ten. Look, the occupants of that blinking red light concur!" She laughed when he sent a wave skyward.

Roman shook off the rivulets that coursed down his face. "God, but it's good to watch you move around without a limp and to hear you laugh and talk again."

"Ten weeks of a bedridden, grunting woman scribbling nasty, nagging notes and horrific emoji's got to you, huh?"

"I prefer listening to you exercise your tongue."

"My barbed tongue?"

"Has it ever turned me off?"

"Not yet."

"Is that what you've been waiting for? Is that why you've packed and unpacked your suitcase every day for the last week?" Moonlight reflected her widening eyes. "Must I keep reminding you what a great detective I am?" His grin was brief. "I would like to know why, Nik."

"The price tag."

"On our relationship?" He saw her nod. "That's up to you. I'm letting you set the terms, the length, the depth." Roman hoped he appeared relaxed on the outside because on the inside he was coming apart. "Have you made some decisions?"

"Yes. Am I supposed to do stuff?"

"Stuff?" He arched a dark brow. "You know, for a woman who's always so direct, concise and outspoken, you certainly make broad arcs. What stuff?"

Nikki scrunched lower in the swirling water. "Dammit, Roman, this is all new to me. We just happened so fast. I don't do relationships. I don't stay in one place long enough to warrant more than a hotel room. I've always lived alone."

His palm wiped the moisture from his face. "All right, Nikki, what kind of stuff has been nagging at you?"

"Cleaning, laundry, gardening, cooking..."

Roman levied himself into the Jacuzzi pool. "You mean 'earning your keep' stuff."

Her expression lightened. "Yes."

"Well, the Garcia's might take offense. Manuela has been doing the cleaning, the laundry, some cooking and the shopping around here for the last three years. And you know how Santi feels about the lawns and gardens." Roman settled next to her. "Of course, if you'd like to contribute to their salary..."

She nodded quickly. "And the phone bills, internet, TV, all the utilities, food, general upkeep."

"Whatever you want is fine with me. Make any changes in the décor, this place came furnished so if you want to add more...frilly things..."

"Do I look like a froo-froo woman?"

Roman shrugged. "Well you did go crazy with the sea shells so I just thought maybe you might want...hell, I don't know...more pillows or something other than a leather sofa or..." When he saw her disgusted expression, he sighed. "Whatever you want. Except, well, about the food. Your specialty is junk food, frozen meals and ordering take-out. On occasion, we'll let your fingers do the ordering, but I'll retain rights to the kitchen." His grin was smooth, his manner confident. "See how easily we disposed of all that stuff'?"

She watched him surface dive back into the main pool. There was considerably more occupying her mind. A partner. That's what Roman Cantrell wanted out of this relationship. Someone to share the good and the bad, the profit and the risk. Nikki readily acknowledged that Roman was an exemplary partner.

The last twelve weeks replayed in her mind. The first two had been spent confined to the hospital. Nikki knew her stay would have been longer if Roman hadn't intervened. He hated hospitals as much as she did and resolutely set about convincing the doctor that hospital surroundings were severely detrimental to this particular patient's healing process.

Roman had transformed his large master bedroom into a hospital room, complete with the necessary medical and rehab equipment. He hired a day nurse, a physical therapist and, designating himself the dietician, created gourmet meals she'd slurped through straws.

Then came the nights. No nurse, no therapist. Just Roman Cantrell, secure and tangible. Lying next to her, his strength transfusing into her, his arm and body were a protective barrier shielding her from the nocturnal demons from her past that frequently haunted her sleep.

Roman Cantrell was a hard man. A tough man. He was also a man who demonstrated, at least with her, gentleness, understanding and an especially caring nature.

She wasn't used to that.

Her thoughts drifted back fourteen years, when, at seventeen, she had been paroled in Matt Cortlund's custody. His wife, Becky, had tried taking care of her. Nikki had resented it.

Yet, right now, right here, she wasn't resisting and it troubled her. Her career and her free, independent lifestyle were her proudest achievements. As for relationships and men...Nikki's lips thinned. Her mother had been a hooker and men quickly lost status. There had been very few over the years and never for any length of time.

So what happened? She could have recuperated in Chicago with the Cortlunds, but it had only taken one simple sentence to stop her. What if you never see this particular man again? That question kept haunting and—

"Earth to Nikki. Earth to Nikki." Roman pushed his face in front of hers. "Say, you aren't trying to transcend time and space by mentally projecting an interview with a UFO tomorrow?"

Nikki blinked.

Twice.

She remained silent.

While his hand was able to wipe the moisture from his face, it couldn't wash away the resurgence of anxiety. "You're thinking again, right, Nik?" His fingers captured her chin and her full attention. "And I know exactly what's troubling you now."

He blundered on urgently. "I was hoping you hadn't noticed. Obviously you did. Okay, okay, I'll admit it. I couldn't control my tone or my expression, and my blood pressure tripled when I heard Teresa Hutton say she had an assignment for you.

"I've been expecting this. Promised myself that I would behave. That I wouldn't say one damn word." Roman shook a wet finger at her. "Technically, I did not speak any of the damn words I was thinking. And I'm sorry as hell those unspoken words became so obvious that you saw them.

"Frankly, I'm damned ashamed. I gave you my solemn oath that I would not interfere in your career. That I wouldn't swallow you up. That you'd never have to report your comings and goings to me.

"But when I heard you had an assignment and thought about you leaving, I...well, dammit all, that dose of reality packed one helluva punch." Roman heaved a sigh. "There. It's out. I said it. Panic. Plain and simple. The idea of you vacating my premises made me crazy. The funny part is I really didn't have much to panic about.

"The detective business is not the way it's portrayed on TV. I don't get a new case every week that can be solved in sixty minutes less commercial interruption while I'm running around in time to a music score. In fact, it's been pretty damn dry around this office. Thankfully, my other offices are busy. So, even if this assignment of yours had been to say Pago Pago, I could have accompanied you."

He leaned closer to gauge the expression on Nikki's face. It proved quite enigmatic. "Only for a short time. Just to make sure your health stayed um...healthy. It's not that I don't think you're ready to get back into harness. Hey, didn't I bring home pizza? I won't get in your way. I—fuck! This is not coming out right at all." Roman disappeared underwater until a knock on his head brought him quickly to the surface.

"You are a romantic, Cantrell."

"Don't sound so accusing and disgusted by it, Holden."

"Don't you sound so smug."

His voice was blatantly affected. "We former soldiers of fortune have an image to uphold."

"You mean the swashbuckling vigilante, pseudo-romantic, go-ahead-get-in-my-bed credo?"

"There ya' go." He gave her his best leer, then turned serious. "Besides, Nik, I find you match me quite well."

"There you go, Cantrell. Building fantasies, making me your cause." Her tone and expression were stony. "All your excitement, all your anticipation, all your fascination with me will dissolve when the newness and the romantic magic in your mind fades. Then, you know what you'll have?" Her finger stabbed his chest. "I'll tell you what you'll have. Boredom. Worse. Mechanical boredom."

His hearty laugh acted like a flint to her anger. Nikki's fingers closed together, and she sent a swiping rebuke toward Roman's cheek.

Still laughing, he ducked and floated out of reach. "Boredom is a catchword and means nothing to either one of us. Besides, I know what you're doing, Nik, I'm wise to your logic. You get all tight and angry. But you're not angry with me, you're angry with yourself."

His voice was low and gentle. "You don't like to admit to even owning any emotions. When you do relax, you run scared, get confused and turn that confusion into anger. I understand. I know where you're coming from. You lived in hell for the first seventeen years of your life, abused by your own mother. The scars are still there, visible and invisible. You can't handle love and affection."

Nikki's features remained stoic. "Is that what you're offering, Cantrell? Love?"

Instead of moving closer, he drifted to the far side of the Jacuzzi and kept his tone light and breezy. "Now if I said yes, you'd only throw it back in my face."

"I'm throwing it back anyway." She took a deep breath. "Look, Cantrell, I'm me. I won't change to fit an image you want. Yes I had a hard-knock life but I'm no red-haired Annie in need of a Daddy Warbucks."

"Please...I have no intention of being your daddy."

"What if this doesn't work out?" She hated sounding so dramatic when his tone was relaxed.

"That's the price of living."

"You can't get back the time you wasted on having me in your life." *Damn the man, he had an answer for everything.* Suddenly,

Nikki couldn't get enough air. She felt she was drowning in the warm, bubbling water and easily swam over the tile step, back into the main pool.

Her body turned into a torpedo – quickly going the distance from one end to the other. She was glad Roman didn't try to stop her. After five laps, she settled on the middle pool step and made her tone as cool as possible. "I know I'm intense and I probably drive you crazy. I am not the easiest person to even like. I'm loaded with bad habits."

"As I recall, you once stated that bad habits are the only habits to have. Besides, I've experienced all your bad habits."

"Think so?" She watched him walk-swim to stand in front of her.

"Well, let's see," he drawled. "You seem to grunt your way through the mornings and that's with or without a wired jaw. You have a little coffee with your three sugars and cream, hate to wear shoes and are too neat, except when it comes to your desk. You have a cast-iron stomach. Hell, wasn't I the one who had to figure out how to whirl together a wet burrito and nachos in the Cuisinart?

"You have abundant self-confidence when it comes to your work but none at all on a personal level. You take too many chances, push people too hard. You're iconoclastic and tenacious. Of course this..." his hands dipped beneath the water and captured her left ankle, pulling it to the surface, "...is also a factor."

"My foot?"

He smiled at her contemptuous tone. "Ahh, but we're not talking a standard size nine-and-a-half foot here, my dear Miss Holden. You have a Greek foot."

"Pray tell, Dr. Scholl, what is a Greek foot?"

"'When one's second toe is longer than one's big toe." Roman planted her foot flat against his chest. "In your case, though, your third little piggy..." his fingers sculpted the digit, "...is also longer than your big toe. That, of course, is the reason for your stubborn, irreverent nature."

She wiggled her toes in the wet hair that matted his broad chest. "Where did you get this? *Scuttlebutt*? It sounds like tabloid material."

The hint of amusement that colored Nikki's sarcasm made Roman relax. "Medical fact," he continued seriously. "You also have a high plantar arch." His fingernail made a delicate sweep from her heel to the ball of her foot. "That indicates bossiness.

"Now, your lateral arch is rough-skinned." His thumb stroked the outside curve. "That denotes willfulness. As does your equally calloused metatarsal."

"I wonder what Freud says about a man with a foot fetish, Cantrell."

"He'd probably compliment me on my exquisite taste. Because this foot happens to be attached to one gorgeous length of shapely leg."

Nikki watched her left foot and leg disappear through the opening formed by Roman's arm and body. She felt his warm hands glide effortlessly along the curve of her calf and the tendons of her knee as they headed steadily up to her thigh. When his hands slid across her hip to her belly, she quickly struggled to shape another rebuke. "I knew it. This relationship is nothing more than physical attraction."

Roman effectively changed the tempo of his movements from erotic to impersonal. "Physical attraction? I'd say yours is a face of character rather than beauty. Forehead's too high. Mouth too generous. Cheeks too soft. Jaw too strong. And a nose broken so many times that it's hard to tell whether it was originally patrician or pug.

"Then, too, there are your eyes. Dangerous eyes. Eyes that analyze and brutalize, envelop and dismiss, linger and laugh." His deep voice roughened. "I like watching them change from icy to warm. The way they just did."

"Sex and cigarette talk, Cantrell."

"Neither of us smokes. As for sex so far it's been just one magical night, twelve very long weeks ago. Hmm...and as I recall, the next day you invited me to move in with you." His next question caught her completely off guard.

"Wh-what?"

"I want to know why you stayed with me. Cortlund was ready to charter a medical plane to get you back to Chicago. Borgianno was ready to buy the trauma center and a rehab unit."

"You checkmated them both."

Roman shook his head. "No, even though you couldn't talk, you were quite emphatic about staying here. So I'll ask again, why?"

"Don't think I haven't asked myself that same question hundreds of times. It would have been easier to run away than to face you."

"Have you ever taken the easy way out?"

"No."

His smile was quick, brief, "What's your best guess?"

"Roman Cantrell, you have complicated my life. My view of people was totally fucked up at an early age, with the exception of Matt and Rudy. I've never had a problem bending the law to get information for a story. I never thought I possessed a conscience until I met you."

Nikki exhaled a dramatic sigh that transformed her lips into a smile. "You make me laugh. You never tell me that I can't do something. Even when I was just starting my therapy and falling all over the place. You never tried to prevent me from falling. I appreciated that. I'm also glad you thought of using the pool as therapy. I really think that's why I gained so much ground so fast."

"Anything else?"

"I feel comfortable here. Comfortable with you." Her blue eyes leveled into his dark brown ones. "That's why I've been thinking about leaving. I'm getting too comfortable. I don't like it. I live my life in the here and now. I try hard not to let the past intrude. I don't plan for the future. Day-to-day was it for me. I was alone but never lonely.

"I seldom make attachments. You got under my skin. Damn it all...I made those stupid shell lamps. Now I've got anchors...I'm happy...a feeling I seldom have and...hell...I don't trust it. I'm prattling on like a crazy person and ..." Nikki's wet palm slapped her cheek. "Damn you run a tough confessional, Cantrell."

A burning in his stomach made Roman wince. "Do you trust me?"

"If I didn't trust you, there would have been no magical night as you like to call it. Yes, I trust you and I like the way you make me feel about myself." Nikki was surprised when that private admission rolled out. She forced herself to continue. "You've made me very satisfied with being a woman. That's something I never thought possible considering that there's no female organs left inside me.

"I thought I knew who I was on every level but you changed that especially sexually. I never felt the need to be touched, stroked, held – you brought that into my life. I'm not sure if I should thank you or just leave. Then you can go back to your bevy of beautiful, healthy women."

Roman shook his head. "You have completely lost me."

Nikki wagged a finger at him. "Alex told me about your endless supply of fashion models when you were doing security for that South Beach fashion shoot."

"Lazarus is a jealous bastard and not just of the models. I see the way he looks at you."

"When I want variety, Cantrell, I open the freezer and choose from a dozen Klondike Bars." She pushed a spray of water at him.

"You deserve more than me. You'll want a family and I can't give you that, so..."

"A bevy does not fill a void." His large hands cupped her face. "I'll checkmate your ice cream bars with Paul Newman's quote: why would I go out for burgers when I have steak at home.

"I lied." He smiled into her narrowed eyes. "When I said you weren't a physical attraction. You are beautiful on the inside and on the outside. I'm glad you realize your worth as a woman is not linked to reproduction. You are who you are because of where you've been and what you've gone through. I understand that, Nik—"

"Don't understand me so fast."

The ensuing quiet began to hurt Roman's ears. But it didn't hurt as much as the pain that seared deep inside him. He'd had that pain since the first day he'd met Nikki. Sometimes it burned with pleasure; other times with anger. Right now it twisted with fear. Fear of loss.

Primitive emotions surfaced within him. Nikki was an unknown quantity. Day-to-day was all he could count on – if that.

He was restless.

Tense.

Charged.

Aroused.

"I do believe my handball days are finally over." Lunging forward, his hands slid through the water and under her ass. He laughed at her shriek and lifted her up in a two-handed butt squeeze, adding a couple of hard shakes. "Awe...damn, you don't glow in the dark."

Gasping, Nikki's fingers curled around Roman's broad, muscular shoulders as his lips locked onto her right nipple. The erotic play of his tongue and teeth turned her rapid breathing into low throaty guttural moans. "It's a good thing you have biceps of steel and strong legs, Cantrell, or we'd both drown."

His hands slithered over her slippery curves. "I know mouth-to-mouth." With that his lips moved with gentle force against hers. "It is so good to kiss you again. No wires or bands."

Her tongue traced the sensuous curve of his lips. "I almost forgot what a good kisser you are." She could feel his heart beating against her palm.

"Can't have that." Roman felt the wild pulse in her neck under his lips. Then it was his turn to gasp when she grabbed his butt. Her fingers rubbed slowly, moving to slide between his thighs and tease the back of his thick cock. "Oh, fuck."

"Yes, please."

"The first one is going to be fast and furious. It's just been too damn long." He guided her backward against the pool wall. Her legs easily wrapped around his waist. His tongue was hard and purposeful against her parted lips, duplicating the action as his cock thrust deep inside her.

Roman savored the moment, storing it away just in case. His hands gently mapped her spine, settling in the indent of her waist. Pulling her tight against him, his body began to move. Long, deep strokes that made her shudder in his arms and cry out.

His need was intense.

His response fierce.

Roman felt everything blur as he pumped every ounce of cum into her. With a groan, he collapsed on her breasts, his head in the curve of her neck loving the way she was holding him. His teeth teased her earlobe. "Can I at least tell people we're going steady?"

Her fingers traced the death before dishonor tat on his left bicep when she felt him harden inside her. "No, but you can brag about the sexual power of pizza."

Chapter 5

"Ain't we up with the roosters?"

"At least roosters have feathers that fit."

Snapping on the lamp, Roman blinked into focus the pile of clothes on the bed. "When did you become so fashion conscious?"

"I'm not. I just didn't realize how much weight I'd lost until I tried on work clothes. I've been living in athletic shorts and T-shirts for the past ten weeks once I got out of the attractive bare-your-ass hospital gown." Nikki stood centered in the closet doorway. "As you can see underwear is it."

He wiped the sleep from his eyes and grinned. "That'd make a great tabloid headline."

Nikki winced, pulling the last pair of khakis off a hanger. "That tabloid...I'm regretting my decision more and more. While you were snoring, I was reading through that UFO material Teresa left and mining the internet."

"How the hell long have you been up?"

"Since four. Questions woke me up. I just couldn't sleep."

He shot her a wicked grin. "As I recall there wasn't much sleeping going on." Roman patted the mattress. "Come here, tell me what's bothering you."

Shoulders drooping, Nikki sat on the bed next to him. "That tabloid is pure sleaze, Cantrell, sleaze, garbage and the bizarre."

"How sleazy? How garbagy? How bizarre?"

"Let me just say their so-called ufologists can be classified as psychopaths or frauds."

He snapped the elastic at the waist of her dark blue bikini briefs. "Be more specific."

"Specifics? You want specifics? How about...how about the Ph.D. expert who claims lint balls, those under-the-bed dust bunnies, are cosmic spies? Alien private eyes. Tiny, fuzzy competition for you, Cantrell.

"And since you brought up poultry, one expert says chickens, roosters and ducks are aliens who've been watching us for centuries and have invaded our bodies..." her fingers waved in the air "...courtesy of our appetite for their little bodies and eggs.

"I used a magnifying glass on that collection of UFO photos. They're all blurred, out of focus, totally invalid. They look more like Frisbees or the planet Saturn. One appears to be an inverted cup on a saucer. I'll be damned if the clearest UFO photo is anything more than a rally-wheel hubcap!"

Nikki slapped his exploring fingers that had slid under the elastic leg of her briefs and was teasing her pubic curls. "You can't still be horny after last night. I've got a hickey on my ass." Ignoring his lecherous grin and bouncing eyebrows, she pulled on her slacks, stood up and zipped them into place. "Damn...these are the skinniest jeans I own and...oh...hell...if I have to run they'll end up at my ankles."

"Run?"

She smirked. "From an alien with a ray gun of course." Rolling the waistband down, Nikki hoped it would tighten around her waist. "Double damn. I don't even have a belt. Do you have a bungee cord someplace?"

"Wait a minute...when I unpacked your clothes, I remember seeing a..." He leaned down and pulled open the bottom nightstand drawer. "Ahh...this will make a perfect belt. Come here."

"You are a genius." She sighed in relief as he threaded the long narrow silk scarf through the belt loops. "I see working security for all those South Beach fashion shoots have made you the perfect handmaiden."

Roman tied the blue and yellow nautical rope design scarf with a perfect slip knot. "I'm good at getting you into clothes but I prefer getting you out of them." Giving her a playful slap on the ass, he leaned back against the black leather headboard. "What else did your research find?"

Nikki finished buttoning on a short-sleeve white shirt and tucked it in. "The truth on the rest of her stories. Her big claim on UFO sightings in Ohio and Wright-Patterson Air Base, well guess what? There were also eight Bigfoot sightings in that same time period and the solar plane was also on a night flight in that area.

"Her alien ruins off Greece? An update was posted by the archaeologists who dove down to the site. The truth of that story it's not a sunken city at all. Microbes did it. Just one of those strange but totally natural phenomenon's courtesy of Poseidon if you must attribute it to a Greek God." Nikki looked up from zipping her feet into white leather Vans. "Well at least my Greek feet have not shrunk."

Opening the middle nightstand drawer, she pulled out a tan crossbody bag and checked its contents. "Oh, good this still has my reporter's notebook and recorder. Battery's still good."

Nikki smiled at him, finger-combing her long hair back off her face. "I normally let Darnie do all my research but in five minutes on the internet I was able to buy a flux capacitor. A levitating hover board. And choose from an assortment of drone kits so you can build your own UFO. I swear drones have become replacements for Barbie and Ken, there are outfits for the damn things."

"There were over a dozen social media groups on UFO's and those wanting to connect up with other people who'd been kidnapped by aliens." Nikki rubbed her forehead. "I sent a list for Darnie to hunt down now that she's back home in L.A. I'm sure a lot of things can't be explained and, frankly, that's perfectly normal in my humble opinion.

"As for the two hundred sightings here in Florida? Wouldn't the Pentagon's satellites have recorded something? A blip? Static? High radiation levels in the atmosphere?" She massaged her temples.

"I did learn that the new electric plane has been doing some test runs in our area. At the Cape, a company is testing jet packs. There was a Cosplay Convention in Tampa, a laser light and antique car show in Hialeah, a dress-up Scifi and Comic-Con at the Miami Convention Center. Barring that, I'm betting the chamber of commerce is trying to whip up the tourist trade after that green algae mess closed a lot of beaches...you know...the way Nessie does for Loch Ness."

She plopped on the mattress and stared at Roman. "Then there's *Scuttlebutt* itself. Teresa left a dozen of them. Until this morning, I'd never really read a tabloid, just gaped in amazement at their headlines."

His hand squeezed her thigh. "And?"

"They have no poverty of imagination. All the sentences are eight words or less, with two of those words being 'mind-boggling.' The rest are breathless adjectives and a generous supply of exclamation points. They constantly call up 'national surveys.' Over and over. National surveys say this. National surveys say that. Now what are you grinning at?"

"Your throaty growl."

She made a face. "I cannot write monosyllabic, adjective-laden sentences, nor do I know how many g's are in boggling. But I would like to know what nation has done all those national surveys.

"When you read a tabloid, you get disinformation. You get lies. You get checkbook journalists searching for the bizarre, the juicy, the inspirational!" She pushed off the bed and paced. "I must have been crazy to agree to this. No. Not crazy." Her fingers raked through her hair. "Just bored. That's what I told Matt."

"You called Cortlund? It's only six A.M. in Chicago. And it's Saturday."

"I'm up. You're up."

"I'm up because you're noisy." Roman ran a palm around his neck. "Hell, I'll bet Matt was damn noisy."

"His answering machine took the call."

"And your four-letter expletives."

"I only left eight," she said sweetly, "and two were mind-boggling. Stop laughing, Cantrell!" She threatened him with a hairbrush. "My laptop, files and all Teresa's paraphernalia are spread across over the dining room table so don't touch a thing."

Roman massaged the dark stubble on his jaw. "You need an office, how about the bedroom next door?"

"Already in the works." At his inquiring expression, she elaborated. "Rudy put Duncan and Edgar on the task. Duncan's been taking an interior design class to help with the restaurant. When Rudy was here last week, he took measurements, showed off paint samples and office furniture choices. I want things simple but the email he sent me this morning..." Nikki's hand fluttered in defeat. "I'm donating all that hospital and rehab equipment to a VA center." She cocked her head. "All that's okay, right?"

"More than okay. I told you before whatever you want to do, change, buy, move around, is perfectly fine with me."

Nikki ignored his masculine smirk. "Do you have any jungle juice?"

"Bug spray's in the utility room. Why?"

"Teresa's scheduled a tramp through a swamp and a sugarcane field looking for UFO residue and little green men."

"You're going? After that ten minute diatribe?"

"Of course."

"Of course," he mimicked. "Nik, you are—"

"Bored." She locked the flap on her messenger bag. "Bored with lying in the sun. Bored with recuperating. Bored with TV and movies. Bored with —"

"Me?"

"'Cantrell, we covered that last night." Arms folded across her chest, her voice and manner were impatient. "If I was bored with you, I would not be standing here. I'd be gone."

"Just don't fake it. I know how well you lie."

"The inference being I should have no trouble writing exotic tabloid news?"

"You bet your asteroids!"

"Please, you're making my breakfast sour."

"I hope you ate something decent. Something healthy. Something..." Roman grew suspicious at her broadening smile. "You ate cold pizza, didn't you?"

"I did not eat cold pizza."

"Good. Very sensible. Because you need...you warmed the pizza, didn't you?" Her laugh provided his answer.

"What are your plans, Cantrell?"

He made a big production of neatening the navy sheets. "I'm going to go back to sleep, wake up at a decent weekend hour, eat a healthy breakfast and watch *They Came From Outer Space* and *Alien Autopsy* on cable."

"What, you're going to forego your usual three hours of cartoons? Wait till Marvin the Martian hears about this!"

"Very funny. We all have our ways to relax and mine happens to be cartoons. What do you want me to tell Matt when he calls back?"

"Tell him that I'm going to take this UFO assignment and turn it into an exposé on sensational journalism. Tell him I can't believe he bought a tabloid. Tell him if he expects me to write gee-whiz stories he ups my salary. I know how much those tabloid reporters make. Tell him...tell him I'll call him back." She winced when she heard the gate buzzer echo from the intercom. "That's Teresa. Damn, my clothes are..."

"Don't worry, I'll rehang everything." Roman grabbed her arm and splayed her hand against his bare torso. "You look great. That's a perfect alien-hunting outfit. There's that growl again. I thought you were staying open-minded?"

"I gave my brain an enema this morning. Can't get more open-minded than that!" She tugged his chest hair, then wriggled her hand free and headed for the door. "By the way I couldn't find my cell so I took your extra sat phone and I downloaded some apps on it."

"Say, Nikki," he called after her, "just in case you do find a little green alien, ask what he and his buddies did with Judge Crater and Jimmy Hoffa." Roman laughed when she gave him a middle-finger salute.

Chapter 6

"Beauty of a morning, isn't it?"

Nikki returned Teresa's beaming smile with a noncommittal murmur, promptly busying herself with the Mini Cooper's seatbelt. Abruptly, a heavily marked road map was quickly spread across her knees.

"Here's our itinerary. We'll be heading up to West Palm Beach for our first interview. It's with Muriel Feinburg. She opted for this early morning conference, by-the-by. Owns a chain of beauty salons and Saturday's her busiest day so she said eight thirty or nothing. Just a few miles from Muriel, I've got a couple of other people, both in the same neighborhood, who have actual photos of the UFO that buzzed their homes.

"Then we'll head inland to Belle Glade. We've got a very reluctant farmer who witnessed the boomerang object. But according to our news stringer, this farmer's got solid evidence to show us. This is where all the landings have been reported."

Teresa inhaled deeply. "Let's be off." She shifted into drive. "I've got a new digital camera in the boot with close-up and wide-angle lens attachments. There are some plastic bags for taking ground and plant samples. I've got a well-stocked ice chest in the back seat, so help yourself.

"Sorry about garnering only those interviews for today. Weekend, you know. But all those orange dots on the map are sightings and that blue index card stapled to the back has more names and phone numbers. You can see by the green markings that the sightings are concentrated in a triangular area from West Palm to Okeechobee to Belle Glade. Interesting.

"I say, Nikki, is it cool enough in here for you? Just fiddle with the air-conditioning. These controls..." her fingers tapped the black buttons set in the silver-gray transmission console, "will adjust your seat. It's a fun auto, rather like sitting in an airplane cockpit." Teresa cast a quick glance at the still quiet redhead. "There's chewing gum in the glove compartment if you're carsick. Am I driving too fast?"

Nikki exhaled loudly. "Don't worry. Your very new, elegant gray leather upholstery is safe with me."

"Sorry. I wasn't worried. I..." Teresa cleared her throat. "Ah, what a total twit I am. Listen, I'm certainly not trying to take command here. I'm more company than director. Just thought I'd acquaint you with all the information we've compiled. I'm just the bowler. It's up to you to finish the cricket match. Finish it any way you wish."

"Does that mean I can use compound sentences? Three-syllable words?" Nikki shifted sideways toward Teresa. "Deal with the definite and the probable, not the disposable? Nothing overwrought or parodic? And forget that exclamation points and the word mind-boggling even exist?"

Teresa watched the odometer click off a mile before she spoke. "I guess you noticed that I can still blush." She sniffed then cast a glance at Nikki. "Actually, the only writing requirement I do have for you is to remember to capitalize UFO."

Nikki's coughed laugh eased the tension. "Why do you do it?"

"Why do you?"

"Love of the job." Nikki's lips pursed. "You can't possibly claim that you love all that sensational weirdness."

"But I do. Loved it when I worked on Fleet Street in London. I get excited about talkies, stories that can't help but be talked about. Like you, I have a great sense of mischief. I was always trying to create chaos in school. Two headmistresses offered to pay my father not to have me attend their boarding schools. Honestly." Teresa's voice and smile were full of memories. "My father, God rest his soul, was blessedly wealthy and didn't mind paying my way out of scrapes. He spoiled me outrageously.

"Then I discovered the tabs and decided to channel my disruptive energies into dirt-stirring. Ah, but lately, we're getting less and less sensational and into more service stories. Health, how-to's, personal advice. Bloody respectable, actually. Cortlund's going to be a cautious publisher. He wants to attract the monied name-brand advertisers."

Nikki arched a titian brow. "What, no more breast enlargers, waist cinchers, hair growers, hernia trusses, exotic insect diets and psychic phone help?"

"Fewer and fewer. We're almost as boring as regular newspapers."

Teresa's sigh was so genuine, it made Nikki laugh. "I can see arguing with you is next to impossible."

"Good. Because you have a reputation for winning arguments."

"I just have a reputation." Nikki lifted the heavy curtain of copper hair off her neck.

"The gossip that surrounds you is very interesting."

"Now that was a nice piece of British understatement. I suppose, since you've become my boss..."

"Only in the widest possible sense."

"You would, however, like to know if the gossip about my police record, my parole and my shady friends like Miami crime boss Rudy Borgianno is true?"

"Well....yes."

"All true. I have vacationed in jail numerous times when the penal code was my to-do list. But...oh...for the past ten weeks I've been a model citizen."

Teresa frowned while resetting her cruise control. "For the past ten weeks...I say Nikki you were recovering and out of commission for the last ten weeks."

"Exactly." Snapping the road map closed, Nikki turned to Teresa. "How'd you get from London to Florida?"

"I married an American professor on sabbatical."

"What's he think of your *Scuttlebutt* managing editorship?"

"We're divorced." Teresa's fingers twisted against the plain gold band on her left hand. "Probably should take this off. It has been three years." She sighed. "Still, when you're in love, it's bloody difficult to shed this final link."

"He didn't care for your tabloid career?"

"Actually, my career didn't bother him at all. It was my scars. I had breast cancer and opted for a radical mastectomy."

"I'm sorry."

"Not to worry. After five years of being cancer free, I'm a very vocal worker for the Cancer Society. I think of it as ongoing therapy. The loss of one's breasts is nothing when you put it in context with the great scheme of life's potential tragedies. My very learned spouse experienced more pain and discomfort than I did.

"I was no Duchess of Cambridge before the operation, but my figure was a source of pride. Especially for him. He loved perfection in all things and the scars marred my body. My body was imperfect and I, therefore, became unlovable. That was after I had reconstruction surgery and barely a scar was visible."

"The man needed help." A muscle twitched in Nikki's cheek.

"Quite typical. The perfect female form is what everyone, women included, is after. It's in the movies, on the telly, in magazines, on billboards and heaven help us all over those reality TV shows. Instagram, the internet, twitter...bloody hell, there are more naked perfect bodies for viewing than if you were on a nude beach or watching porn.

"Polished, smooth, satiny skin whether it's on voluptuous curves or model thin bodies. That's what being a real woman is all about. Talk about reverse chauvinism. I've even come to excuse his reaction.

"What a twat! But all that changed when he started snogging other tarts in public and then going full-on with a slapper and not even having the decency to keep it quiet. Bloody hell, I was the one in need of more therapy." Her deprecating smile turned into a frown. "Sorry, you probably didn't understand a word of what I just said."

Nikki rubbed her jaw and didn't even try to hide her smile. "Your ex was into public displays of kissing and cuddling before he had a very public affair."

"I see you do speak the Queen's English." Teresa readjusted the cruise control. "Hmmm, that's the third patrol car in a mile. Probably aiming their radar guns right at my little red hardtop. Red cars are a flag for the coppers. I think I'll take the next exit and head up A1A. Much more scenic."

Polished, smooth, satiny skin. Teresa was right, Nikki thought. The photos were everywhere. She didn't own it either. She inched her spine away from the leather seat. From her shoulder blades to her buttocks, she possessed scars that were gifts from an abusive mother. Some had faded into white netted lines; some were taut and shiny; the raised, red keloids were forever.

Roman Cantrell made love to her scars. Last night, he'd kissed each one. "That's something to think about."

"I say, what was that, Nikki?"

"I...I was just wondering..." she flipped though the note cards, "Muriel Feinburg? What model UFO did she see?"

Chapter 7

Roman Cantrell aimed the remote and snapped off the television. "Nikki was right, I should have stuck with Marvin the Martian and the Bugs Bunny crew. Both are more realistic than *Alien Autopsy*." The ringing bedside phone had him sitting back against the pillows. "Hello?"

"A friendly voice. Where's my snarling redhead?"

"Hello, Matt. How's Cortlund Publishing doing these days?"

"Fine, fine and she was right, I should have called and told her I bought that paper. Hey tabloids are pure profit and I need that. These racehorses eat me out of house and home. Besides, *Scuttlebutt*'s headed for a Spanish edition and a cable TV talk show. Christ, the language Nikki knows! Let me talk to her."

"You've been given a reprieve." Roman grinned at hearing Matt's exaggerated sigh of relief. "She's out hunting for UFO's and little green men with Teresa Hutton."

"Bet she bitched her head off at me and the whole assignment."

"You bet right and she wants a raise."

Cortlund laughed. "She needed this. Don't you agree?"

"Reluctantly. You're right, she did need this. I'm very glad the aliens decided to land so close to my home."

"Very funny, Roman. How's our girl really doing?"

"She ate pizza for breakfast. And, be prepared for this one, for the first time ever, Nikki couldn't find anything to wear."

"No!"

"Yes. She's lost so much weight, everything's too big."

"Don't worry, that'll make Rebecca happy. My wife loves to go shopping for Nik. Oh, there goes my other line. Have her give me a call."

"She intends to." Smiling, Roman cradled the phone and headed for the shower until the shrill tone thwarted his efforts. "Hello?"

"Roman Cantrell, please."

The female voice that invaded his ear was thick with tears. "Speaking."

"This...this is Ellen Mackey. To...To...Tony's wife."

An image struggled forward. Ellen was twenty, barely five feet tall, shoulder-length black curly hair framing petite features. Roman remembered she was pregnant and due in three weeks. "Yes, Ellen, what's wrong?"

"It's Tony. He...he called. He's been arrested and he's hurt and he said to call you, Roman. That you'd know what to do. You got him this great job and now he's been arrested and I couldn't find your phone number. My Tony's in jail and I...it...it took forever to find your number and...and...and..."

The rest of her words were flooded in tears. "Easy, Ellen. Relax. Take a couple of deep breaths, that 'a girl." His deep voice sought to soothe. "I'm sure we can get everything straightened out. Tony's a good man. An honest man. Hartwell Armored Services only hires the best." When her sobs turned to sniffles and the sniffles became less violent, he tried again. "Ellen, tell me exactly what Tony told you."

"Well, he had an armored car run early this morning. He left home at his usual time, around three." She sniffled, swallowed and cleared her throat with a cough. "Then I got a call from him about...let's see, what time is it now?"

"Ten-thirty."

"He called about half an hour ago. It took forever to find your phone number, Roman and..."

"Shhh...easy, Ellen, you've got me now. What did Tony tell you?"

"Well, not much really. Just that he'd been hijacked but wasn't hurt too bad and that the police were holding him and...and...oh, God, Roman, I keep thinking, wondering...what if he was shot?"

"Whoa, Ellen, if Tony had needed medical attention, he'd have been hospitalized. He's probably been checked by doctors and the cops are just questioning him to get all the facts." He heard her blow her nose and hiccough. "Listen, Ellen...Ellen?"

"Yes?"

"Where did Tony say he was?"

"I...gosh, I don't remember him saying. Oh...that's bad, isn't it?"

"No. No problem. Nothing for you to worry about. I can find Tony. Hey, Ellen, that's the business I'm in." Roman hoped his laughed sounded more confident than forced. "Now, listen to me...Ellen, listen, I want you to fix yourself a nice cup of hot milk, sit down, put your feet up and relax. Have you got someone who'll come in and stay with you?"

"My neighbor. I don't dare call my folks. You know how they feel about Tony since that other trouble."

"Okay, you call that neighbor and leave everything to me." Cantrell was thoughtful for a long moment. "You know what Ellen, I'm going to send Louise Coughlin over, she's the best. A grandmother to six kids and a fabulous cook. I'll make sure she comes prepared to just pamper you." He heard another round of tears and sniffling. "I'll get back to you as soon as I can with...Say, Ellen..." Cantrell teased, "I'll just drive Tony straight home."

Roman pulled his cellphone out of the drawer and punched in Louise Coughlin's number. She was one of his best operatives and the perfect person to calm Ellen down, pamper her and make sure no reporters added to her stress. Louise was quick on the uptake, said she'd handle it all and would be at Ellen Mackey's in thirty minutes with both catered food and cooking supplies.

"Saint Anthony, what in hell's happened to you now?" Cantrell's grimace was slowly replaced by a wry grin of remembrance.

More than camaraderie was formed in the mountains of Afghanistan. He'd met Mackey and six other soldiers who were manning *Minehounds* and *Gizmos* as they swept the roads for IED's ahead of their convoy.

He had been on a lone, special ops assignment and told them about an area two kilometers ahead that harbored way too much lumber for a dusty rural road. His warning had been right. The *Minehound* with its ground penetrating radar had been able to locate a non-metallic cache of IED's that were hidden in the wooden debris.

Mackey especially welcomed him to share their camp. After two days with Mackey, Roman had given him the nickname of Saint Anthony because of his innate ability at finding IED's and saving a lot of lives.

A throbbing pain made Roman's grin fade. Wincing, he rubbed his forehead. But the quick images of the war refused to disappear.

He focused – hard – on the present. First was to find where Tony Mackey was being held. He reached for the phone and punched in a text. An answer came just as he'd finished dressing. "How's the best FBI man in the country?"

"Busy. Nikki okay?"

"Off and running on an assignment. A local assignment."

"That's why you're still civil. Listen, I'd love to chat but –"

"Tony Mackey." When the silence stretched beyond fifteen seconds, Cantrell added: "You've been called in on this hijacking."

"Fuck!"

"Alex, the world just keeps getting smaller and smaller, doesn't it?"

"How'd you hear? There's been a blackout on this."

"His wife called me."

"Fuck, I didn't realize the locals had let him use a phone."

"I got him the job, pal. I want in." Cantrell took a deep breath. "Look, Alex, I'm gonna level with you. Tony's had a rougher time than most since coming home from Afghanistan. He's been in and out of VA hospitals, rehab groups. Hell, you know the drill. Things began to turn around for him when he put together a small trucking business. Then, well hell, the entire economy went sour."

"We've all been kicked in the gut when we came home, Roman. We were all hostile. Most of us rebounded and not while we were in prison."

"Fine, Alex, but Tony paid his dues. He's been clean ever since. You know Ed Hartwell's reputation. He'd never hire Mackey to drive his armored cars if he wasn't sure of the guy."

"How hard did you push that assurance, Roman?"

Now it was Cantrell's turn to run silent. "Alex, the guy's turned around. I'll stake my life on that. He's married with a baby on the way in three weeks. Tony's been a solid, employed citizen for the last three years."

"Well, maybe he's turned around again."

"Hijacked himself?"

"Don't sound so skeptical, Roman. This is the screwiest damn thing I've ever heard."

"Give."

"You want all your work done for you?"

"It is Saturday."

"I should make you work for this, Roman."

"Didn't I let you stay with Nikki for two days when I had to go to New York?"

Alex laughed. "Yeah, but you never mentioned that she was a card shark. She took me and the guys for a bundle when we let her sit in our poker game. And she still had her mouth wired. At least Rudy and his merry band brought in a fine catered buffet and Cuban cigars."

"I'll get Borgianno to cater next week and make sure she loses," Roman laughed. "Come on, give, Alex."

"Okay, okay, here's the long and the short of it. Mackey and his partner, Glenn Ennis, were hauling an armored tractor-trailer loaded with an eight thousand pound prize." His voice lowered. "Roman, we're talking nearly five million dollars in gold bars, industrial diamonds and silver that run between three and ninety-seven percent pure."

Cantrell whistled. "The outlets for that are innumerable, just in terms of the jewelry industry."

"Yeah, the metal's very attractive loot. All of it was headed to Arcadia where it was going to be transferred to three smaller armored trucks that would transport it to Attleboro, Massachusetts, which is a major hub of jewelry outlets. At five this morning in a heavy fog, Mackey says they were hijacked by –" Alex's laugh was coarse. "You'll love this one, buddy. Mackey says he was hijacked by the army."

"Whose army?"

"Our army. I don't know any other army that has an M1A1 tank?"

"An M1A1 tank?"

"That's right. And that's not all. Your friend Mackey claims not only was there a tank but there was also a nice crowd of...oh, about sixty masked men wearing camo jumpsuits and carrying a variety of weapons including MAC-10, AR-15's, a bazooka, an M203 grenade launcher, a flame thrower and..." he paused for effect, "my favorite a Stinger."

"A missile launcher?"

"Thought you'd like that one." Alex cleared his throat. "Come on over, bring some decent coffee and a couple dozen donuts. Frankly, I've seen more information on a dog bite. Maybe you can get more out of Mackey and find out what really happened."

"What the hell does Tony say happened?"

"That he stopped the armored car, cooperated and –"

"And? And what?"

"And woke up half an hour later, handcuffed to a drain pipe. The truck, his partner and the five million dollar cargo all missing."

"You don't believe him?"

"Believe him! That he was hijacked by the fucking army? Hell, no. Do you? You know, Roman, I'd believe Mackey more if he'd told me he'd been hijacked by a UFO and a band of fucking Martians!"

Chapter 8

"Well...it was circular and I'd say a good fifty feet across, made of some shiny metal and it glowed red. Didn't make a sound when it hovered over the house and...whoops! There goes the alarm on my new cappuccino maker. Wait until you taste the lattes. I'll be right back, girls."

Nikki winced, as she had at least a dozen times in the eight minutes she'd been in the company of Muriel Feinburg. Muriel was a lot like West Palm Beach. Pink. Neon. Silver. Trash trove. Her plastic surgeon had been heavy-handed leaving her with trout-pout lips, a face that barely moved when she talked and a too obvious butt and boob job. Very theatrical.

As was her large tract house. Nikki's gaze kept wandering from one outrageous piece of decor to another. Stacked stone covered by coquina shells formed the fireplace that was flanked by two four-foot gold Buddha's surrounded by silk palm trees. A leopard skin rug seemed to track Nikki's every movement with its gold glass eyes.

She stifled a laugh at Teresa's mutterings in the oversize hot pink bungee chair surrounded on three sides by enormous silk ferns. "Comfortable Teresa?"

"Bloody uncomfortable. Nikki how are you sitting so perfectly? I can't keep my knees from hitting my chin." Teresa tried shifting forward, but the chair refused to release its hold on her petite body. "Do you believe this place? She must have cornered the stuffed parrot market." Teresa waved her hand. "I've counted nearly two dozen in assorted plumage and sizes tucked in every nook and that's not including the flock of pink flamingos on the front lawn."

"Ahh, Mrs. Feinburg, can I help with that tray?" Nikki stood up watching as her hostess teetered on neon pink stiletto-heeled fringed sandals.

"No, no...sit...sit. I've got it, I live in these things. Make it Muriel. Mrs. Feinburg's my mother-in-law. The bitch." The deeply tanned, leathered skin of her face barely registered a smile. "'Moved down from New York just to get away from her. Betcha couldn't tell, right? Hardly got an accent anymore."

Nikki accepted a glass mug of perfectly layered crème and coffee with no comment about her hostess' diction. "How clever, I see these mugs carry an ad for your beauty salons." She smiled watching Muriel pat her bleached, pink streaked flat-ironed hair that shimmered down to the middle of her back.

"Yeah. Nice, huh?" Muriel shrugged off Teresa's refusal of coffee and resettled in a rattan fan chair. Adjusting her black off-the-shoulder crop top and leopard leggings, she smiled at Nikki. "Love your hair. That's Clairol number?"

"Mother Nature number too much." Nikki opened her notebook. "Now, about that UFO. Let's see, you said there were no sounds. Nothing at all?"

"Not even a hum. Funny, you'dda thought something that big would make a noise."

"Mrs. Feinburg...ah, Muriel." Nikki's smile was innocent. "You weren't drinking that night by any chance, were you?"

"Sweetie, the only thing I drink is coffee, cola and that Frenchie mineral water with plenty of fruit." She batted exaggerated false black lashes, "I'm not into drugs either. I was stone cold sober. Maybe a bit depressed."

"Depressed about what?" Teresa struggled to lean forward.

Muriel turned toward her. "Hugo had been gone about a week."

"Sorry. I hadn't realized you were recently widowed."

"Widowed!" Muriel's ringed fingers slapped against her over-sized breasts. "I'm a very happy divorcee. No, no...Hugo's my dog." She tapped the pink feather framed photo on the coffee table.

"He's a teacup Bichon. I sent him off to a stud farm. Hey, if I can play, he can play."

Muriel winked at a rapidly blinking Teresa Hutton. "So anyways, it was a week ago yesterday that I was lying in my new outdoor Jacuzzi spa, staring up at the stars. Ya know, that's what I thought it was at first, a star, until it began to move. Then I thought it was a plane in trouble, until it came down weaving and bobbing. Then I saw it didn't look like anything we had."

"We?"

Muriel leaned toward Nikki and whispered, "The United States of America. I thought that maybe it was a Russian spy plane. But it wasn't. Not unless they've got something that looks like that planet, the one with the rings—Saturn—and can dance around the skies before it disappeared. Disappeared just like that." She snapped her fingers.

"Did you get any pictures?"

"Miss Holden, who has a camera in a hot tub?"

Score a point for Muriel. Nikki nodded. "About how long did this sighting last?"

"Mmmm...maybe ten minutes."

"Anything else?"

"Like?"

Nikki paused, wondering if her questions might cause Muriel to manufacture events. "Did the power go out?"

"Nope."

"Lights flicker or dim inside the house?"

"No."

"Notice any burn marks on the lawn? On your roof? Did any coral paint peel off the concrete block and stucco?"

"Uh-uh."

Nikki cleared her throat. "Muriel, you didn't receive any type of telepathic message from the UFO by any chance?"

"Good grief, no."

"Well, okay then..." Nikki snapped her notebook shut. "Thank you so much. You've been very straightforward." She stood up. "Would you mind if I looked around outside? Checked your backyard, examined the house, the grounds? It would be very helpful if there was some physical evidence."

"Oh, there will be some soon."

"I beg your pardon?"

"Physical evidence. I mean, a baby is pretty physical."

"Baby?"

Muriel's smile was dreamy as she patted her stomach. "I'm hoping it looks more human than alien."

Nikki sat down. Hard. "An alien baby?"

Muriel nodded, looking very complacent. "I'm sure the commander thought he was the most handsome figure in his silver metallic suit. When he took off his helmet, he did look a lot like that old movie actor, Yul Brynner crossed with a bit of that movie creature, ET. Only he had grey skin and big green glowing eyes. But a wonderful calming smile. They all looked like that. There were six of them. Round heads, no hair, large eyes. Really long, thick fingers."

She shivered. "And did he know how and where to put his fingers to make a woman feel good! I am the adventurous type, sexually I mean. My ex was pure vanilla which was why I dumped him.

"The commander...oh my god...he just climbed into the hot tub, slid his long index finger right up my ass...then...then cupped my pussy and jammed his thumb right up there. Ever so slowly, he worked them both at the same time. I thought I'd died and gone to another planet. I...I just never had so many orgasms at once. He kept increasing the finger thrusts. The hot tub water was bubbling like crazy. I was trying not to shout in pleasure. The neighbors you know. Then I just collapsed in his arms...he had four and made sure I didn't faint into the water. He was very tender afterward.

"That's how they mate. Very different, huh? But effective. That's why they came to earth, to mate. They need to impregnate choice female humans in an effort to continue their own race. That's what one of his soldiers said. His English wasn't perfect but I understood every word. They'd been watching me, thought I was the perfect vessel to birth one of their own even though I'm forty-five."

"Sort of 'Beaming Up Baby'?" Nikki muttered.

"How's that?" Muriel blinked, then continued. "Now, I want to make one thing perfectly clear," she said firmly. "They treated me very politely through the whole thing and nothing was done without my consent. Even the baby."

She rubbed her stomach again. "You'll probably want pictures. The other tabloid said they'd want pictures. Of course, I haven't decided who will get those pictures." Her voice lowered, and one lopsided false eyelash winked involuntarily. "I guess whoever writes the biggest check will get the baby pictures."

"I see." Nikki pushed herself off the chair. "Well, Muriel, you will really have the definitive baby pictures. Teresa, I think we'd better be going. Thank you so much." She literally pulled Teresa free of her webbed chair. "No, Muriel...don't get up. Rest...rest and put up your feet. Can't be too careful now that you're pregnant. Muriel, have you figured out which end the baby will come out? We'll see ourselves out."

Teresa massaged her temples. "I am bloody sorry. The stringer felt Mrs. Feinburg was a reliable, hard-working woman with no...no..."

"Delusions or duplicity?"

"Well, yes...she never mentioned a thing about being pregnant with an alien baby. And...hold on..." she plucked her cellphone out of her purse.

Opening the car door to let the heat escape, Nikki watched a myriad of expressions cross Teresa Hutton's face. "Problem?" When

Teresa hesitated and looked more embarrassed than anything else, Nikki shook her head. "Just. Tell. Me."

Teresa cleared her throat. "Well that was my other stringer on the UFO sightings that we had interviews for in Delray Beach. They weren't UFO's they were UAS's..." at Nikki's arched eyebrow, she added..."Unmanned aircraft systems...err...drones. It seems the FAA and the sheriff's department raided both homes and made some arrests. They found a group of college students had been flying drones equipped with lasers that were being aimed at pilots. In between doing that, they outfitted the drones with 1500 lumen flashlights with adjustable beams from spot to flood that went 800 feet down, so they'd appear to be flying saucers."

"How were they caught?"

"They bragged about it on social media, actually had a *Facebook* group that was pulling the same stunt in numerous cities that were close to major airports. The stupid little arseholes posted *YouTube* videos. That's the way it goes sometimes." Teresa blotted the perspiration off her face with her fingertips. "Onward to that farmer in Belle Glade, he's got proof. He's got the physical evidence you want."

Nikki's eyes narrowed. "Teresa, if that farmer claims he's pregnant, the only ones who really got fucked today are you and me!"

Chapter 9

"You look like ten miles of bad road."

Tony Mackey's brain registered a new voice. "Roman? Roman!" He jumped up, only to be forcefully pressed down into the molded plastic chair by an armed guard.

Cantrell saw relief chased off Tony's perpetually bloated face by fear. "Take it easy, I've got the FBI's approval." His thumb jerked toward a lagging Alex Lazarus. "Besides, that's no way to treat a material witness. A very cooperative material witness." He placed a fresh cup of steaming coffee and a bag on the narrow table in front of Tony. "Apple crullers."

"You remembered."

"Mind like a steel trap. I talked to Ellen and calmed her down. Your neighbor's coming over to make sure she stays off her feet and I sent one of my operatives, Louise Coughlin over to help out as well." He snapped a finger against the white bakery sack. "Go ahead, indulge. And relax."

"Thanks." Mackey stared into the black depths of the coffee. "That seems to have become your first name." Through heavy-framed glasses, his brown eyes concentrated on Cantrell. "You're always there to save my scrawny ass. If you hadn't alerted me to that IED trap in Afghanistan —"

"Everybody was trying to save everybody's ass."

"Don't sound so goddamn modest."

"Don't you sound so goddamn beholden. Eat."

"Yes, sir!"

"Can the salute." Pulling out an extra chair, Roman turned it back to front and straddled it comfortably while Lazarus lounged in the shadows. "They treat you all right? Ellen said something about your being hurt."

71

Extending his arms, his white bandaged wrists showed from underneath the sleeves of his gray uniform. "Lacerations from the handcuffs the hijackers used. Had to shimmy up a ten-foot drain pipe to get free. Damnedest thing.'" He sighed deeply. "I still can't believe what happened."

"I want you to tell me exactly what you told them." Cantrell removed a small notebook and pen from the pocket of his black knit shirt. "Step by step. From the time you woke up. Don't leave anything out, no matter how trivial."

"That's just the point, Roman, nothing peculiar or out of the ordinary happened." Mackey insisted. "This morning was routine. Alarm went off at three A.M. and I was heading for the armored car dispatch forty-five minutes later. "

"Any odd calls to your house or cell the previous day or even last week?"

"Nope. Not even a wrong number." Mackey's fingers splayed through the dark hair that grew thick only at the sides of his face. "And I wasn't followed. I'm damn careful. This job means everything to me, even more so now that a baby's on the way." Abruptly, he raised his voice. "I'm not in debt, or in any trouble, or being threatened, or blackmailed, or...or anything else. That's what these guys think." He nodded toward the guard and Lazarus. "That's the bone they keep gnawing. But, Roman, I swear, I'm clean."

"I never doubted that fact, pal." He squeezed Mackey's forearm. "Okay, so you landed at Hartwell's dispatch at..."

"Mmmm, Glenn Ennis and I were in the armored cab at four sharp. That's when we opened the computer generated route." Mackey squared his shoulders. "That's another thing they don't seem to understand, the drivers don't set their routes or even know the cargo. The computer handles it. We don't know where we're going or how we're to get there until we pop the seal on our instructions. Hell, the computer doesn't even put the package together until one minute before we're ready to roll."

Cantrell nodded toward Lazarus. "I know. I set up the computer system."

Mackey looked over at Lazarus and his voice was taut. "Maybe he'll believe you. Maybe he'll finally believe me when I say for the millionth time that I don't even see the fucking computer. I don't even know what's being hauled!"

"Take it easy. Chill out. Don't let them get to you. They're just doing their job." Cantrell caught sight of Lazarus's wry salute. "Now, you and Ennis got your route instructions..."

"On the dot of four. We were to use Route 27, connect to 29 then take 70 into Arcadia. That was our destination, a transfer point in a secure facility just outside Arcadia. The computer plans it all."

Mackey shrugged, then gave a rueful chuckle. "Frankly, that mechanical brain's done a damn good job. This route was like all the others: clear, dry and radar-free." His gaze slid from Cantrell to the guard and back again. "When you're assigned a three-hundred-mile round-trip run, you get damn thankful for a quiet stretch where you can wail and make time."

"What about breakdowns? Or medical emergencies?"

"The armored cab's equipped with a radio and—" Mackey hunched forward. "See, that's another thing that bugs the hell out of me, Roman. The damn radio was totally useless. Static. Transmitting and receiving, all we got was an earful of shitty static."

"Okay, back up a few miles."

"Yeah." Mackey rubbed his face and grimaced. "I didn't shave this morning, no wonder these guys are treating me like a bum. I look like a damn bum. I sound like a crazy man. I—"

"This isn't a beauty pageant, pal. You got your route and..."

Mackey inhaled noisily. "Right. Nothing strange there. Envelope was sealed as usual and—Hey! When they find the truck, the cops can check on that." He raised his voice again. "Maybe the seal had been tampered with. Hell, I just ripped it open, automatic like, didn't even look. Are they checkin' out the dispatcher? The loaders? The—"

Lazarus's terse "yes" sliced apart Mackey's words.

He sniffled once more, cleared his throat and refocused on Cantrell. "We followed the route instructions to the letter. No problems. At four fifteen in the morning, the few cars we encountered paid no attention to us. We were on the lower end of Lake Okeechobee, went about twenty, twenty-five miles and ran into fog. Fog! Hell, it was more like a...a big, thick cloud that fell from the sky."

"Hold on a sec." Cantrell tapped his notepad. "Fog?"

"I know, I know." Mackey scratched the wide bald spot on his scalp and the confusion in his voice matched the bewilderment in his eyes. "It sounds crazy but it's the damn truth. The fog was there. Boom! Like a curtain had fallen. No misty buildup, no rolling haze. One minute the road was crystal clear and the next, we slammed into an opaque wall.

"Let me tell you, I reacted. Fast. But careful," he quickly added. "I didn't want to jackknife. While I was slowin' down the rig, Glenn was using the radio. Trying to use the radio," he amended. "Like I said before, all we heard was static. Couldn't raise anyone. Just got an earful of garbage. Glenn even tried his cellphone and got a no service message. I remember we looked at each other, said nothing but made damn sure the cab's security system was working better than the radio."

"Was it?"

"Our call panel showed it was."

"What happened next?"

"I kept the truck moving. Crawling, actually. Glenn had the shotgun across his lap and was still fiddling with the radio, we both stared straight out the windshield into the fog. On alert."

"Stay alert. Stay alive."

Mackey nodded vigorously at Cantrell. "Right on. Just like over there." He leaned forward, tapping his index finger on the table top. "That's just the way I felt, too. Pumped up. Waiting. Then the enemy appeared. And...and for a minute I thought—" Suddenly his mouth clamped shut.

"The truth, Tony."

"All right." His abrupt laugh was dry, forced. "Fuck it...I thought they were..." His next word was whispered, "Martians."

"Martians?" Cantrell shook his head, "Did you say Martians?"

"Yeah. Martians. Men from outer space." Mackey twisted around toward Lazarus. "Go ahead, snicker. It's the damn truth. That's exactly what Glenn and I thought they looked like. In fact we both said the word at the same time."

Lazarus pushed out of the shadows and moved to Cantrell's side. "Now this is a new twist in his story...no, his tale of the century. I can't wait to hear this new, improved version." His invitation was sarcastic.

"It's the goddamn truth," Mackey spat. "What stepped out of the fog were six hulking, silver-suited bodies with glowing, goggley eyes. We nearly pissed in our pants." He swallowed hard. "Then, as they surrounded the truck cab, we were able to figure out what they really were."

"Is this where we go from Martians to commandos?" Lazarus asked derisively.

"Well, that's what they proved to be," Tony snapped back. "Their eyes were goggles. Some sort of fancy new high-tech ones that were attached to standard chopper pilot helmets. You remember those helmets, Roman. They're football style with big padded earphones and the tiny boom microphones. You add all that plus the goggles and well, hell, there was no way to see a face."

Lazarus's scornful "How convenient" taunted Cantrell's ear. Massaging his stubbled face and jaw, Roman shifted his eyes from

Mackey's earnest expression to Lazarus. The FBI agent's blond, boyish features were etched in polished granite. His usually affable demeanor had turned equally callous.

Cantrell turned back to Mackey. "You said there were just six of them?"

Mackey nodded. "At first. Two in front and two on either side of the cab. Glenn and I immediately put on masks in case they tried pumping tear gas or another inhalant inside. We watched them. They stared at us. Suddenly, somehow, some way that thick curtain of fog vanished. Vanished just as quick...just as fast as it appeared. That's when we saw the rest of them."

"Now here's where he segues from commandos into an entire army tank battalion." Lazarus crushed the empty bakery bag and proceeded to toss it idly back and forth from hand to hand.

"It was an army battalion, Roman," Mackey rushed on. "I know a fucking M1A1 tank when I see one. Seventy-two tons of precision fire power." Mackey stared at Lazarus with narrowed eyes. "I can take a tank apart. You probably wouldn't know an M1A1 from..." The pressure of Cantrell's hand on his forearm silenced him. "He was there?"

"I was there," Lazarus' voice was hard. "Cantrell and I went through Army Ranger School together. Did more than a few special Ops assignments and some odd jobs for the CIA. Shared deluxe accommodations with Cantrell in Guatemala, nothing like a tent during the rainy season."

"Sorry."

"Ain't we all." Lazarus kept bouncing the paper ball. With each toss the sour expression that contorted his mouth grew more pronounced.

Mackey exhaled sharply before he went on with his story. "Then...then what the hell is your problem? Why don't you believe me? I was staring at that M1A1 tank, with its turret aimed right at our windshield. If that wasn't enough, those sixty army guys were packed. Each had his own weapon. Drawn and aimed.

"Now the armored car would have easily handled a spraying by a Mac10 but not from the tank, or from the bazooka or the grenade launcher, and certainly not the new version of our old Redeye Sams. Those babies are antiaircraft, antitank. They'd blow us off the face of the earth.

"Sure, we had the capability to emit a smokescreen or tear gas, but that wouldn't have put sixty well-armed men out of commission. We could have even taken off on four flat tires at seventy miles an hour, except that damn tank stood in our way.

"I know Glenn. He was thinking about the same things I was." Mackey swallowed hard. "And I was thinking about Ellen, our unborn baby...never knowing if my new baby would make death before dishonor meaningless. So call us cowards but that's why, that's exactly why we opened the cab doors."

"Okay, take it easy. I can understand." Cantrell pushed Nikki's image from his mind. "No one's calling you anything."

"No?" Twisting around in the hard chair, he nodded toward Lazarus. "How about liar? That's what he's thinking. It shows." Mackey turned back to Cantrell. "What about you, Roman? Before I saw concern. Now there's nothing. Your eyes are stones. They trained you well."

Cantrell pushed the untouched cup of coffee toward him. "Take a drink and a deep breath. What happened when you and Ennis got out of the truck?"

Mackey washed the weariness from his face with his hands, letting the last dregs of coffee wet his throat before he spoke. "There's not much left to tell. I don't know what happened to Glenn, but I can tell you what happened to me. Sort of.

"Two of the helmeted men moved on either side of me, threw me against the cab door, patted me down and cleaned the thirty-eight out of my holster. They even found the Swiss Army knife I keep strapped against my calf. Then they turned me around, each holding an arm while this little guy patted my shoulder.

"No one said a word. Even that close I couldn't make out any features. He just kept patting me. I remember feeling dizzy, light-headed. My knees buckled. I remember them saying 'hold on' or something close to that. I was wobbly as hell and then everything went black."

Mackey's lips compressed into a thin line. "I woke up, maybe fifteen or twenty minutes later. I was handcuffed to a standpipe. Nowhere near the road. Took me another dozen minutes to figure things out. I was...disoriented. Confused." His laugh was rueful. "Hell, I even remember I was drooling. Slobbering like a teething baby.

"My brains slowly returned. I shouted for Glenn. Kept shouting, even as I inched my way up the ten-foot pipe and got free. Then I started walking. The sun was lightening the sky. I took a chance and headed east.

"I kept yelling for Glenn, zigzagging through the sugar cane, hoping to spot him. Never did. Seemed like forever to finally strike macadam. When I did, I just kept walking, always on the lookout for Glenn. For the truck. Hell for anything familiar.

"I ran into the police who were out hunting for us. We were long overdue in reporting to dispatch and when they couldn't raise us on the radio or our cellphones, they contacted the authorities. A police doctor bandaged my wrists after the handcuffs were sawed off and I've been sitting here ever since."

Lazarus smiled as Cantrell rubbed the back of his neck. "I told you it was a fantastic story, pal."

"Well, when you find Glenn he can vouch for this fantastic story," Mackey retorted.

"I bet he will. Especially if you two planned this heist. He's probably very busy right now hiding the truck. I'm betting he'll be turning up soon, looking a little worse for wear."

"Jeez, what the hell does it take to get through to you? We are the victims. Why won't you believe me?"

Lazarus ignored Mackey's pleading and circled him like a vulture. "Because your story just doesn't wash. A rogue army unit? The National Guard gone berserk? I'm betting the tank, the weapons, the commandos are all up here." He gave Mackey a hard rap on the back of his head. When Mackey tried to strike back, Lazarus danced out of reach with the finesse of a prizefighter.

"Tony!"

"Hell, he has no right. Roman..." He shifted around, breathing hard. "Roman, you believe me. You've got to believe me."

"The only thing you'd better believe, pal," Lazarus sneered, "is that there's a man and a five million dollar cargo missing."

"Roman, I didn't have a thing to do with it. I don't know about Glenn. But I am clean, man." He gripped Cantrell's hand. "On the life of my unborn baby, I am clean."

Roman stared into Tony's brown eyes for a long moment. "Okay, Tony, let's go back to the beginning. Step by step. I want you to remember every sound. Every smell. Every movement. Every word. One more time."

Chapter 10

"Well?"

"You want to know if I think this guy's for real or a con job."

"Right."

"I believe him. Now you're looking at me as though I'm crazy."

"I'm bloody stunned. Here you sit admitting -"

Nikki held up her index finger. "The only thing I'm admitting is that I believe Farmer Earl."

"So you do think he saw a UFO?"

"Let me qualify my statement," Nikki spoke carefully. "Earl Cordman convinced me that he saw an unidentified flying object hover over his house before landing in his sugarcane field."

"At least you agree that UFOs exist."

"No, Teresa, I agree that unidentified objects that fly exist."

"Bloody hell isn't that what I just said?"

"You're presuming they come from outer space. I'm saying they are objects. They fly. And, at one particular moment, unidentified but will eventually have a logical explanation."

Teresa stared blankly. "You are confusing the bloody hell out of me."

"I must admit I'm a little confused myself," Nikki admitted, "especially after interviewing Muriel Feinburg."

"Let's go back to that one. Alien baby aside, why are you dismissing Muriel's story? Her sighting matched detail for detail the descriptions by fifty others."

"Fifty others? Any of them pregnant? Okay, okay, drop that eyebrow down to its normal height, Teresa. I suspect Muriel jumped on the UFO bandwagon once she found out that tabloids pay for stories. She instigated this interview, obviously loves to be center stage, embellished her supposed close encounter with an alien baby. That, Ms. Hutton, is one of the dangers of checkbook journalism."

"Now look whose bloody eyebrow has arched," Teresa countered, then sighed. "Your point is well taken. Unless, by the by, Muriel does indeed deliver."

"If *that* happens, I'll pick up the tab on the alien baby photos." Nikki reclined the car's bucket seat slightly. "I am sure there's a simple explanation of what Muriel and fifty others witnessed. It could just have been one of those man-made drones dressed up to look like a UFO."

"You sound like the Air Force."

"Please, Teresa, no insults until you know me better." Nikki's smile came easily. "And never insult me on an empty stomach."

"Buggers, almost forgot about unpacking lunch." Teresa twisted around and opened the picnic cooler. "Do you feel what Earl Cordman told us will also end up having a simple explanation?" Teresa handed Nikki a bottle of ice tea and a sandwich wrapped in aluminum foil.

"No, what he saw was completely different and..."

"Illogical?"

She twisted the top on the bottle. "You know, Teresa, I get the feeling *you* don't believe Farmer Earl."

"Truth is, I'm just not really sure." Teresa looked up from her egg salad. "What turned you 'round?"

"A lot of little things." Nikki tore open a bag of potato chips. "How did you find Earl?"

"One of our stringers happened to stop in a local pub...err...bar and heard workers talking about the unusual destruction they found in that field. Beer flowed and, finally, so did Cordman's name. He was a very hard sell for an interview. Not that he accepted any of our monetary offers," she added hastily. "I think what made him speak out were his sons. They kept pushing for him to get an answer to what happened to over half an acre of their valuable crop."

Through the windshield, Nikki focused on a seemingly limitless tract of sugarcane. "He resembles his name and the stalks of sugarcane."

"How's that?"

"Cordman. He's tall, close to seven feet, reed thin but with a surprising strength. You can feel it when he shakes your hand. Watch it in the working muscles in his arms and back. See it in the clear blue of his eyes. His face is as furrowed as his land. Farmer Earl's a cautious man. Very discreet. Very careful, especially with words."

Teresa's eyes widened. "Goodness, he seems to have made quite an impression on you. To me, he came across quite...mmm...frugal. I know sugarcane is extraordinarily profitable but you couldn't prove it by Mr. Cordman. Everything about that man was, well, threadbare. His clothes were at least a decade old. His gray hair was in a fifties buzz cut. And that disgusting baseball cap on his head had to be held together by grease and sweat. His house is total bollocks. In absolutely frightful condition and I'm sure when the next hurricane hits it will be leveled."

"I thought his home was very comfortable, very cozy, full of character. Now, why are you wearing such a disgusted expression?"

"Because my trousers and blouse reek of mothballs. That chair I was sitting in was covered with crocheted antimacassars and doilies that smelled and were yellowed with age. He didn't even have air-conditioning. Just those twenty-year-old ceiling fans that circulated dust and mildew." She sniffed. "I much preferred Muriel Feinburg's melodramatic decor. At least it was modern, air-conditioned and—"

"Antiseptic?"

"Clean." Teresa studied Nikki. "I am puzzled. Cordman, his house, his manner...frankly, the minute we set foot in the door, I just didn't see the man or his surroundings appealing to you."

"Well, he did." She crunched another chip. "You called Cordman frugal. He is with himself. He has one of the few commercial fields not owned by a corporation and not totally machine harvested.

"I guess you failed to notice the housing he'd built for the migrant workers he employs come the October harvest. They weren't typical cardboard-box shacks. Prefab, yes, but they were durable and large enough to hold families. They had solar panels, sewer, water and air conditioning.

"Earl Cordman's no gaffer. He gave a succinct account of the UFO sighting. I must admit it provoked my interest." Nikki pulled her notebook onto her right knee and riffled the pages. "Hmmm, here it is. He said it was right after sunset Monday night. The sky was still pink but clear. He was outside, getting ready to burn trash when some lights caught his eye. Yellow, amber and green. Not red."

She looked up at Teresa. "That's odd, because red is the international color for aircraft beacons. Yellow, amber and green lights in a crooked, moving pattern. Again, no sounds. Although, Cordman hesitated on that point. I caught him muttering something about hearing whispers.

"As the lights moved closer and their speed was picking up, he began to see the shape more clearly. A bent elbow." Nikki grinned. "Your boomerang shape. A good three hundred feet from tip to tip, another fifty or so foot wide. It hung over his house, over him, for maybe five minutes at roughly one hundred feet.

"The object drifted east to the cane fields. Cordman followed cautiously, watched it descend and sit on his sugar stalks for ten minutes. Then it blasted off. No flames. No rumbling. No smoke. Just a sudden burst of speed. Then...gone. Gone except -" she jerked her thumb toward the cane field, "a huge leveling of cane stalks. Leveling. Not burning. In fact, Cordman said the cane was bleached white and lifeless. Twenty-four hours later, a wide swath was brown and shriveled."

Teresa stared out the windshield. "I wonder why they landed in the sugarcane field? Why didn't they make contact with Cordman? He was highly visible."

"For argument's sake, let's say this UFO was controlled by aliens. Perhaps man isn't what they seek."

"Why not, Nikki? We're the most intelligent life force on this planet."

"That, at times, can be quite debatable," came Nikki's wry rejoinder. "Besides humans may not be the single most important thing on the earth, at least from an alien's point of view."

"Are you trying to tell me that sugarcane is? That the aliens have a sweet tooth?"

"I'm telling you that sugarcane produces green renewable energy that replaces nearly two million barrels of fossil fuel a year."

"Yes...but really...I say..." Teresa turned suspicious. "You are pulling my leg with all this rubbish, aren't you?

With a grin, Nikki picked up her crossbody bag and opened the door. "Come on, grab those plastic bags and let's check out the UFO landing site for hard evidence."

Chapter 11

The noon sun hit like a fist when they opened the car doors.

"I don't understand how Earl Cordman can survive without air-conditioning in this inland steam bath," Teresa muttered. "We've only been out here five minutes and my clothes have welded to my skin. I was barmy to wear linen." Despite sunglasses, she shaded her eyes with her hand while squinting at the endless rows of sugarcane. "How far in do we have to go?"

"About a quarter mile."

"Loverly." Teresa licked the salty perspiration from her top lip. "Why couldn't these aliens have landed in a drier, cooler location? Oooh...I should have worn sensible shoes like you. This swampy ooze has managed to creep between the toes of my sandals. This air is not moving." She fanned herself with the plastic bags. "God, what I wouldn't give for an ocean breeze. What are these wretched little bugs swarming all over my head?" She batted at them. "Oh...Lord...did you see that...that snake? Nikki! How can you keep walking in this beastly mess?"

"It's just a non-poisonous king snake." Nikki turned around and handed Teresa a small spray bottle of *Bug Off*. "Here use this."

"Thank you...can't be too careful with this Zika virus." Shielding her eyes, Teresa carefully misted her face, neck and clothes before handing back the sprayer.

"I get the feeling you haven't left the comfort and safety of your desk in quite a while."

"Two years and that was in the relative safety of a concrete jungle." She winced as the wet, rich soil sucked at her shoes. "I thought cane fields were dry."

"They are in October during the harvest, now with all the rain we've had..."

"Good God, this must be like walking through hell."

"No, hell is much worse."

"I say, how's that?" Teresa flailed her arms, staving off insects and creating air currents. "I hope you know where we're going because I am totally lost. The road and car have completely disappeared. All I see are these damn stalks. I don't even use sugar! This should have been a Stevia field. Those plants are just a foot tall. In a planter. No snakes...and...what is that horrible wailing? Nikki? Did you hear that...howling?"

"It's just a bird."

"Are you sure? Maybe it's..."

"A werewolf? Teresa, what a *Scuttlebutt* headline that would be," Nikki peered over the top of her sunglasses and grinned. "Martians versus Werewolf in a Florida sugarcane field."

"That was beneath you." Sniffing, Teresa knocked aside the long narrow leaves that reached out to her. "I can hardly breathe and I'm so hot." Her hands wiped bugs, sweat and hair off her forehead. "Don't you ever complain? Lord, woman, you're not even sweating!" Teresa squinted at Nikki.

"Matt Cortlund calls me his cold-blooded reporter."

"Knowing the way he feels about you, I'm quite sure he meant that in the nicest sense."

Nikki laughed. "He did and I take it as a great compliment. I readily adapt to all conditions and climates. Overnight, I once exchanged sunny Baja California for a frigid expedition to Prudhoe Bay, Alaska. A month later I went from a hurricane in North Carolina to a boron mine in the Mojave Desert."

"I can hear in your voice that you loved every minute of it, too." Teresa sniffled and blew a beetle off her nose. "Sorry about being such a sniveling, whining twit. Hadn't realized how wretchedly spoiled I'd become."

"A desk job will do that to you. Maybe you should get out into the field more."

"As long as it's not a sugarcane field. This has been a very humbling experience for me, in more ways than one."

"What do you mean?"

"Confession time? Well, Nikki, I'd become very envious of more than your writing talent after reading the clippings Cortlund sent. Story after story was filed from a different location. It was exciting reading and, frankly, my daydreams merged with your articles. I thought this excursion into the field would...well, I guess the truth of the matter is I find I'm not the intrepid roving reporter I'd always fancied myself to be," Teresa reluctantly concluded.

"That's because Fleet Street's muck and mire was a paper swamp. This is the real thing especially since we've had so much rain."

Teresa neatened her chignon. She struggled to keep the tears out of her voice when her palms came away from the back of her neck covered in bugs, dirt and sweat. "You are quite right about my journalistic career. All the dirt, so to speak, has been print. Even my early interviews were neat and tidy, done in apartments, houses, occasionally in a pub. That, to me, was field work and...Whoa." She stumbled against Nikki. "What happened? Why did you stop?"

"Because we're here."

"Bloody hell that sounded quite eerie."

Nikki turned sideways and gestured. "This looks eerie." Her arm came up to block Teresa. "Hold on, I want to snap a few shots."

Through the sat phone's camera, Nikki documented a picture of destruction and the sharp contrast between life and death.

Row after furrowed row, the sugarcane grew thick and tall, with a double tier of long narrow leaves springing from solid yellow-green stems. Abruptly, in a fifty-foot-wide swath that stretched horizontally into the distance, the thriving crop had been annihilated. Beyond the razed section, the bamboo-like cane flourished again in healthy, valuable acres.

"What a terribly profound exhale, Nikki."

"I wasn't sure what we were going to find, Teresa. Frankly, I didn't expect this." Nikki quickly sent the photos to the safety of her email and just for good measure another set to her research assistant, Darnie. "Hmmm...look how the ground has changed. Where the cane grows, the loam is dark and rich with moisture and nutrients." Nikki crouched and poked into the dirt. "Here the topsoil is a burnt ocher crust that crumbles." Her fingers splintered an arid mass.

"I say, should you be touching that stuff?"

"Why?"

"Cordman said his field hadn't been burned and I've asked myself what else could have caused such a bleaching of crops."

"What answer did you come up with?" Nikki filled two plastic bags with the iron red earth.

"Radiation. It could still be hot and you could be getting bombarded by all sorts of rays and...what is that you're holding up?"

"A radiation badge. I clipped it on my purse this morning and so far no color change. This area, as well as Muriel Feinburg's house, is perfectly safe."

Teresa's lips twisted into a moue. "You do think of everything."

"We intrepid types are always prepared." Nikki grinned. "Come on...you can let your toes dry off on this desert pavement while you load up a couple more plastic bags. Take soil samples from the live cane, too. I want at least three independent labs testing our findings."

Teresa nodded. "*Scuttlebutt* has one on retainer."

"I'm sure you do. I'll find two labs of my own choosing." Nikki answered smoothly. "I'm no geologist, but even I can see the dissimilarity in what should be the same soil." Picking up a handful of wasted cane, she slowly walked along a devastated row, searching. A few yards away, she was back on her knees examining the ground. "Here's something else."

"More?" Teresa scrambled upright and hurried to join the photo-taking redhead. "What is that?"

Taking a pen from her purse, Nikki pushed it into the narrow displacement and pressed down on the cap. The pen quickly vanished into the earth. "A fault line. It appears the entire ground structure shifted. I'd be interested to know how deep this goes."

"Let's try for a more accurate measure." She aimed her laser measuring app and the sat phone's camera into the crevice. "Wow...it's over ninety feet. I'm emailing this and the measurements to the cloud for safety. I'm going to keep on this trail. Teresa, go back to where you were and head east. See if you find a fault line at that end. Or anything else out of the ordinary."

"This entire thing is bloody extraordinary," Teresa muttered, carefully searching her way along the withered track. She spied a blue-gray mass of stone that proved quite heavy as her fingernail cautiously urged it into a plastic bag. A dozen steps later, a cluster of small, irregularly shaped weighty silver-white pebbles were added to her specimen collection. Despite close observation, Teresa was unable to find any ground fissures in her section. She did assemble five more bags of unusual nuggets before reaching the end.

Using the shirt tail of her brown linen blouse, Teresa cleansed an insect-riddled sweaty film from her face. "Quite a haul," she murmured with satisfaction. "Maybe I am the intrepid sort, after all." Examining her valuable evidence, she preened with achievement. "Wait until you see what I've discovered, Nikki!" Turning, she was startled to find she was very much alone. "Nikki! Nikki!"

Her shouts increased in volume as she ran back along the ruined cane path. "Nikki, where are you? Nikki, can you hear me?" Gasping for breath, she searched for a pennant of copper hair or a flash of Nikki's yellow and blue scarf-belt amid the towering sugarcane stalks. "Nikki!" She screamed. "Bloody hell...I'm lost...I...I'm...scared...oh, my God...there's more snakes...a nest of vipers. Nikki! Nikki!"

"Calm down, Teresa, you're only about twenty feet from me around that bend."

"I'm quite all right. Honest...just went a bit barmy for a minute." Teresa pulled free the other side of her blouse to wipe her eyes. She straightened her clothes and tried not to gulp so much air. "Just very anxious to show you my swag. I didn't discover any ground cracks but I've accumulated the most fascinating assortment of odd pebbles. Did you find something?"

"Oh, you could say that."

"Bigger than pebbles?"

"Much bigger. Teresa just...please...wait."

"I'm fine...really...all under control." Teresa quickened her pace. "Ah, here you are. My goodness, Nikki, the expression on your face. I say, you've found something of great scientific significance, haven't you? Well, what is it? Part of a UFO? An actual alien? Don't be so mysterious. Move just a bit so I can take a look..." Teresa peered over Nikki's shoulder. "Oh, bloody hell!"

"Bloody hell is right." With a sigh, Nikki unclipped her sat phone from her bag and pressed the red emergency button. "Fuck, now I've got two bodies to deal with."

Chapter 12

"That's the fourth time in the last thirty minutes your G-man buddy's left the room." Tony Mackey's gaze traveled from the slowly closing door to Roman Cantrell. "What do you think's going on?"

"Maybe the lunch I had sent in didn't agree with Alex."

Mackey's responding smile was weak. "It agreed with me. Thanks."

"We all needed nourishment."

"I know I did." As Mackey rubbed his jaw, short, sharp whiskers rasped his palm. "I could use a shower and a shave and a chance to personally talk to my wife. Are you sure she's okay?"

"Doing just fine," Cantrell repeated. "I talked with my operative. Louise said Ellen had eaten a good lunch, downed two cups of warm milk and fallen asleep. Maybe you should pick up another half-gallon of moo juice on your way home."

"Home..." Mackey exhaled heavily. "That's where I'd like to be right this minute. I'd like to roll off our living room sofa, hit the rug and find this was all a nightmare. I want to feel Ellen's arms around me and hear her teasing laugh.

"She's got the sweetest smile. A little girl's smile." His lips curved. "We decided not to find out the sex of the baby. I'm hoping for a girl, Roman, one with a smile just like Ellen's. I don't know that baby's got quite a punch. Could be a little boxer. A son. My son. I won't let him make the same mistakes I did. A new life is a miracle. We just finished those Lamaze childbirth classes and..."

Cantrell's attention wandered from Mackey's litany on Lamaze to focus on the new life that had enhanced his own-Nikki Holden. She had survived a brutal beating by her mother that had made it impossible for her to ever have children.

Nikki had once told him he deserved someone brand new. Someone who could give him a family. Someone who knew how to make a real home. Yet, he never felt the loser. He wouldn't be unless she left.

When Mackey's glasses clattered on the table, Cantrell was assailed by a pair of defenseless brown eyes and a dejected voice. "This probably sounds crazy, but sometimes I think that Ellen, the baby, the job, the house, all of it, isn't real. It's just a dream and I'm going to wake up and be back in prison. Or worse, be back in Afghanistan."

Mackey wiped his eyes. "You know, Roman, what I went through today brought back strong visions of the war. Everything was nice and normal one minute, then I was pumped up and hyper-alert the next. There I was facing an enemy that melted out of the fog and I had no place safe to run.

"I come here expecting help and what do I get? Frustration. I go over and over and over the same ground and know I haven't gained an inch. Now? Now, everything's quiet, relaxed, boring." He gnawed his lower lip. "What's your best guess about how much longer they can hold me?"

Cantrell rubbed his temples, hoping his fingers would erase his own invading memories. "I think it's time we pushed. You've been cooperative."

"Damn cooperative!'" Thrusting the heavy frames back on the bridge of his nose, Mackey shifted his gaze to the ever-silent guard in the far comer. "It seems to me that they're the ones breaking the law. This is hardly a righteous call. Here I am, the victim, being treated like a crook."

"Calm down, Tony." Cantrell had witnessed Mackey's cocky attitude transformations before and was never quite sure what had been the catalyst. Today, it could have been the fortification from food, worries about his wife, images of the war, or fear. Cantrell had a hunch it was a compilation of everything. "Now look, Tony..."

"No. Now hear me out." His voice was loud and clear. "I think I did score some points. More than once, I offered to take a polygraph test. They fail to understand that Glenn and I didn't even know what our cargo was. Hell, it could have been turbine parts or electronic components or scrap metal for all we knew. Plus, as drivers, we did not have the code to get into the cargo hold.

"Thank you for pointing out to your friend Lazarus that military weapons are on the streets. Drug dealers and gangs are armed with Uzis and Mac-10's and you can buy a flame thrower on the internet. Doesn't your G-man friend read the news? In under thirty minutes anyone can own an AR15 assault rifle. "

"But not a tank." Mackey jumped up to face Alex Lazarus. "Or as you so succinctly pointed out, an M1A1 Tank," Lazarus continued. "A tank that left no tread marks. Nor did any of your sixty Martian-looking, commando army unit leave souvenirs. No footprints, no cigarette butts, not even a wad of chewing gum." He balanced on the balls of his feet. "We've fine-combed that entire area. Your hijackers proved to be a neat, tidy bunch."

"Damn it to hell, isn't the truth enough for you?" Mackey pleaded. "Everything I've said happened. When you find Glenn—"

"Glenn Ennis was located about two hours ago."

"Well, that's great!" Mackey sighed. "Now he can tell you."

Cantrell pushed up from his chair, his keen eyes never leaving Lazarus's expressionless face. "Alex, what is it?"

"Would you like to see him?" Lazarus asked Mackey.

"Of course."

Lazarus walked over to the table, his right hand reaching into the pocket of his gray suit jacket. "Here's your partner." He snapped down four glossy black-and-white photos. "He's not in a position to talk."

"Oh...my...God..." Mackey's hands shook as he lifted a close-up photo. "How—"

"You're so good at giving detailed descriptions of other ammo, I'm surprised you don't recognize your own gun."

Mackey dropped the photograph. "Wait a minute. You don't think I shot him?"

"Our lab boys have been working very hard and very fast. It's your thirty-eight with only your prints."

"But...but..." Mackey rumpled his hair. "They took my gun."

"The hijackers?"

"Yeah. They did something to me. Remember? I told you about my shoulder and then fainting and—"

"Strange, but the doctor who checked you didn't find any needle or dart marks. No knockout drops or other drugs were in your system. Hell, you didn't even have an insect bite on your body."

"I didn't kill Glenn. Hell, I was handcuffed." He extended his bandaged wrists. "The police found me stumbling out of the swamp. I didn't have the time -"

"So you say. But you'll have time, lots of time, to create another hijacking story. Or maybe you'll play it smart and really tell the truth. How you and Ennis hijacked yourselves, hid the truck and then greed set in. One thief killed the other. You know the drill, Mackey." Lazarus snapped his fingers for the guard. "Read him his rights and —"

"Hold on, Alex." Cantrell stepped between Mackey and the guard. "All you've got are paper-thin conjectures. Why not give him that polygraph test he offered to take?"

"Because too many people can fool the machine. Besides, if the courts don't consider their findings admissible, why should I?"

Cantrell faced Mackey. "Did you fire your gun today?"

"No."

"A gunshot residue test will prove that," Cantrell challenged Lazarus.

"Not after the doctor sterilized his hands and arms when they treated his wrists." Lazarus held up a hand to stop Cantrell's next suggestion. "Checking his uniform would be equally useless. It was soaked from his so-called exploits in the swamp."

"Have you checked out Hartwell's other employees? Loaders? Radio dispatcher?"

"We're working on 'em, Roman. As for today's hijacking, they're all clean. None of them were in the vicinity."

"That doesn't mean they couldn't have engineered the whole thing."

"Which is exactly what your friend here did. Like I said before: thick as thieves until the haul and then Mackey whacked Glenn Ennis."

"Since when are you so arrogant you think only you have all the answers?" Cantrell watched the angry workings of his best friend's facial muscles.

"Take Mackey on an extended tour of the new men's room," Lazarus ordered the guard. He paced off the interrogation room a dozen times before he finally spoke. "Roman, what's the deal with you and this guy?"

"He's a good friend. Murder is not in his wheelhouse."

"Mackey's got a record."

"And our mercenary days in Africa got us the *Good Housekeeping Seal of Approval*?"

"We were running food and medical supplies."

"You conveniently forget about the guns and helping train those guerilla units before you came home. As for Tony's arrest record just once. He was eighteen and he did his time. Alex, think of the rap sheet I'd have if the details of my ten years in Central America were ever enumerated."

Lazarus's hand brushed through his military-cut blond hair. "Do you really believe his story?"

"I find it interesting that nine tons of army weapons were confiscated from a Miami drug dealer just three months ago."

"It's only interesting to you."

"Damn it, Alex, you know very well that high-tech military equipment is available to anyone who's got money. Drug dealers. Survivalists. Terrorists."

"And you want to add hijackers?"

"Why not?"

Lazarus shrugged. "No reason not to. But, Roman, it's not the weapons I disbelieve. It's the damn tank." As the silence stretched, he smiled. "No comment, pal?"

"The only one I can come up with is why would Tony invent the tank? Hell, I sure would have left it at a band of well-armed hijackers and not added such a preposterous finale. Of course, there have been a few other preposterous events. Like that Tomahawk missile that went astray and hit Walton Beach, or all that Soviet ammo that washed ashore from Coral Cove to Jupiter Inlet."

Lazarus yawned. "Two in a billion."

"The tank isn't?" Cantrell shoved his balled fists into his pants pockets. "You said you were checking on the other employees."

"Yup. Nothing remotely suspect so far."

"Say, where's Ed Hartwell? Cooling his heels in another room?"

The agent shook his head. "He just might prove interesting."

"Give."

"According to the misses, he's out of town. Odd thing, though. She wasn't able to get ahold of him when she called either his cell or his hotel room at seven this morning."

"How far out of town is he?"

"Atlanta."

"Could be a lot of things, Alex, from his cell being turned off, to him being in the shower, to an early breakfast meeting to the clerk ringing the wrong room."

Lazarus settled in a chair. "Talk to me about Hartwell."

"He was one of my first clients when I opened up shop here. His thirteen year old son, Randy was having problems with his parent's divorce, turned to booze, moved on to hash, was constantly stoned and on a complete downhill slide. Between troubles at home and at school, Randy split. Hartwell called me and I tracked the boy to Hollywood. Got him before the pimps were able to do more than buy him food and clothes."

Cantrell sat down across from Lazarus. "The Hartwell's tabled their divorce, turned their attention back to Randy and enrolled him in a private hospital rehab program. Things began to turn around for everyone, including husband and wife. They got back together.

"A couple years ago, Ed called and wanted to know if I could install one of the new computer security systems. His armored services operation was expanding. I went in and did the job. He was hiring and I introduced him to Tony. I picked up the tab on Tony's training program; Hartwell cut through the bonding maze with his personal backing. It proved to be a good marriage."

"Until today," Lazarus countered.

Cantrell massaged the kinks from his neck. "Back to that are we?" He pulled the photographs of Glenn Ennis closer. "What about him?"

"Ennis? He was forty-two, six feet and hefty. He topped two hundred fifty on the scales. Family man, wife, three kids, big mortgage. This was a second job for him and only his third trip out. The other two were also with Mackey. And before you ask," Lazarus added, "we are checking Ennis's background. It's a little difficult trying to talk to the widow right now—"

Cantrell waved him silent. Fingers drumming an abstract beat, he studied the photographs. "Where was Ennis found?"

"In Belle Glade."

He frowned. "But they were hijacked on the way to Arcadia."

"About fifty miles on back roads. It's certainly not unusual for bodies to be dumped some distance from the actual crime. The ME should be phoning in his preliminary autopsy soon. There's really no doubt that this..." his forefinger tapped the close-up snapshot of the gun, "put that bullet hole in his chest."

"Did you ever think the person who found him could have destroyed or tampered with valuable evidence?"

"No, they didn't. Actually, we were lucky. Care was taken, what little evidence was preserved and these excellent photos were turned over to us. Say, I bet you'd like to interview the person who found Glenn Ennis's body." He stood up. "I'll be right back."

As Cantrell stared at the pictures, Tony Mackey's voice echoed in his mind. Hijackings weren't out of the ordinary. Neither was a band of well-armed, well-shielded commando types. But then there was that tank. "That goddamn tank."

"Talking to yourself is the first sign of madness, Cantrell."

Chapter 13

"Nikki!"

"Brilliant deduction." She saluted him with her soda bottle. "I thought you were spending the day in bed with old movies."

"I thought you were out hunting little green men."

"Found a dead one instead."

"You?" Cantrell leveled a cold stare at Lazarus. "Alex, why in hell did you keep her..."

"Don't blame him. I've been enjoying private time with Agent Hurley. A very informative man."

Lazarus arched an inquisitive brow. "Ted is nicknamed 'the clam.' That's the reason I picked him to entertain you."

"I'm quite a clam opener." Her smile was very slow and very satisfied. "Agent Ted Hurley is the proverbial chatterbox."

"I beg your pardon?"

"Never underestimate the power of cleavage, Alex. I just unhooked the top three buttons on my blouse, bent slightly forward and deep-breathed a lot. Using curves to get all the angles never fails. Between gasps your clam spoke volumes." She flipped up the ends of Lazarus's muted striped tie. "How's that, Alex? You're babbling."

"Ted is gay that's why I put him in with you."

"He's bi, we're having lunch next week."

"Excuse me a moment." He disappeared out the door.

Roman smiled. "You shocked the poor boy."

Nikki shrugged. "It's that bureaucratic wardrobe the government forces on Alex. He thinks everyone else is equally dull and uninventive."

"A major mistake in your case."

"Too true, Cantrell." She sauntered to his side. "Say, my photos look great, don't they? So crisp and clear you can pick those bugs right off that body."

"You all right?" His hand covered hers. "This was not a pretty sight."

"Hell, I've looked worse alive after a beating than Ennis does dead. Teresa didn't fare too well."

"Where is she now?"

"After the EMT's checked her out, she's safely resting in her air-conditioned home." Nikki settled in a chair. "Teresa tried hard but she's definitely a desk jockey. In fact she said she wasn't leaving her desk ever again." Her laugh was brief. "When she first saw Ennis, she fainted. I got her back on her feet and pointed her toward the car. She insisted on another look. She kept mumbling something about supervising the printing of a tabloid photo of some celebrity in a casket. One more look had her throwing up and blacking out." Nikki tapped a photo. "I think Teresa was hoping that he'd been shot by a cosmic ray gun. He wasn't." Nikki's smile was sly. "How long have you known Ennis?"

"Never met the man except through your photos." Roman studied her for a long moment. "See anything you didn't share?"

"Would I do that?"

"Yes."

"Cantrell, I'm dealing with those of the federal persuasion."

He released the bottle from her hand and drained the soda. "Now we can dance around for a while or you can play it straight."

Nikki made a face. "I emailed other photos to the cloud and Darnie. Nothing else remotely relates to your hijacking case. I'll be glad to share when we get home."

"I'll hold you to that." He grinned. "Don't worry, the government will believe you. You haven't lost your touch when it comes to lying."

She grinned back. "So, you don't know Ennis?"

Roman shook his head.

"Then it's that driver...ummm...Mackey. I know they're holding him." Nikki leaned forward. "Come on. Give. Let's discuss the bust."

"It seems to me your bust has been discussed enough." Roman re-buttoned her blouse. "I know I went over it pretty thoroughly last night, then there was Agent Hurley's free peek and we wouldn't want poor deprived Alex to get a hard-on for no reason. Hey, if you want more..." He stroked the swell of her cleavage with one finger. "I'm up for an instant replay."

She slapped his hand. "Don't hold your breath."

He laughed. "What were you doing in a sugarcane field in Belle Glade anyway?"

Nikki pushed the photo at him. "See this dead area? It runs close to three hundred feet on a curve and fifty feet wide. All profitable cane until a UFO used it as a parking lot." She chucked Roman under the chin. "How about it, Alex? Is this the same expression you wore when you heard about the M1A1 tank?"

"It is and I see you really did get Hurley to talk."

She turned to face Lazarus. "One way or another, Alex, I get everybody to talk."

"How did you know I was in here? I move pretty quiet."

"Sixth sense."

Roman exhaled an exaggerated sigh. "I thought you reserved that for me?"

"My radar never shuts down. So, boys, have you found the five million dollar cargo yet? That armored tractor-trailer wasn't hiding among the sugarcane."

Alex swore under his breath as he advanced toward her. "Nikki, you've got to keep this quiet. Roman..."

"Don't look toward me, pal. Even a wired jaw couldn't keep her completely shut up."

"Flattery, flattery." Nikki shook back her copper hair. "Relax, Alex. I take in a lot of information that never gets printed." She patted his cheek. "While this hijacking is intriguing, I'm involved in a story with global significance." She winked at Roman. "Of course, if more tank hijackings occur..."

"You'll be the second person I call," Alex promised.

"The first being?"

He straddled a chair. "A psychiatrist."

"Don't close the book on the well-armed commando unit," she continued knowledgeably, ignoring his wince. "I did a story last year about six hundred incidents of weapons and ammunition thefts from the army.

"We're talking hundreds of millions of dollars in ammunition, weapons and military gear that's stolen annually from army and marine bases. One million dollars in combat gear was stolen from Camp Pendleton, nineteen thousand pounds of explosives was heisted by an army reservist in Texas and at Fort Bragg...well, I think they've given up."

She leaned forward. "In one case, an army noncom stole a military truck, backed up to the supply depot, loaded it with fifty grand worth of light antitank rockets, Claymore mines, hand grenades, C-4 plastique and drove, sweet as you please, right off the base and sold it to a white supremacy group.

"The market for anything pilfered from the army is enormous and they're lousy at bean-counting. Their massive supply system is so flawed that any level of computer literacy can gain access to the system. Soldiers and others can walk away from any installation virtually unchallenged. They're just waved out the front gate. They sell it to drug cartels, neo-Nazis and other extremists who use mainstream issues as fronts for a thin veneer of respectability."

Alex turned to Roman. "Did you tell her to say all that?"

"No, but we both know it's a fact."

"Of course, there is that tank," she added. "I've heard of jeeps being smuggled out piece by piece. I once interviewed a motor pool staff sergeant who claimed he ate his favorite cycle so he could bring it home. An M1A1 tank...that's a bit hard to digest."

"You told her to say that," Roman accused Alex.

"No, but we both know that, too, is a fact," Alex parroted.

"Then there's means and opportunity," Nikki continued. "The computer-generated route was done a minute before Mackey and Ennis left the loading dock with their extremely valuable cargo."

"The drivers didn't know what they were hauling nor did they know the security code for the cargo." Roman reminded them.

"Maybe they didn't have the code but there's always a way to break into the armored trailer," Alex countered.

"Plus they had the opportunity to hijack themselves along that lonely stretch of road," Nikki added. "In fact, they could have easily used a burner cell to contact the rest of their gang."

"How thoughtful of you to create a gang," Roman muttered.

"That was Mackey's MO before," Alex reminded him. "He boosted cars for a chop-shop ring."

Nikki nodded. "That's what Agent Hurley told me."

"Could you imagine what Hurley might have told Dolly Parton?" Roman rubbed his forehead. "I vote we send Hurley to Guam."

"DC is much worse and fuck we all thought Hurley was gay," Alex muttered.

Nikki polished her fingernails against her cleavage. "I defy gender classification."

Alex held up his hands. "Face it Roman, you're backing a dead horse when it comes to Tony Mackey. Pardon me, I should have said killer." His finger flicked the nearby crime scene photo of Ennis' body.

"Still, I wonder why he invented the tank." Nikki shook her head. "I would have left it at the very plausible commando unit."

Alex patted her arm. "No accounting for intellect."

"Be interesting to find out if the government ever sold any tanks to..."

"They sell them all the time, Nikki," Alex interrupted, "to Iraq, Egypt, Saudi Arabia, Kuwait and Australia. Hell, I don't know why I'm wasting any more time on this." He stood up. "Sorry Roman, I'm booking Mackey for the murder of Glenn Ennis. If you know a good lawyer, I'd – "A sharp rap on the door silenced him.

"Thanks for your help," Roman groused to Nikki when Alex walked across the room. "I've been trying to prove that everything against Mackey is circumstantial."

"Might have been easier if he hadn't insisted about the tank."

"Please, that word must be on a leash, it keeps following me around."

Nikki laughed. "Frankly, it falls into the same category as my first UFO interview did this morning. Mmm...maybe I should amend category to crackpot." She rubbed the soreness in her jaw. "Say, your friend Mackey isn't into pharmaceuticals, is he?"

Roman stood up and faced her straight on. "Nik, he says he's clean in all areas and I believe him. Tony's finally got everything he's ever wanted. He's devoted to his wife, there's a baby on the way and he loves his job. He just wouldn't jeopardize all that by..."

"Heisting five million bucks?" Her tongue clicked. "That sacred-a-sum corrupts even the most pious."

"*I* believe him. Tony is innocent."

"So *you* keep repeating. Shall I have that cast in bronze or carved in granite?"

"Whichever is more expensive."

"I get the impression that you're expecting me to agree." Her eyes narrowed into icy slits. "Just because I share your bed doesn't automatically mean I'll cast my vote for your point of view. The world according to Roman Cantrell is *your* world, not mine. I happen to side with Alex."

"Christ, you two are opening the guy's palms and nailing him to a cross."

"He's no sacrificial victim, Cantrell," she argued. "Your personal feelings are compromising your judgment. Mackey's got more negatives than positives. The biggest being he shot Glenn Ennis. Maybe *you* just don't want to see him as a killer."

Alex Lazarus' booming, "The hell he says!" had them both turning toward the door. They watched Alex grab a file folder from a scurrying clerk.

"I think the proverbial shit just hit the fan." Roman turned from Nikki to Alex. "Problem?"

"Only for me." Alex exhaled sharply. "Take Mackey and get the hell out of here."

"You've found the truck and the real hijackers?"

"I found that Glenn Ennis was already dead when he was shot with Mackey's gun."

Nikki whistled. "No kidding."

"How'd he die, Alex?"

"It wasn't from a bullet," Alex repeated, tossing the folder on the table. "That's the preliminary results of the autopsy. The ME thinks heart attack because there was no hemorrhaging around the wound. His early tests indicate that Ennis was shot after we'd taken Mackey into custody.

"Don't keep that smile on your face too long, Roman." Alex's voice was thin and tight. "Mackey's not off the hook yet. I still think he organized and planned this whole deal and I'll damn well prove it."

"Than we'll be on opposite sides," Cantrell stood eye-to-eye with his friend. "Because I'll be working damn hard to find the real hijackers."

"I wish somebody would work damn hard at providing me with dinner. My lunch left a lot to be desired." Nikki patted her growling stomach. "Cantrell promised to grill steaks. Join us, Alex."

"Maybe he'd like his raw, Nik."

"Medium rare will be just fine." Alex shook the tension from his head. "I'll get Mackey for you. Just remember, Roman..." He paused at the door. "I'm only letting him walk temporarily. You're his appointed guardian. The guy doesn't leave the county."

"Alex's right," Nikki shouldered her purse. "You really should wipe that smug smile off your face."

His arm slid comfortably around her slender waist. "Didn't the ME's report alter your opinion of Tony Mackey?"

"You can choose to believe him and his crazy tank story. I am not convinced. While he may not have pulled the trigger on Ennis, that doesn't mean he didn't coordinate the hijacking. It's right up his alley." She edged into the hallway. "Mackey's got a police record for working with a chop-shop gang and boosting cars."

"So he's presumed guilty because of his past? Hell, Nik, *you've* got a police record for boosting cars."

"That's a low blow, Cantrell."

He bent his head slightly and with his lips at her ear whispered, "No, a low blow is what I hoped you'd give me tonight."

"The only thing you're getting tonight is your mouth washed out with soap."

"I've got something else you might enjoy washing and I'm certainly up for experiencing more of your crude but effective wiles."

Nikki took a step away from the husky voice that tickled more than her ear. "Christ, Cantrell, sometimes you can act like such a...such a..." She glared into his grinning face, "Man."

A commotion in an intersecting hallway drew their attention. "Just remember what I said Mackey," Alex's deep voice ordered. "Don't leave the county. You're not clear of this yet."

"That's harassment, Mister G-man," Mackey taunted with cocky superiority. "Pure harassment. The law says I'm innocent and you can't prove me guilty and that just sticks in your craw, you bastard. The way I was fucked around—"

"Tony..." Roman's hand settled heavily on his friend's shoulder. "Come on. I'll drive you home. We can stop and pick up some flowers for Ellen and some milk. Didn't she say she needed more milk?"

Mackey pushed his heavy framed glasses up and pinched his nose. "Right. Ellen. Yeah, milk." He pulled off the FBI visitor badge, spat on it and threw it on the floor. "Let's get the hell out of here, Roman."

Cantrell's hand went up to ward off Alex's determined response. It was Nikki's dulcet tones that quelled the tension. "Alex, you lucky guy." Wrapping strong hands around his well-muscled forearm, she turned him in the opposite direction. "You get to drive me back to the house in your new agency car.

"Now don't tell me, let me guess. I bet it matches your suit. Gray. Right? Wasn't too hard to figure," she chattered glibly, pulling him out the rear office door. "See, your backlot is filled with new gray sedans. Oh...wait there are a few black Chevy's and, be still my heart, even a couple SUVs."

Nikki held up his car keys, ignoring his "how in hell" and pressed the remote entry button. "Ahhh...there she is, right up front, blinking at us." Guiding him to the driver's side, she opened the door, pushed his head down and deftly shoved him onto the seat.

"You know, Alex, there's a vicious rumor going around that the government really buys red sports cars, then does a complete auto-lobotomy on them." Nikki yanked the shoulder harness across his broad chest, pressing against him to lock it into position. "Inquiring minds." Her right eye executed an outrageous wink.

Chapter 14

Alex was still grinding his teeth when she settled in the bucket seat beside him. "No inquiring minds, Nikki," he warned her, starting the car. "No questions on the hijacking. No questions on the cargo. No questions on the autopsy. And if you mention the word tank—"

"The way you're strangling that steering wheel? I wouldn't dare." She adjusted the air conditioning vents before relaxing against the headrest. "Besides, Alex, I'm already hard at work on a story of global significance."

"Global significance? A sugarcane crop?"

"Not the crop. What destroyed part of it."

"I can't believe Matt's got you doing a feature on pest control." Nikki's husky laugh eased away the last of his anger and lightened his mood. But when she said "Oh, Alex" in that sultry timbre, his tension returned.

It was a pleasurable tension.

Too much so.

Easily ignited.

Difficult to dismiss.

Alex kept reminding himself that she now belonged in his best friend's life. Belonged? No, Nikki would never belong to anyone but herself. He could tell Roman knew that, too.

That was why, on occasion, Alex allowed his feelings and his imagination latitude. His eyes shifted from the stalled traffic to stare at Nikki. More than her copper-gold hair and chameleon eyes made her distinctive and vital. He'd been impressed and intrigued with her from the instant they'd met. Nikki Holden uniquely blended the talents of a consummate con artist and liar with charm, delivering both with the provocative punch of wholesome sexiness.

A smile curved his lips as he remembered her warning. "One way or another, Alex, I get everybody to talk." And she did. He really couldn't blame Ted Hurley for giving her information. She fooled the best.

Himself included.

And his father. Jake Lazarus had been the circuit court judge in Saratoga that Nikki had inveigled to keep sending her to juvenile detention centers. For her, a cell and a matron were safer than home and her mother.

"Alex, the traffic light's gone from green to red to green again."

"Right." Hand brushing through his hair, Alex laughed with embarrassment and returned to the business of driving. "So, what kind of pest did you find in the sugar field?"

"The exact same pest J. Edgar Hoover noted in a top secret FBI memo." Her head jerked sharply when his foot smashed the brake pedal. "Jeez, Alex, I just got out of a neck brace!"

"Damn! Nikki, I'm sorry." He grasped her forearm. "Are you..."

"Fine." She squeezed his fingers. "The car behind us, however, is bleating a nasty comment about your driving ability."

"My driving ability is a direct result of your comment." He stepped on the gas. "Now what's all this about a Hoover memo?"

"Since you asked..." She unzipped her bag and pulled out a slim notebook. "Let's see...here it is. The year was 1950 and the Air Force recovered three flying saucers that crashed in New Mexico. Aboard were three bodies that were humanoid but only three feet tall."

She ignored his incoherent mutterings and continued. "According to Hoover's memo, the saucers were circular with raised centers, approximately fifty feet in diameter. The small bodies were dressed in, and I quote, 'metallic cloth of a very fine texture.' Each was, quote, 'bandaged in a manner similar to blackout suits used by speed flyers and test pilots.' The crash was blamed on, again I quote, 'very high-powered radar set up in New Mexico,' that could have interfered with the controlling mechanism of the three saucers. The White Sands Missile Range is there."

"Where did you get this memo?"

Nikki smiled. "Alex, the Freedom of Information Act is the Fourth Estate's greatest gold mine. This is one of thousands of now declassified government documents that prove the existence of UFOs."

"Shit."

"Of course, the memo doesn't say what Hoover did with the alien bodies or the saucers."

He turned his head. "Hey, wait just a damn minute, Nikki. If you think you can get me to check into such an asinine, obviously phony memo—"

"Alex, it's a proven fact that UFO sightings increased after World War Two with the birth of the nuclear age. I can show you copies of numerous other government documents that refer to UFOs repeatedly nosing around nuke labs and ICBM sites and frequent aerial interceptions of UFOs by military jet aircraft. Probably one of the biggest draws for them in New Mexico is the Manzano Mountain nuclear weapons storage base. Then there's this." She quickly flipped through her note pages. "A 1977 article in *U.S. News and World Report* speculated that then President Carter was expected to make, quote," 'unsettling disclosures' about UFOs based on CIA data."

"Well, you should have said that in the first place," Alex smiled.

"What?" The word was laced with suspicion.

"CIA. Completely different agency. Completely different focus. I've got a man for you."

His twinkling blue eyes and affable expression made her shake her head. "No, thanks, Alex. I can get my own man."

"I'll say prayers for him."

"Very funny."

"Come on, Nikki, this whole schmear is a joke, right? You? Matt Cortland? UFOs? I can't even think of a publication Matt owns that would print such garbage."

"*Scuttlebutt.*"

"No? Really?"

"Pure profit."

Alex nodded. "That'll do it. What about you?"

She arched her brow. "What about me, Alex?"

Her tone made him shift uncomfortably. He blundered on. "Is that your story of 'global significance'? What the hell has it got to do with a sugarcane field? I can't get you information, Nikki, if I don't have more facts."

Head turned toward the window, Nikki allowed herself a brief, satisfied smile before acquainting Alex with a few discreet details of her UFO assignment. She was still discussing Farmer Earl Cordman's boomerang-shaped visitation thirty minutes later as they walked up the steps of Roman's house.

"Why the frown?" Alex leaned against the carved wooden front door "Doubting your UFO stories?"

"No. I knew you had the gate code, I was hoping Cantrell would be here to let us inside."

"Don't you have a key?"

"Never needed one. Today was my first day out." Nikki tested the knob and rang the bell. "Maybe Manuela or Santi is still here. No such luck. Hold this." She shoved her bag into his hands and sifted through its jumbled contents.

"What are you doing with all these plastic bags?" Alex held up three for inspection. "Are these...rocks? What's this weed?"

"Nothing noxious." Nikki returned to the lock. "Ahhh...there we are.

"You did have a key."

"No, I have a lockpick."

"Christ, Nikki—"

"It's air-conditioned in there, Alex, plus food and cold drinks."

"Bribery." He slammed the door. "Now, what about these bags and their contents?"

"They're samples from Cordman's cane field," she reluctantly admitted, adding hastily, "None of them came from anywhere near Glenn Ennis's body."

He stared at her for a long moment, then smiled. "I believe you. Why'd you collect them? You must have felt they were important evidence."

"A couple of things in that field didn't make much sense and these were part of it. I figured I'd get an analysis from an independent lab and—" Nikki snapped her fingers. "That reminds me. I want to give Rudy a call. He'll be able to fix me up with a good lab and...Now, why are you wincing?"

"I always wince when Borgianno's name is mentioned." His hand settled on her shoulder. "You don't have to call on a mob boss to find a lab. Besides, I doubt if it would be a legal one."

"Alex, you're a bigot. I thought you liked Rudy."

"I like the way Borgianno likes you. I know you used to run numbers for him when you were a kid and I know how well he's treated you through the years. I will admit he's an entertaining, charming character. But, Nikki, I spend a major part of my life trying to get rid of organized crime."

She patted his cheek. "Don't worry about that. Rudy doesn't take your efforts personally."

"Gee, thanks. Now, about these samples. Let me take them in and have the FBI lab analyze them."

"How nice. That'll be a big help." Nikki's smile and eyes were warm. "However, I did promise *Scuttlebutt* could also run tests and I do want to keep a control group, so let me sort some of these out for you and repackage them."

"Fine." The relief in his voice matched his expression. He dropped the bags into her outstretched hand. "I could swear you bribed me with the promise of something tall and cool."

"You know where the kitchen is." Nikki casually pocketed the plastic bags. "If you'll excuse me for a few minutes, Alex, I'm going to freshen up."

He nodded. "You had quite a day for your first time back at work."

"Excitement feeds the soul and diminishes the aches and pains." When she stepped from the partitioned foyer into the living room, dozens of department store packages claimed her attention. "What the hell is all this?"

"Appears somebody bought out Saks, Nordstrom's and the entire Bal Harbour Mall. You found time to shop between UFO tracking and finding dead bodies?"

"Very funny. I never shop. I hate shopping. Although, I will admit to needing new clothes with all the weight I've lost." She investigated the boxes. "The only person I know who'd do this is—"

"Roman?"

"He probably would. I've got a hunch that this is the work of...Ah-hah!" She held up an invoice. "Rebecca Cortlund. Amazing how an American Express Card and a phone can overcome a thirteen-hundred-mile shopping distance. Knowing Becky, she's purchased each garment in three sizes."

"Come on, I'll give you a hand carrying all of this to the bedroom."

"Don't bother. I'll do it tomorrow."

Laughing, he slapped a pink-and-black parcel. "You're the only woman I know who can let packages like these just sit. Most women would die of curiosity about what's in all of them. Speaking of packages. I want those rock samples."

Nodding, she walked toward him. "You know, I am curious about one thing, Alex."

"What's that?"

"How many women do you know?"

Her probing eyes rendered him powerless and he struggled for something intelligible to say. "I...I...think I'll go fix us those drinks." He stepped around her and headed for the kitchen.

Nikki watched him long-leg it across the expansive living room and disappear under the arch into the dining room. Guilt tinged her expression. It was a brief, superficial acknowledgment. There was absolutely no registration on her ever-dormant conscience.

Conscience? Nikki shuddered at the very word. Her conscience had only been disturbed once, by Roman Cantrell.

Ignoring Roman's image, she focused on Alex Lazarus while she headed down the hall to the master bedroom. Nikki liked Alex, trusted and respected him, but pushing his buttons was easy.

She knew why. She could see the way he held himself in check whenever she got physically close. The pulsating nerve on the side of his neck gave him away.

On certain occasions, she mused, playing to his fantasy might be useful. "Just not with these," she murmured, tossing the pebble-filled plastic bags on the bed.

Alex's knowing about them didn't faze her. It was the government laboratory probe she found disquieting. Alex was still under the illusion that the government dealt in truth and excellence. She knew better. She wasn't about to become the victim of classic disinformation. Or worse. The ever popular alternative facts.

"What if they do prove to be something other than common stones?" She hefted the bag of heavy silver-white pellets. "Hmmm...I have to give him something to analyze."

She emptied one baggie into Roman's spare-change dish, covering the pebbles with coins. Heading into the spacious bathroom, Nikki eyed the lush, verdant garden that surrounded the sunken tub. From the pots Nikki extracted a variety of ornamental gravel. Her final choices, near-perfect matches to the specimens from the cane field, were sealed inside a bag. "That should satisfy Alex and the government. Now I just need to give my favorite fed something else to think about."

A devilish smile peered back at her from the mirror. "Perfect...let's give that pulsing nerve on the side of his face some exercise." Thirty seconds later, she was wrapping a bath towel around her naked body and heading out to the kitchen.

"Alex...Alex...there you are." She ignored his rapidly blinking dark blue eyes. "I just wanted to tell you to check the fridge, Manuela always leaves some wonderful appetizers in there. So munch away while I grab a shower."

Nikki sniffed her bare shoulder and wrinkled her nose. "Gosh I didn't realize how...umm...fragrant I was from slogging through the sugarcane field. Please...please relax...dump that suit jacket and tie...oops..." hastily, she grabbed the front of the falling towel. "I'll be back in a flash."

Alex leaned as far left as he could without falling onto the gas cook-top to get the full rear effect of her short blue towel, long legs and tumble of copper hair. Then he remembered she'd picked his front trouser pocket for his car keys. Her fingers had been *that* close to his cock. And he'd never felt a thing. "Damn..." Rubbing the ice-filled glass of gin and tonic against his forehead, he hoped the cold would deflate the bulge in his trousers before she returned. "I should just stick my dick in the freezer."

While her shower was quick, Nikki took her time rejoining Alex. She needed to keep him off-balance until Cantrell joined them. "What to wear? What to wear?" She replaced the blue towel with a short gray sweatshirt dress, the wide neckline slipping and sliding over bare shoulders.

Her fingers raked her hair into a pony tail before twisting it into a bun, anchored with two long bobby pins. Numerous wayward copper curls softened the effect into a sexy mess. "Purrfect. Well...I'll go one-step further..." She coated her full lips with a soft pink gloss. "Now for a little smoke and mirrors."

"Where are you hiding my gin and tonic?" Nikki watched Alex jump off the bar stool at the sound of her voice when she padded barefoot into the kitchen. "Sorry, I didn't mean to startle you." She neatened the rolled up sleeves of his business shirt. "You look nicely relaxed. I see you found the appetizers. Yum...Manuela did a fabulous antipasto."

He cleared his throat, trying not to let the touch of her hand on his arm effect the tone of his voice. "Yes...umm...I'm afraid I really did help myself." Alex reached around Nikki and grabbed the tall highball glass. "Here you go."

She slid on the stool next to him. "I so need this." Nikki downed half the glass. "It's been quite a day for all of us. Oh...here's a good representation of all the stones I found in the cane field." She pulled a plastic bag from the kangaroo pocket on the front of her dress.

Alex pocketed the stones. "Are you hoping our lab says they're unearthly?" he teased, pulling the antipasto platter between the two of them.

"No, I just want your lab to tell me the truth." She tilted her head. "Cantrell will be joining us in about two minutes."

"I didn't hear—oh, there's the door. That radar of yours should be harnessed. Hi, Roman."

"Alex. Got another one of those?" Roman nodded at Nikki's glass.

"Won't take but a minute." Alex disappeared into the den and the fully appointed bar.

"Make it a double," Nikki called after him. She slid off the chair and moved in front of Roman. Her knuckles tenderly sculpted the deep groove in his right cheek before stroking his ever present stubble. "You look tired, boy."

He pressed a kiss into her palm. "I am. There was quite a scene at Tony's house. His wife was pretty strung out."

"Stress is dangerous when you're pregnant. I'm betting you were easily able to calm her down." Nikki smiled at his raised brow. "Hey, I have my sentimental side, too. I just don't noise it around."

Roman grasped her bare shoulders, pulling her tight against him. "It wouldn't hurt if you did."

"Why spoil perfection? There! Your laugh just erased ten years."

"The feel of you erased ten years." He intimately squeezed her ass. "Maybe I'll send Alex home with a steak and a potato and instructions on how to cook them himself. We can go someplace quiet and you can put your tongue in my cheek and—"

"I don't think he'll go for it. Will you, Alex?" She turned her head and smiled at Alex. "Cantrell, you've made him blush."

"I was trying to make you blush."

"Never happen." Nikki patted his crotch. "I'll go fire up the barbecue. Hmmm...I've got my stuff spread all over the dining room table. Alex, you know where everything is, set up for dinner on the island. Cantrell, you get to show off all those culinary skills your mother taught you."

Roman drained his gin and tonic and handed it back to Alex for a refill. "Ed Hartwell finally called home. His wife told him about the hijacking and he'll be coming in on the first available plane tomorrow morning."

Alex nodded, pulling forks and knives from the drawer. "I want to talk to him."

"We can do that together. I texted him that I want to check on the security system."

"Fine. I'll do the questioning on his employees..."

"I'm telling you Alex, Mackey doesn't have a damn thing to do with this hijacking."

"Right, can't forget the imaginary tank and the Martians!"

"Boys...boys...my stomach cannot take this stress." Pausing halfway out the patio door, Nikki threatened them with barbeque tools. "Let's make a rule. For the rest of the night we discuss only nonviolent topics like politics, religion and sex.

"And speaking of sex," She gave a broad wink, "wait until I tell you about my first interview of the day with the Queen of Botox, butt and boob enhancements and hairstylist to the Palm Bitches. Pink haired Muriel, I've-been-finger-fucked-in-two-orifices-by-an-alien-and-now-I'm-pregnan Feinberg." Nikki winced when silverware and plates crashed on the floor.

Chapter 15

Too tired to sleep.

Too fitful to lie down.

Sliding into the comforting turbulence of the pool's Jacuzzi, Nikki savored not only the silence but squares of a seventy-two percent cacao chocolate bar. She hoped the combination of chocolate, aspirin and the magic fingers of a pulsating massage would dull her aches. Eyes closed, she thought about her day.

UFOs.

Alien baby.

Dead body.

Five million dollar hijacking.

"What more could a reporter ask for! Maybe not so many muscle spasms," she muttered, stretching the heel of her right foot for relief. Funny how pain intensified when adrenaline and excitement diminished.

For a while, Nikki focused on the brightest star in the midnight sky, allowing her imagination to fill with images of spaceships and alien invaders. She hadn't believed Muriel Feinburg's visitation or pregnancy. Earl Cordman's sugarcane field was another matter.

Something had landed.

UFO?

"Dammit, the truth has to be out there...or up there...and I plan to find out." She winced and flexed her right foot again.

Bonus of the day: the hijacking. Despite Cantrell's assurances and support of Tony Mackey, Nikki had filed the 'tank' report alongside Muriel's delusions.

Delusions?

Okay, maybe more people than Muriel did witness the exact same sighting and she would investigate. However, the only corroboration Mackey had was Glenn Ennis.

A very dead Glenn Ennis.

Nikki knew Roman would work long and hard to find out what really happened. The case already consumed him. He'd been oddly restrained and vague during dinner. She had skillfully steered the conversations away from both UFO's and the hijacking to a discussion on the new summer movies and TV shows. Luckily, Alex had joined in with a few reviews and suggestions.

After Alex left, Roman had grown progressively quieter, introspective and preoccupied. There had been none of his usual teasing. While she missed his teasing, she also sensed his need to be alone.

She had cleaned the kitchen while he'd played with the television remote. Through the open archway to the den, Nikki watched him shuffle through the cable channels at least twice, pausing to view NASCAR trials and a few innings of baseball. He had settled on CNN for fifteen minutes before snapping the set silent and throwing the remote on the sofa.

While she'd called to check on Teresa and sent some emails to Matt and Darnie, Nikki could hear him working out in the gym. If he'd hit the punching bag any harder with his feet and fists, it would have deflated. Half an hour later, he'd excused himself, muttering about a headache, a shower and bed.

Maybe he doubted the veracity of Tony Mackey's story? Maybe he doubted their friendship? Maybe...Nikki jerked upright when her nose came in contact with the swirling water.

"Maybe I can finally sleep," she murmured through a yawn. After toweling dry, she quietly entered the bedroom through the sliding doors and eased herself onto the wide mattress. As her head burrowed against the plump pillow, Roman's harsh, almost labored, breathing echoed amid the dark corners.

Chapter 16

Stay alert.
  Stay alive.
    Who's to live?
    Who's to die?
    Peace is hell.
    War is power.
    Besides, there's no place to run where there isn't war.
    And no time to wonder –
    Why you are going to die.

* * * *

"Addler! Addler!" He grabbed the grunt's arm, but instead caught a torn uniform sleeve. "Dammit, Tommy, get over here."

"Please. Just let me go. I've gotta get outa here."

"Where the hell do you think you're going to go?"

"Home. Yesterday I was a normal, fat, happy kid. Now I'm in hell! Just what did I do wrong?" His shaking hand smeared tears, dirt and greased charcoal across his face. "This isn't the way it's supposed to be, Cantrell. They aren't playing by the rules. The good guys are supposed to win. We're the fucking good guys and there's only a dozen of us left."

"Take it easy, Addler. Calm down. Let's go back to the bunker and—"

"And what? I can't hump sixty pounds of gear another inch. And a friggin' inch is all we've moved in a week. I've been here one hundred days. One hundred fucking days of the glamorous Operation Phantom Fury. Sounds like a damn comic book."

His eyes narrowed; his voice was a whisper. "They can hear our hearts beating. That's how they keep tracking us, finding us, killing us.

It's a goddamn game. You...you play well. You're good. The killing comes easy for you."

"Killing doesn't come easy for anyone."

"Liar."

"Addler, let's move it."

"Don't turn into a CO on me, man. You're not even part of our company, Cantrell. Just taggin' along until you meet up with your unit. Adding notches on your sniper rifle."

"Come on. Tommy, let's go get you some food. I know there's some bottles of Efes Turkish beer floating around." His arm settled across Addler's shoulder. He could feel the grunt relax. "Come on. Everything's going to be fine."

"Beer? Yeah, I could use a brew. Two or three." Tommy's laugh was quick. "Why can't it be a Bud? Why can't we be in Pennsylvania, surrounded by brotherly love? I am supposed to love my brother, right? And all men are my brothers, right? Even them, right?"

Suddenly, Addler swung wide and hard, catching him off-guard. He staggered against a weakened wall and found himself smothered by concrete shards. He was clawing his way out of the concrete when he heard Tommy yelling and then the rapid, violent brrbrrbrrbrr of an M60. "The crazy bastard's gone outside the wire!"

And outside the wire, there was no one but the enemy.

He pushed at the blocks and mortar, struggling to gain a foothold, wrestling for control. His arms flailed, searching for anything stable. Just as he connected with something solid, he heard and felt the explosion. And smelled the burning acrid remains of..."Addler!"

Roman became a mass of whirling arms and legs, punching and yelling.

A distant voice called, "No! Not any more!"

"Addler! I'm coming!" Gaining strength, he battled for freedom.

Freedom.

Hit.

Back.

Hard.

Chapter 17

Roman jerked upright.

Eyes open.

Heart pounding.

Gasping for breath.

His sweat-drenched body was snared in the twisted sheet. It seemed forever before the roaring in his ears subsided. When it did, he realized he was not alone.

Someone else was sitting beside him, laboring for air.

Confused, he groped along the headboard for the light switch. Roman squinted and saw a hunched, heavily scarred back and a tangled mass of copper hair. "Christ! Nikki..." He shook his head to clear it. "Oh, Jesus..." Leaning forward, he pulled her close. "Did I hit you?"

When her left cheek rubbed against his shoulder, she felt the cold dampness of his flesh. She sat up and wiped the wetness from his face with gentle fingertips. "It wasn't me you were hitting."

"Never."

The masculine arms that surrounded her were unsteady, almost weak. She realized the man who owned them had just visited his own private hell. Nikki pushed aside her personal demons to focus on Roman.

Tonight, he was the one with wounds that needed ministering and a soul that cried for restoration. She'd experienced both needs. Would she be able to provide the healing strength? She tried to stroke the anguish from his face. "Talk to me about Addler."

"Addler?"

"You were fighting him."

"Addler?" He exhaled forcefully. "Yeah. Addler. Among others."

As her hand slid up his arm and across his chest, she felt the tension in his body. When he tried moving away, her embrace tightened. "What you most want to forget always comes back first."

The laugh that invaded her ears was cruel. "Ain't that the truth."

When she reached up to snap out the light, his harsh "no" stopped her. "Too many dark corners. Too many Addlers hiding in them. I'm sorry about—"

"Why don't we make a rule not to apologize for our collective nightmares? They don't respect the passage of time." She stroked his cheek. "You make me talk them out."

"Does it help?"

"I could lie and say yes."

He shuddered and within seconds, his body was trembling violently. No matter what she did or what she said, she failed to calm him. He didn't seem conscious of her efforts.

His anguish became hers.

"Roman...please...Can I call someone? Do you have any meds?" She clung to him, pleading. "Please, talk to me? Tell me what's happening to you. Roman...I want to help...

Nikki swallowed hard, struggling to regain her strength.

She kept talking.

Touching.

Comforting.

Little by little, she sensed he was becoming more aware.

Returning to this time.

This place.

To her.

Roman began to take control again. By concentrating hard, he made his ragged breathing stabilize and the tremors subside. "I'm really sorr—"

"Shhh...Just relax. What can I do?"

"Be here."

Her hand splayed across his chest. His heart beat heavily against her palm. "Is there any medicine?"

"You're doing just fine."

She kissed his shoulder. "Somehow, I think I set you off."

"Not you. That word. Liar. Addler called me a liar."

"Who is Addler?"

"A grunt in Fallujah."

She leaned over him. "What made you open that door?"

"Today, talking with Tony." He rubbed his face. "Mackey said the hijackers put him on alert and he felt he was back in Iraq. Stay alert. Stay alive. That photo of Glenn Ennis, dead in a cane field...the soil looking for all the world like a desert. I saw too many bodies in the sand. That's where Addler was blown apart."

Roman was staring at her, but Nikki had no doubt he was seeing someone else. When his hand began to tremble, she slid her palm against his, her fingers locking tight. "Is that who you saw? This Addler?"

"I...I heard him. I heard his voice. All the lies I told myself were turned into truths." His eyes closed briefly. "Ugly truths. Addler said the killing came easy for me. He was right. It did. I turned the carnage into a carnival...a shooting gallery. I never missed. Always came away the winner. But most of the good guys lost. Addler lost."

His tongue washed dry lips. "I should have seen he was in trouble. I should have offered him help instead of beer. If I could just go back...talk to him different. I lied, Nikki, I lied and said everything was going to be fine. I even lied to my mother."

"Your...your...mother?"

"Yeah. I...I promised her I'd write. I never did. What the hell was I supposed to say? 'Dear Mom, I killed ten insurgents on Monday. Having a wonderful time, so glad you're not here.' All I knew was that stupid fucking politicians were running a war with an enemy no one could understand. Glamorizing the war with what Addler called comic book names like Operation Phantom Fury."

Hearing the anger in his voice, Nikki tightened her arms around his torso as he continued to talk. "I had just finished another covert mission. My extraction team was delayed due to weather; I hunkered down with a marine battalion in that hellhole Fallujah. Urban warfare is a different animal. We were shot at almost every minute of every day. Bullets. Mortars. Rockets. The insurgents had imbedded themselves on roof tops, in houses, even in the fucking sewers. IED's were hidden everywhere.

Roman leaned his forehead against hers. "Damn it, Nik, the enemy had filled mortars with white phosphorus. I...I can still smell the burnt metal, the rubber...the flesh.

"Troops were coming in and body bags were going out. I couldn't explain the random nature of death. I didn't understand it. We had rules. The enemy didn't. I was tricked too often and got damn sick and tired of living a second at a time. So they got from me exactly what they wanted. I abandoned the rules. I went on one covert mission after another. I was the perfect killing machine.

"I...I lost me. I thrived. I loved it. After a while all the faces blurred and it was a matter of survival. In the end...in the end, you remember each and every face and the horror etched in their death masks. It takes an eternity to become human again."

"Time doesn't stop all the second guessing. There's nothing you can do. What happened happened." Nikki gathered Roman's quaking body against her own. "You do what you have to do to survive. I know. "

She rocked him in her arms like an infant. Soothing. Consoling. Comforting. Gradually, she felt him settle and soften. His jerky gulps for air were transformed into the rhythmic meter of sleep.

Chapter 18

"Nikki, about last night—

"Cantrell, I know I snore." She let the dress boxes she'd been juggling fall on the tumbled navy sheets. "It's this nose. Probably the next time it gets broken the snoring will stop. Of course, if the nose is too much for you..." she arched a brow, "I can always bunk in the guest room on the other side of the house."

"I wasn't talking about snoring and you damn well know it."

"Not that? Then I don't see we have a thing to talk about." Her eyes never wavered from Roman's as he gently curved his hand against her left cheek. "You weren't the one hitting me last night. Because if you had, I wouldn't be here and..." She swallowed hard, "you wouldn't be alive. The hell I lived wasn't my own choice. Living with you is my choice."

"It isn't any easier when the nightmares are about the dead."

"In my case, pure nocturnal bliss." Finger-combing the damp hair off his forehead, Nikki tenderly stroked away the pinched lines that etched his eyes. "I thought that lengthy shower you took would have rinsed away your hair shirt." Hoping to coax a smile, she tugged at the dark curls that matted his broad chest. "Okay, okay, Cantrell, if you feel the need for penance, how about letting me order dinner?"

Her exaggerated wink and cajoling manner diminished his remorse. Roman tucked a copper ringlet behind her ear. "Are we talking fast food?"

She nodded and smiled.

"Lots of grease, salt and calories?"

Her smile turned into a grin.

"Heartburn is my second favorite dessert." His arms secured her. "By the way, I find your snoring..." he kissed her nose, "soothing, seductive and..." his tongue traced her lips, teasing them apart, "very stimulating."

Nikki snapped the elastic on the terry shower wrap that was slung around his hips. "I'm getting the distinct impression that you're about to start the day with a bang!"

He pulled off the Yankee's baseball jersey she wore as a robe. "A grand-slam home run," he corrected. Her sun-tanned skin was warm and sleek. He filled his hands with her velvety bare flesh.

Breathing heavily, Nikki gripped his shoulders when his finger slid inside and teased her clit. "I don't suppose..." erratic jolts pleasured her body when a second masculine finger slid deep inside. "I...I don't suppose you'll step out of the batter's box even when I tell you Alex called while you were in the shower."

"You're right. I won't." Roman let the towel fall and sat on the edge of the bed. He pulled her forward, letting his lips suck on her hardened nipples.

A low moan of pleasure escaped. "He...he...said to meet him in half an hour at Hartwell Armored Services and...and not to be late."

"I'll try my best." He lifted her up until she was straddling him. Her legs instantly wrapped around his waist. His hands opened her up, his rigid cock buried deep inside her.

Nikki nipped his earlobe, moaning when he lifted her hips and slid in and out. "You are going to be very late."

"Are you complaining?"

Chapter 19

Alex Lazarus did all the complaining.

He started with expressive hand gestures Cantrell could see through his windshield as he waited for Hartwell's security guard to check him into the Doral area facility. Alex's silent flailing's were quickly replaced by a whining verbiage that had Roman supplicating: "*Mea culpa, mea culpa, mea culpa.* I guess I should have worn sackcloth and ashes."

Lazarus pulled his head turtle-like into the collar of his gray suit jacket. "Sorry, pal." He shrugged down his shoulders and frowned at the black-bellied clouds that comprised the midmorning sky. "It's this damn on-again off-again drizzle. I feel royally pissed on."

Cantrell grinned. "You could have started talking to Hartwell without me."

"He hasn't shown yet."

Cantrell's grin faded. "I see what you mean about the weather." He wiped the fine mist from his freshly shaven face.

"Of course, Hartwell's seeming lack of concern over a five-million-dollar hijacking, coupled with the great difficulty in finding him yesterday, makes me add his name to the top of my list."

"Meaning Tony Mackey's been—"

"All it means, Roman, is that your friend Mackey gets to share top honors with his boss and..." Alex sniffled, "...that fucking tank." He leaned against the trunk of his gray sedan. "I've had time to take a few turns around this place."

"And?"

"Looks damn tight to me. You've got your inside armed guard stationed behind an impregnable gate. There's a heavy-duty, electrified twenty-foot fence with a topping yard of barbed wire encircling the warehouse."

Lazarus nodded toward the complex. "The building's good. No windows. Business offices in the front, biometric retina scanner on the main door, top-notch backup alarm system. I checked the rear loading dock area and that's equally secure. Hey, why the face? I just paid you a compliment. You did a great job setting up the security on this place."

"Yet somehow, some way, somebody managed to get around the system."

"Inside job."

"You're back to Tony again?"

"Maybe you need to run a check on your client." Lazarus nodded toward the new Mercedes-Benz that was being waved through the front gate. "Hell, maybe we should both check on Ed Hartwell."

In the few minutes Hartwell needed to park the silver sedan, the fine mist turned into a warm drizzle. Cantrell watched Ed press open a large golf umbrella for protection as they all sprinted for the canopied front door. He felt the need to reacquaint himself with Ed Hartwell.

Ed Hartwell made him believe in the *Dorian Gray* legend. Hartwell never seemed to age, although Cantrell knew he was in his late fifties. His deeply tanned, pretty-boy face teamed perfectly with an enviable mental vigor and physical agility.

Hartwell and his wife, Judith, were perennial favorites in the society column. Besides co-captaining a polo team, he was forever being touted as the chairman of this or the host of that charity event. His energy, time and money never seemed to wanc. The man was a multitude of admirable traits.

Although they'd had many personal associations, including aiding Tony Mackey, Cantrell had never counted Hartwell among his inner circle of friends. He wasn't quite sure why he made that distinction. Certainly not because Hartwell was a client and he'd come to know a few skeletons. Cantrell shook the rain from his hair. There was just something...

"No golf today." Hartwell joked, leaning in to the retinal scanner.

Lazarus's eyes narrowed. "I'd have thought the hijacking of a five-million-dollar shipment and the murder of an employee would have dampened your golfing appetite."

"Oh, dear...Agent uhhh..."

"Lazarus."

Hartwell nodded. "I apologize for the shallowness of that remark. I'm just, well..." He blotted precipitation off his forehead, cheeks and jaw with a crisp white handkerchief, "Frankly, I'm overwhelmed and confused and overwrought and..." His manicured hands made a defeated palms-up gesture.

"We're all overwhelmed and confused," Cantrell repeated.

"Nothing like this has ever happened before," Hartwell continued, motioning them inside. "Left me at a loss. I've sent my executive assistant to the Ennis house to handle all the arrangements for Glenn's widow. We carry insurance on all our drivers, so she and the three children will be well provided for. Someone will be checking on Tony and his wife later today, also. And Roman..." Hartwell's hand pressed urgently against the detective's shoulder. "Despite the fact the FBI is on this, I want you investigating. My plane landed very late last night and my wife...well, Judy was so incoherent, I still don't know all the details."

While proceeding through the elegantly appointed reception area, Cantrell related Tony Mackey's statements on the hijacking. Lazarus added the medical examiner's report on Ennis once they settled in Hartwell's executive office with its gray flannel walls and strong white-on-white furnishings.

"So, you're saying that Glenn actually died of a heart attack before he was shot?"

"That's just the preliminary autopsy," Lazarus cautioned. "We'll know more tomorrow. In any case, it's still murder."

"Yes...yes, of course. Now about Tony's story on the...ummm...the commando unit and tank?"

"The bureau's got big problems with Mackey's tale, too," Lazarus muttered, his gaze sliding to Cantrell.

"Not enough evidence to arrest or even hold," Cantrell cautioned, draping his damp tan sports coat on the coat rack. "For my money, Tony's report was just too damn brazen to be a lie."

"It's not your money—"

"It is mine." Hartwell's polished voice interrupted Alex. "Or at least entrusted in my care." He pressed his fingertips together, forming a pyramid. "However, I really must agree with you, Roman. Why would Tony concoct such a wild story?" He shook his head. "I don't envy the FBI in tracking down such a well-armed group, Agent."

Lazarus turned a snicker into a cough.

"While we are insured," Hartwell continued, "I'd much prefer the cargo be found than to file a claim. I'm certain you won't mind if Roman also works to that end, Agent."

"Not at all. In fact, I personally hope he discovers the M1A1 tank first."

"What I'd really like to discover is the breach in security," Cantrell did his best to control the anger in his voice. Looking from Lazarus to Hartwell, he continued, "For the moment, let's all agree that Tony Mackey and Glenn Ennis were victims. That implies a vulnerability right here. All your employees are being rechecked and it appears that external security is intact. So that makes me question your internal operation."

Anxiously, Hartwell leaned forward. His voice was low and quick. "Are you saying that we've been bugged?"

"Had any repairmen in here lately?"

"All the time, we've initiated all the repair orders and they've all been validated at the gate."

"That makes you careful but not necessarily safe," Cantrell said matter-of-factly. "Using a computer to set your routes and giving the drivers cellphones makes you susceptible to electronic spying. There's always a way to get into any electronic device. I've got four men ready to sweep this place." At Hartwell's rapid nod, Roman reached for his cell and punched a button to his office.

Alex Lazarus looked at Hartwell. "Any objections if we make this official and doubly efficient?"

Chapter 20

Hartwell visibly relaxed once his private office had been electronically sanitized. "It's a great relief to know I wasn't bugged." He nodded toward the boat-shaped gray conference table that had been set for a brunch buffet. "Please, gentlemen, help yourself. If I don't eat at certain times my digestive system just rebels."

He refilled coffee mugs for the sixth time. "Frankly, I doubt they'll find anything. Roman, you installed such a secure computer system for us. It's been constantly upgraded. Hell, with the combination fingerprint and retina biometric scanners handling the main access to the building, someone would need to carry around an eyeball...my eyeball or one of my employees' thumbs." Hartwell shuddered. "I just don't see how someone could gain access to our cargo manifests and intercept our hauling routes."

Roman looked up from adding mini-muffins and wrapped sausages to his plate. "Very easily, WiFi hotspots can make all computers vulnerable. Hackers live for the fun and power of getting into the impenetrable. Landlines and cellphones are all fair game.

"But you're probably right about not finding any bugs. In the old-tech days, you could usually find physical traces of tampering. Now..." Roman shrugged. "The newer devices are impossible to detect."

"Nothing is ever completely secure," Lazarus agreed. "International phone calls that are beamed up to satellites can be intercepted with a satellite dish anywhere within hundreds of miles of a ground station. In fact, many of the new high-tech spying devices fall into a legal no man's land."

"ATM machines, gas pumps, hospital records, hell, even critical care hospital equipment have fallen victim to hackers. I've lost count over how many federal agencies and banks have been hit.

Cantrell pushed himself out of the white leather wing chair and began to pace the room. "Frankly, Ed, changing the entrance code on a daily basis is just not secure enough. I really feel a more elaborate encrypting is needed, plus a new scramble phone system in the office and in your vehicles. We can also install a TEMPEST program, electronic shielding, around your computer system."

"That sounds like a major investment," Hartwell murmured. He combed through the gray wings at his temples that distinguished his wealth of dark brown hair. "But —" His palms slapped down on the white marble-topped desk, "it's an investment I'll willingly make. Carte blanche, Roman. It'll be a relief to know that no one can ever break in again."

Cantrell shook his head, his tone brusque. "All we can do is make sure nothing gets out."

"Are you telling me, no matter how much money's spent or what devices are put in place, I'm still vulnerable?"

"Hell, the federal government gets hacked on a daily basis. All we can do is stay ahead of the threat."

"What shall I do in the meantime?" Hartwell's arms flailed in desperation. "I certainly can't afford to shut down this entire operation. We have contracts on at least a dozen valuable long-haul cargos, plus our regular day-to-day money transferals."

"Maybe the sweep will get lucky and find something."

"Lucky? What do you mean by lucky?"

"We might be able to run a trace or just leave the bug in place and..." Cantrell inclined his head toward Lazarus "see if another million-dollar cargo might prove alluring bait, with the FBI as a fisherman."

"Interesting suggestion," Lazarus said. "I'd like an up-close-and-personal view of that tank. How about you?"

Cantrell grinned. "I wouldn't mind coming along for the ride."

"If we could just return to the current problem," Hartwell snapped. "While I certainly am grateful for the tight lid you've placed on the hijacking. I need to know what's being done to find the cargo. I've got to contact Perry and Daniels, owner of the shipment."

Alex nodded. "The search for the truck began immediately. We had police helicopters in the air and roadblocks set up. Unfortunately, we couldn't spot a thing. Your green tractor-trailers are very easy to camouflage, especially in that overgrown area."

Lazarus leveled a hard, inquisitive gaze at Hartwell. "Of course, it would have helped us considerably if we could have gotten in touch with you much sooner. We need to know what made up the shipment and how it was packaged." He allowed himself a quick side glance at Cantrell. "Your wife couldn't get in touch with you until late and—"

"Yes, well, nothing unusual in that," Hartwell's tone was cool. "I was booked from breakfast to dinner with either business meetings or charity considerations." He pushed a heavily inked appointment calendar toward Lazarus. "Wall-to-wall. I try to plan my trips so I can kill the proverbial two birds with one stone. That way, I only have to spend a couple of weekends a month away from my wife and son.

"As for the precious metals shipment, the cargo's always packaged the same way for these weekly hauls. You'd be looking at about a dozen huge drums and large metal sheets." His dark eyebrows rose expressively. "Four thousand pounds of precious metals plus our armored truck. Seems to me it would be very difficult to—" A sharp rap on the door startled Hartwell.

Cantrell admitted one of his operatives who, along with an FBI technician, reported the offices, computer, and interior loading area of Hartwell Armored Services contained no electronic eavesdropping devices, nor was any evidence of tampering discovered.

Hartwell's gray eyes were bleak. "What do I do now?"

"Business as usual with double the guards," Cantrell said. "If someone has hacked into the computer routing system, why not let the computer print half a dozen suggested routes, then simply have your driver select one at random? I'll start installing the scrambler phones in your offices and vehicles tomorrow and get the TEMPEST equipment here as soon as possible."

Lazarus stood. "Since you've got more of those multi-million-dollar shipments contracted, the bureau will be glad to provide escort service. I'll have someone here in the morning to work out the details. Meanwhile, we'll double our efforts to track down the missing cargo and Glenn Ennis's killer. I'll get my men together and head back to the office to see if there's anything new."

Turning to Cantrell, he added. "Bring Tony Mackey in tomorrow. Just for a few questions, pal." Lazarus was half out the door when he veered back and spoke quietly to Cantrell. "By the way, tell Nikki that I'll call her on that lab report later tomorrow."

"Lab report?"

"She asked me to have those rock samples she found in Belle Glade analyzed."

"Right...I'll tell her" Cantrell was successful at hiding a broad grin until Lazarus closed the door.

"Was that anything I should know about?"

"Hmmm? No, Ed, another matter."

"Oh. Well, Roman. I'd appreciate it if we could discuss the new security improvements you'll be installing. And I'd like to talk about Tony." Hartwell gripped the back of his neck with both hands. "I know I said I agreed with you about his version of the hijacking. Frankly, Roman, a tank? On a back Florida road? With, what was it? Sixty armed commandos?" He waved Cantrell toward the white leather wing chair. "This is all so confusing. And poor Ennis. Dead! I just don't know ..." His voice faltered, his gray eyes appealed for answers.

Walking to the desk, Cantrell nonchalantly picked up Hartwell's appointment calendar before settling comfortably in the matching chair Lazarus had vacated. "Bizarre as Tony's story may sound, I trust him. Besides, hasn't the bizarre become front-page lately?" His smile came quick and faded fast.

"My God, Ed, you were booked solid all day yesterday in Atlanta." Cantrell's finger guided his eyes as he carefully studied each notation. "And today and..." he flipped the page, "... tomorrow."

Hartwell shifted and cleared his throat. "Doing a lot of business up there, Roman. Need to keep bringing in the contracts, bringing in the work, bringing in the dollars. Costs keep going up. So does the payroll, vehicle maintenance, taxes, insurance, my personal expenses and now with these additional security measures I go back to the drawing board to re-budget."

"Mmmm...Atlanta must be very profitable. I see you've got the city inked in twice a month for the rest of this year." Cantrell snapped the book shut and tossed it onto the free-form sculpture desk. "I hope yesterday's appointments will be exact with times and places when Lazarus checks on them." He focused on Ed Hartwell's pinched expression. "Alex will check. He's trained to be thorough."

"You...you're making it sound as though I need an alibi."

Cantrell's left eyebrow arched at the shrill thread that twisted Hartwell's affectedly refined speech. "You don't, do you, Ed?"

He lunged to his feet. "Good God, Roman, why would I steal from myself?"

"Well, it's not really you you'd be stealing from," Cantrell returned easily. "That precious-metal cargo was a nice score and relatively easy loot to dispose of. If you did arrange to have your own truck hijacked, you'd get back the tractor-trailer. The insurance company will pay off the shippers and, since this is your first claim, you won't be dropped. Your premiums will go through the roof, though."

"You...you're joking. Right?" Hartwell's laugh was tight, nearly choking.

"Relax, Ed, you've got yesterday covered. I'm sure the background check the FBI's doing on you will come out squeaky clean." Cantrell reached into his shirt pocket for a notebook. "Well, let's talk about some of these new security measures."

"Yes." Hartwell cleared his throat. "Yes, good idea." He straightened his pastel green monogramed dress shirt and settled on the edge of his leather contour chair. "So...uh, when do you think the FBI will...uh, start their checking?"

"Yesterday. Why?"

"No reason. It's just..." Hartwell nervously slicked back his hair. "I'm just, well, concerned about the...all that old stuff with Randy and the drugs. My boy's been through a lot. This is his last year in a very exclusive college. I'd hate to have all that dredged up and publicized. It could send him right back and...and, I know it's been eight years, but Judy's still seeing a psychologist –"

"Listen, Ed," Cantrell leaned forward. "I've helped you out before. I'll go to bat with you again. So, if you've got any *new* skeletons, tell me right now."

"No. Nothing. Nothing at all. I...I guess I just overreacted. Probably all that coffee." His laugh was hollow. Quickly, he cleared his throat again, yanked open a desk drawer, pulled out a leather-bound legal pad and fumbled for a pen. "Why don't you tell me more about the...what was it? TEMPEST system?"

Cantrell stared at Ed Hartwell. The man had aged. His bronze complexion had taken on an ashen cast. The taut skin of his face had suddenly become flaccid. Dark hammocks of flesh under his eyes were shockingly pronounced. Even his posture had changed. His shoulders had lost their strength and a dowager's hump had appeared.

Hartwell was lying.

Cantrell knew it wasn't the first time a client had lied and wouldn't be the last.

Was Ed Hartwell's a five-million-dollar lie?

And did it cover up a murder?

Chapter 21

Roman's watch showed quarter to six when he entered the house through the garage door. He was hungry, tired and damp to the bone. Then he heard Nikki laughing.

She had a great laugh. It matched her vibrant voice.

Sexy.

Sultry.

Provocative.

A rejuvenating grin transformed his weary features.

Deciding to sneak up on her, Roman shed his shoes and padded soundlessly down the hall to the den. He expected to find her curled on the sofa, enjoying a program on the TV.

The tube was on.

The sound muted.

The room—unoccupied.

Another seductive laugh tantalized his ears. Tossing his blazer and tie on the kitchen barstools, he released the top four buttons on his shirt. "Ahh...she's probably on the bedroom phone talking with the Cortlund's." However, the master bedroom also proved to be empty. Roman opened his mouth to call her name when feminine laughter became entwined with words.

Words delivered by a deep voice.

A masculine voice.

An unfamiliar voice.

Frowning, Roman long-legged it down the hall to the spare room.

The door was half closed.

The people inside could be heard but not seen.

The instant Roman's fingers curved around the door knob, he felt the insistent pressure of cold steel against his nape together with a nasal voice that droned in his ear, "Don't move or I'll blow you away."

Chapter 22

Two heartbeats later, the door opened and Roman came face to face with a smiling Nikki Holden. "Didn't they teach you the dangers of skulking in detective school, Cantrell?" She chucked him under the chin.

"Not in my own home." His thumb jerked backward. "Am I allowed to straighten and breathe?"

"Sure Mr. Cantrell, I just wanted to show you that I took your suggestion." Duncan popped back his bubble gum.

"My suggestion?"

Pushing a wide lock of blonde hair off his angular face, Duncan grinned. "Check out my new Sig P238, you were right, it's perfect for conceal/carry. This one doesn't spoil the cut of my suit jacket."

Nikki exhaled an expansive sigh. "Men...holster that gun Duncan so you can show off your decorating skills."

"Where's your companion? The three-hundred-pound physical therapist?"

"Edgar's gone on an errand."

"Probably a terminal one."

Nikki laughed. "Rudy's here."

"So I see. How are things Rudy?"

Rudy held up both hands. "Don't ask."

Roman looked at Nikki for an explanation. "Issues with the restaurant remodel. It's taking three times as long due to some surprise problems with the plumbing and wiring and a crack in the foundation on the beach annex." She patted Rudy's shoulder when he let out an uncharacteristic groan. "Everything be fine. October's when the snowbirds start heading south and they'll be hungry for both the main restaurant and the beachside extension."

Borgianno rubbed his forehead. "Tell him the rest...I can't...I can't even talk about it."

"It's just a fad, Rudy." She arched a titian brow. "The restaurant next door is serving–"

"Not just serving," Rudy shouted, "they're turning culinary masterpieces into...into...I can't say the word." He slapped his hand over his mouth.

"Plastic."

Roman echoed. "Plastic?"

Nikki nodded. "They set up this display in their bay window of a 3-D printer that is printing edible canapes and..."

"It's fucking standing room only." Rudy interrupted. "Lamb drumsticks on a ginger-maple edible plastic bone. I nearly had a heart attack when I saw they printed bite-size black truffle polenta –"

"They had to cook that with a blowtorch," Nikki reminded him.

"Which made it even more theatrical. More entertaining." Rudy's arms were flailing in disgust and anger. "The people were packed in there like sardines. Which they'll probably print next. Sacrilegious punks."

Roman turned a laugh into a cough. "Someone please explain to me how you print food?"

Nikki stepped in when Rudy's mutterings were mostly profanities. "Frankly, it was quite interesting. Works like a regular printer only the cartridges are filled with edible pastes, food powders, herbs and sauces. The printer head goes back-and-forth, layer-on-layer, creating exotic looking, computer generated shapes. The food needs to be cooked but one of the chef's did mention that someone was working on a printer that will do just that."

She patted Rudy's shoulder. "Total fad. Right now it's getting fifteen minutes of fame but..." she snapped her fingers, "gone and forgotten by the time your restaurant opens." When he failed to respond, Nikki tried another tactic. "Rudy, why not try a game of checkmate?"

At his interested expression, she continued. "I mean that printer took a lot of time making that teeny-tiny polenta cube plus the blow torch. Create another one of your *YouTube* videos showing off quick summer food ideas. Your calamari in spicy cocktail sauce is a perfect example." Nikki watched the anger drain from his tanned face as he finally stopped pacing. "I'm sure there are a lot more recipes and...and... Why not post the recipes and your *YouTube* link in the front window of the restaurant. In fact you can play the cooking video in a loop on a big screen TV in your front window. Perfect coming attractions promo. Plus add in the link to the free app for direct connection to your cooking channel."

Rudy ran his fingers through the dark curls laced with silver that sculpted his head. "Hmmm...Nikki that is a brilliant idea." Borgianno smiled, "It's been too long since I added to my *YouTube Channel* of recipes."

Cantrell looked at her pleading expression and nodded. "I doubt any 3-D plastic food could have such a heavenly aroma."

Nikki patted his stomach. "Hungry?"

He held her hand against his body. "Not for printed food. Rudy, what delicacies have you brought that will save me from one of Nikki's microwaved burritos."

Borgianno gave a little hand flourish. "Roman, I brought antipasto." He lifted the silver cover on a heated chafing dish. "Linguini with clam sauce. The garlic bread is still warm and..." Reaching for a glass pitcher, Rudy arched a dark brow. "The perfect Manhattan to lift the gloom of this very rainy day."

"You are the ultimate guest," Roman complimented him, reaching for a dinner plate. "I trust you were able to get Nikki to eat something decent for a change."

"Yes, Nikki ate something decent," she mimicked.

"Nikki also ate her way through the food court at the mall." Rudy shuddered. "Including one of everything on the all-day breakfast menu at McDonalds."

"You two went shopping?" Roman settled comfortably on the sofa, balancing a fully loaded plate on his knees.

"Rudy went shopping. I went returning and exchanging," Nikki explained. "I kept a few things that Becky sent. I intend to eat my way into my old wardrobe."

"Well, I like that denim dress you're wearing and...oh...wait...you didn't return that lacy little *Victoria's Secret* negligee? I really liked that—"

"You should have said something, Cantrell. I would have given it to you, although I don't think peach is your best color."

Laughing, Rudy topped off his and Roman's cocktail glasses. "Do you sometimes wish the wiring was back in her jaw?"

Cantrell eyed Nikki, then grinned. "Never."

"Right answer." She wagged the tack hammer at him. "You haven't said a thing about my new office courtesy of Duncan's decorating skills."

"Between calming my nerves with a drink and my stomach with food, I really hadn't noticed. I do like this new white leather sofa."

Nikki crooked a finger at Duncan. "Let me present to you a future *HGTV* design star, former Blackpool footballer extraordinaire, Duncan Gladstone." She grabbed his arm, pulling him front and center. "Stop blushing and tell Cantrell how you created this fabulous room." Leaning in, Nikki stage whispered: "His home office needs a major overhaul."

"Mr. B?"

"Nikki's in charge." Rudy nodded, adding more smoked meat, olives, peppers and garlic bread to a second plate for Roman.

Duncan cleared his throat, smoothing the front of his black silk dress shirt and adjusting the shoulder holster. "I've been working up a design plan since Mr. B took pictures and laser measurements of the room the last time we were here. There've been lots of back and forth emails on things. And...well...my mates along with Edgar of course, came in so we could do this in one day.

"First thing was to take-up that old carpet and put down this bamboo floor. Eco friendly, renewable, easy for Manuela to take care of and so durable Miss Nikki could race around the room in her new office chair without worry.

"The walls got a fresh coat of paint. I made sure it was VOC free, environmentally friendly. Miss Nikki liked this light gray-green tone and I paired it with white crown molding and wide baseboards. Solar sheer shades are on the back window and the skylight. All are remote controlled. That's basically all I did, except maybe..." Duncan cleared his throat, averting his perpetually pink-rimmed eyes, "referee about the office furniture. Mr. B cancelled what Miss Nikki wanted, had this wall unit set up and...well...that was it."

Roman stood up and walked around the room inspecting the wall system, wide L-shaped desk and bookcases all in a distressed white oak finish. One interior wall had been armored in corkboard and held a pushpin-studded map of Florida, along with the photos Nikki had taken of the purported UFO landing site in the Belle Glade sugarcane field.

The end-cap bookcase featured more of her favorite conch shells and the blown glass animal collection that was one of Rudy's gifts. A six foot file cabinet was on the other end. The wall hutch held an impressive array of tech gear: a new all-in-one desk-top computer, both a laser and an optical printer, scanner and fax machine. He turned to Nikki, "I see you've joined the ranks of the tech savvy."

She wrinkled her nose at him. "I retired my typewriter to the closet. Duncan hooked all of this into our WiFi. I will admit the printed photos look pretty damn good. They were easy to download from the..." her fingers wiggled..."cloud."

Roman faced the rangy footballer turned designer, whose eyes blinked rapidly in panic. "Duncan, you did an outstanding job. I'm impressed enough to hire you to do the same for my in-home office."

He swallowed a laugh at Duncan's pronounced sigh of relief. "Why don't you work on an update for my office next door. I like everything in here but the white furniture, let's go darker wood, no sofa, a couple client chairs, more file cabincts...oh, and my desk chair is perfect. The room's a bit larger, has a side window and an outside door." He pulled a business card from his dress shirt pocket. "Hell, just go in and make some preliminary notes and take measurements, you can email me your design ideas, questions and an invoice." He slapped Duncan on his back. "Congratulations, you did an outstanding job."

"Now what are you grinning at, Cantrell?" her tone suspicious.

"I like the permanency of all of this."

"So do I," Rudy slipped a fatherly arm around Nikki's shoulders. "I want her to stay here. I enjoy doing things to help her and I like watching over her. It reminds me of the old days in Saratoga." His index finger tenderly traced her broken nose. "I should have taken you out of your house and put you someplace safe instead of just having you run numbers for me and—"

"And feeding me and giving me clothes and more than a few times ignoring the fact that I was sleeping on the couch in your poolroom." Nikki shook her head. "I hate giving power to the past. I have no interest in reliving my history. Even if it's just through old memories. I prefer the here and now, Rudy. The good old days just weren't, at least for me."

"Yeah, kid, I know." He kissed her forehead before turning his attention to Cantrell. "So far, Roman, you seem to be doing well by her. She has no complaints."

Roman smiled his thanks but didn't miss Rudy's implication of how he might view any failures. "So you two came to verbal blows over the furniture?"

"I just ignored her selections and chose this wall unit. One piece that does it all. It was a fight that I won. At least she didn't fight me on this ergonomic chair to help support her back. I don't like all the aspirins she keeps chewing."

"It's just the rainy weather," Nikki patted his arm. "The only reason I relented on the furniture was so you'd stop badgering me. I was flooded with emails showing off room after room of selections. You wore me down. Besides, tell the truth, Rudy, you'd already ordered it and scheduled the delivery." His tell-tale blush was all she needed to see.

Roman laughed. "I'll have to remember that approach when she gives me a problem. Who did the installation?"

"I did, with some help from Duncan and Edgar." Rudy declared proudly. "The upper wall unit is solid and secure enough to hold even Edgar." They all laughed. "You've got a well-built home, Roman, on a very nice piece of property."

"Actually, this house was my first fee. I was just starting out, taking on any legit job I could find and did some repo work for a client who turned out to be plastic rich. He was letting this place go into foreclosure, so I took it over in lieu of what I knew would be a bounced check."

Nikki cocked her head. "What did you repossess?"

"A seven passenger Cessna Citation CJ2."

"I didn't know you were a pilot."

"I'm a man of many talents." His dark eyebrows jiggled suggestively.

"And little modesty," she added quickly.

Rudy rubbed his jaw as he studied the antipasto platter. "Hmmm...I think that plane goes for around four million dollars."

He selected a prosciutto wrapped square of cheese. "Hardly in league with what you're currently trying to reclaim." His even white teeth sliced through the canape. "Five million, isn't it? Plus Hartwell's armored tractor-trailer."

Nikki shook her head at Roman. "He already knew."

"I trust you." Roman's smile was warm. "I'm really not surprised that you heard, Rudy. Just for my own information, do you have any idea who-done-it?"

"No." Rudy carefully wiped his hands on a linen napkin. "But I want to know. I need to know." His fist landed hard against the new credenza and perked up the dishes. "I don't appreciate these punks coming into my territory and pulling off a heist of this size. Hell, of any size.

"I've got enough trouble with the drug cartels bringing heroin into the Miami suburbs. People stupidly think it's just a party drug and they can't get hooked. There are too many teachers, too many professionals, too many teenagers..." Rudy's fist punched the air. "My end of the business is clean, Roman." His dark eyes focused on Cantrell. "No drugs. Never. Just gambling."

Crossing her arms across her chest, Nikki's eyes narrowed. "You told me you were retired and just mentoring."

"I am. I am. Officially I'm still in charge of the younger crowd and I make sure they don't even dabble in drugs. A few of my...business associates are...dabbling in...well, let's call it merchandising. That's why I want to know about these hijackers. They're treading on thin ice." Rudy inhaled deeply, then turned to smile at Nikki. "I apologize for the outburst, my dear. Sometimes business makes me"—he waved his hand—"forget my manners. Have you any new leads, Roman?"

"Nothing you probably don't already know."

"Do you still believe your friend Tony Mackey's story about the tank and the armed commandos?" Rudy's dark brow lifted skeptically.

"You do have big ears!"

"I'll take that as a compliment." Rudy delivered another gracious smile. "I have many people firmly in my pocket and my pocket reaches far beyond Dade County."

Roman nodded. "That comes in handy. By the way, I do believe Tony's story." He ignored Nikki's affected cough.

"Well, whoever did the job is going to need a fence. I've put the word out. I'll know the second anyone tries to get rid of the gold, silver and diamonds."

"I'd certainly appreciate hearing about that myself, if you don't mind," Roman nodded. "Hartwell is anxious to keep his reputation intact and his insurance premiums down."

"I think we'd all like to keep our reputations intact," Rudy clicked his glass against Roman's. "I'll be glad to keep you advised if I hear anything. I'd be delighted to share my knowledge with the FBI. Alex Lazarus is so much nicer than his father, isn't he, Nik?"

"The judge needed a lobotomy," she retorted, pushing another green pin into the wall map.

"Speaking of Alex..." Roman cleared his throat. "He said he'd be giving you a call about the lab report on those stones you found yesterday."

"Nikki," Rudy interjected, "I just set you up with a chemist for tomorrow at—"

"At *Prime One Twelve* in South Beach," she finished. "I know, Rudy. What I have Alex doing is—"

"Jumping through hoops," Roman finished. "Duplicity becomes you, Nik. Your skin glows, your hair shines and your brain goes into overdrive behind those chameleon eyes. You're much too Byzantine."

"Puhleeze..." She blew an errant copper curl off her forehead and faced him. "Alex wanted to help, so I compiled...well...substituted flowerpot gravel for the stones."

"Nikki, just because the government did a damn good job screwing you doesn't mean you can screw the government."

"Save the pontifications, Cantrell. My conscience is going to remain unconscious." Her upraised hand stalled any further comments. "It's not Alex I don't trust. Although he does have his head far up the government's ass."

"You don't trust the government lab?"

"Right. Any resemblance to the truth is purely accidental with them." She settled on the edge of her new desk. "You should read all those newly unclassified government documents Teresa gave me copies of and then tell me where to place my trust. Hell, if those rock samples turn out to be something, the government will confiscate, deny and bury."

"Then you admit to believing in those UFO sightings?"

"The same way you believe in Tony Mackey's tank and commandos." She walked over to the wall map. "While the guys were installing, I called over two dozen people who reported sightings that were on Teresa's list. They all said the same thing: a big, red, silent, glowing object that resembled the planet Saturn that hovered then disappeared. All but three of the two hundred sightings parroted that same description."

Her knuckles tapped the pins. "Those sightings I've marked in red and you can see how they cluster in three areas from Boca to Lake Worth to West Palm. Now, these three green pins around Belle Glade represent the odd sighting. That's the boomerang-shaped object that landed in the sugarcane field. Those are the three I believe in. At least, I believe some as yet unidentified object that flies did land and was seen.

"As for the other hundred plus sightings, I don't know...just a feeling. A very strong feeling that the UFO was a hoax. The reason for that scam will be my story."

That wild, unholy look Roman had come to know but not understand glittered in Nikki's eyes. He stared from her to Rudy, who shrugged, and back to her again. "Your story is on the hoax?"

Chapter 23

"Right. A phony UFO that was able to fool two hundred people. I already know the when and where. Now I need to discover the who, the how and the why." Settling back on the desk top, Nikki smoothed the denim dress. "That's what's nagging at me. Who would go to all that trouble? How did they create something that real and frightening? And why? What was the purpose? Maybe it's nothing more than a publicity stunt or a new product promotion. Either way, I'll find out."

Roman pointed at the series of color photos mounted on the wall. "What about the happening in the cane field?"

"Something besides your murdered armored-truck driver landed there, but no sign that a tank dropped him off," she joked. "Oh, come on, come on, Cantrell, stop with that disparaging look. I did some sleuthing today that just might be of interest to you."

"Sleuthing? What sleuthing?"

"Rainy days are great for phone conversations. I let my fingers do some legwork and..."

"Is there a point to this?" Vacating the sofa, Roman moved to her side, watching her stretch to retrieve something.

"Just getting my notes." She picked up a steno pad and riffled through the pages. "I called some contacts in the television and movie industry."

"TV and movies?"

"Right. Florida's got a healthy piece of the entertainment pie and I wanted to see if any sci-fi epics were being shot around here."

Roman lightly tugged her copper braid. "Very smart thinking. Miss Holden. But, I gather from your expression there weren't."

"You gather correctly and Darnie checked to see if Hollywood was doing anything in Florida. I did get a listing of special effects labs, although I seriously doubt the 'imagineers' at Disney would perpetrate a UFO hoax. Still, I'll start checking on the others tomorrow." She flipped over another page. "I did ask about the army."

"Whose army?"

"Our army," she chided. "The Pentagon has supported over five hundred films since World War Two. If they approve the script, feel it informs, is accurate, balanced and real, they'll provide technical assistance. This can be advisors, men, locations and equipment."

Roman exhaled sharply. "The tank and commandos. Did they?"

"They did not. However, when my movie source informed me that the Pentagon doesn't approve ninety percent of the scripts they're sent, he passed me along to a private military consulting firm. They're able to find the same equipment, locations, advisors and even a willing army if you have the money."

"Are they...?"

"They are not. Now, now..." She patted his cheek, noting the smoothly shaved face had been replaced by his sexy stubble. "My source also tells me that that doesn't preclude some B-movie production company from doing some filming. However, when I checked with the state's motion picture council, no permits have been issued. Still, it doesn't mean—"

"Nice try, anyway." He squeezed her thigh.

"I did get some interesting information on your tank, weapons and commandos. Most of this you probably already know." She sifted through the notebook. "Camouflage uniforms can be bought at surplus stores. Those Martian-type flying helmets Mackey claimed they were wearing are available in most toy stores, a place where very realistic-looking weapons can also be purchased. I was told toy stores look like war zones these days. Fun stuff for the kiddies."

Rudy Borgianno's cynical laugh intruded. "The real stuff is readily available, too. Unfortunately, some of it gets into the kiddies' hands." He brushed down the sleeves of his teal silk dress shirt. "Dade County is loaded, no pun intended, with Mac-10's, its smaller cousin the Mac-11, Uzis and a few acquaintances have in their possession Stinger missile launchers and a flamethrower that was bought online. Please, don't ask," he cautioned Roman, then added, "By the way, no one I know owns a tank."

"The good old M1A1," Nikki flipped over more pages. "Named after the late General Creighton W. Abrams, former Army Chief of Staff and commander of the 37th Armored Battalion. It's the backbone of the armored forces of the United States military and several US allies as well. Nearly nine thousand M1 and M1A1 tanks have been produced. About a thousand of them are being reconfigured to the M1A2 series that have all the new bells and whistles.

"General Dynamics[1] acquired the battle tank division of Chrysler and received a contract to build the U.S. Army's M-1 tank. When the first M-1 prototypes were delivered, there were serious design flaws and it went through two years of acceptance trials. After a series of modifications, the M1A1 was delivered in 1985. While it's one of the heaviest tanks in the world, it has tremendous firepower and maneuverability.

Roman neatened the collar of her dress. "Say, does this mean you're changing your mind about the hijacking?"

"I'm just giving you the facts, boy. Besides, you're the detective. You're the one who's supposed to go looking for something that isn't there and find it. I'm afraid that unless you head for the Aberdeen Proving Ground's tank row museum, you won't be finding any M1A1 tanks leaving their seventy-ton footprints on a Florida back road. Of course Alex did say there were no tank prints." Her head tilted. "'Edgar's here."

Roman grimaced. "Even I heard him. That man registers on the Richter scale. Rudy, you've got to stop feeding him steroids."

---

1.   http://www.crocodyl.org/wiki/general_dynamics

"Edgar's a bit over his NFL playing weight. He's a great food tester though," Borgianno shrugged on his jacket.

Edgar's grizzly-bear sized body filled the door frame. Short, black dreadlocks hugged his massive head while dark curls sprouted from the open collar on his white shirt. "Here's a receipt for your donation of all that medical equipment Miss Nikki." He nodded respectfully. "Mr. B. I got everything done. The weather, though, she's gettin' much worse."

"Fine. I'm coming." He raised his voice and called for Duncan. "No, no, you sit, Nikki. Don't bother with the dinner things, just keep them."

Rudy cupped her face in his hands and kissed each cheek. "Now, don't forget your luncheon date with Carlos Alvarez tomorrow. He's a very nice boy. Went to college with my nephew. And an excellent chemist. He'll answer all your questions." He shook hands with Roman. "Nice seeing you again. Glad you approve of Duncan's design work. I know he's thrilled. No, don't get up, we can see ourselves out."

Pausing at the door, Rudy turned to add, "Nikki, one word of caution about Carlos. He's quite the womanizer. If he gets out of hand, just mention my name."

Roman boosted himself onto the desk next to Nikki. "I don't like the sound of that."

"Then I'm glad you weren't here listening to the way I have to flatter and seduce information from some of my sources. I won't have any trouble handling the Don Juan of chemists. Even if I do, it'll be worth getting a truthful, informative analysis." She held up her palm. "Please don't mention Alex again."

"I've given up reforming you."

"What a relief!"

Roman laughed. "I'm curious. What are you going to do if the lab says your rock samples are not of this earth?"

Frowning, Nikki considered the implications. "Well, I guess I'll embrace the ideology of that great detective— Stop preening. Cantrell, I'm not referring to you. Sherlock Holmes is the one who said: 'when you eliminate the impossible then whatever remains, no matter how improbable, is the truth.'"

"Sherlock Holmes?"

"A criminologist of great genius."

"Unlike me, he wasn't real. He's a fictional character."

"That's your opinion, mister messy." She peeled a bite-size piece of linguini off his navy and white striped dress shirt. "How did you do with Ed Hartwell?"

Roman pressed his chin against his chest. "The truth isn't exactly what Ed was speaking."

"You think he hijacked his own truck?"

"I hope not." He stared at Nikki. "Hell...I'm damn sure he was lying about where and what he was doing yesterday. Hartwell's spending half his year in Atlanta. He claims his travels are either business or charity-related, so I'm having one of my operatives do some checking." His expression was bleak. "I hate not being able to trust my own client. Ed should damn well know that no matter how well-hidden, skeletons rattle like hell.'"

Nikki pulled the rubber band from her braid. "Well, maybe old Ed's skeleton doesn't have anything to do with the hijacking." Her fingers pried apart the woven copper locks. "Anybody tamper with the computers?"

"Not that we could find. Alex had his boys sweep the place after mine finished. But with all the new, high-tech eavesdropping devices available, it was really a show maneuver..." His voice faded.

Feeling restless, Roman got down from his perch on the desk and started pacing the room. "I've decided to expand and offer a stronger emphasis on corporate espionage and personal security. The way local law enforcement budgets have been cut, they certainly can't keep up with private-sector demands. Certain businesses are in need of state-of-the-art protection. I'm going to provide it."

"What was Hartwell's reaction to Mackey's story?"

"He's sticking with Tony. So am I." Roman grinned. "I think I'll embrace that great genius criminologist Sherlock Holmes's line about the improbable being the truth."

"Touché, touché."

As his hands combed through her hair, the vibrant curls insinuated themselves around his fingers. "Your French is lousy."

"But my choice of detectives isn't."

"Are we talking Holmes or Cantrell?"

"You decide." Nikki looped her arms around his neck. "I drank too many Manhattans, want to take advantage of me?"

Roman watched Nikki's ice blue eyes darken. Soften. Tempt. His own voice deepened. "Absolutely." He twisted the buttons free on her denim dress, "I know the perfect way to break in your new desk." His mouth swallowed her sexy laugh.

"That would kill my back, Cantrell, can't you be more inventive?"

"Hmmm....hmmm..." after pushing the dress off her body, he unhooked her bra and pulled her upright, "well I've always had this fantasy..." his thumbs locked onto the sides of her navy bikini briefs. "The big bad detective fucking the sexy reporter on a desk." He unbuckled his belt and dropped his pants and briefs. "So bend over and let's make my fantasy come true."

Chapter 24

Nikki patted the dashboard of her twenty-two year old dark blue Chevy Blazer for the tenth time. It felt so good to be behind the wheel again. Roman had the dealership replace all the seat cushions and heavily detail the car inside and out. Not a speck of blood or dirt remained anywhere on the vehicle. Her grin broadening at the new car scent that permeated the air conditioned air.

Navigating through the traffic on Ocean Drive, she headed for the historic Browns Hotel and the scene-stealing *Prime One Twelve* boutique steakhouse. Rudy had warned her that the restaurant was the place to see and be seen, so Nikki had spent more than her usual five minutes on makeup, hair and choosing an outfit. Reveling in the fact that her navy cowl neck halter top and navy and white pleated skirt not only complemented the restaurant's brick interior but harmonized with her sartorially elegant luncheon companion.

"I never dreamed that I would be so privileged to lunch with such a beautiful woman." Carlos Alvarez deliberately assessed her curvaceous body before allowing his lips to languish against the top of her hand.

Ahhh...Latin machismo. With some difficulty, Nikki managed to regain control of her arm. "You're too kind." Settling on the beige leather dining chair at their small table, she kept her tone and manner formal. "I'm hopeful you'll be able to quickly analyze the samples I've—"

"Please, please, must we rush into business?" His manicured fingers plucked the rose from the table vase and presented it to her. "Let's enjoy each other's company. Become intimate with our hopes and dreams." Carlos claimed both menus from the waiter. "First, we must toast the fates that conspired to bring us together. I am an excellent judge of voices, Nikki, and yours says whiskey and soda."

Her eyes glittered as dangerously as his. but with an entirely different meaning. "My voice may say whiskey and soda but I'll be drinking this..." Her fingernail made the crystal water goblet ring. "Rudy Borgianno told me you were one of the best chemists around. And that's all I'm interested in. Do I make myself clear?" Nikki watched his Adam's apple climb his throat a half dozen times before he finally spoke.

"How is Tío Rudy?"

"Anxious not to have me disappointed."

He eased the collar on his light blue shirt. "My policy is to never disappoint a lady in either pleasure or business. Who knows, maybe in this case one will lead to another. "

"Carlos..." Her warning changed into laughter. "I really don't think you can help yourself, can you? You're primed all the time."

"You wound me, Nikki, I...I..." A frown marred his handsome features. Carlos ran his fingers through his thick, wavy black hair. "Am I so obvious that you see right through me?'"

"Don't worry about it," she patted the top of his hand. "You're probably too successful with women for your own health."

He considered that for a moment, then gave her a dazzling smile. "That is very true. Sometimes, I get quite exhausted by it all."

"Our luncheon will be the perfect respite." Nikki took the plastic sample bags from her purse. "I need to know about these."

Carlos took his time with each of the five pebbles. He felt the weight, the hardness, studied the white, silver and blue-gray colors. Finally, he rolled the pellets between his fingers, letting them tumble together in his cupped palm. "Hmmm...where did you find these?"

"In a sugarcane field in Belle Glade." She showed him one of the photographs. "They were scattered along this...I guess you'd call it a fault line. I checked the depth. It went well beyond ninety feet. The cane plants were destroyed as well." She handed Carlos a bag containing shriveled, white leaves. "According to the farmer, his crop was completely bleached. I don't suppose you'd have any ideas about that?"

"Well, I did take quite a few botany courses," he informed her. "A plant becomes bleached or white when it loses its chlorophyll, the leaves turn like these."

"What would cause an entire swath of cane, in an otherwise healthy field, to lose chlorophyll? If it was due to disease, insects or even a reaction to a pesticide, the destruction wouldn't have been in such a deliberate pattern." She showed him another photo.

"Curious. One thing that comes to mind is a high concentration of ultraviolet light." His even white teeth shone brilliantly. "I don't know if that is of any help."

"I'm not sure either." She jotted down his suggestion in her notebook. "What about these pebbles?"

"I must admit I find them of extreme interest. Before I give an expert opinion, a few tests need to be done." Carlos checked his watch. "Yes, now would be the perfect time. Why don't you peruse the menu. The cuisine here is -" he kissed three fingers "...extraordinary. Order a salad and before our main course arrives, I'll be back from the lab."

Sliding from the booth, he tucked the specimen bags into the pockets of his white silk jacket. "You are on an expense account, yes, Nikki?" At her nod, Carlos flipped open the menu and tapped one of the most expensive items. "I like both my women and my Kobe filet very rare." He winked. "Make it a ten ounce portion, with baked potato and grilled asparagus. I always make lunch my main meal."

Chapter 25

Despite the fact the restaurant was filled to capacity, Roman easily sighted the back of Nikki's shoulder length copper curls in a secluded table in the rear of the dining room. With dexterous skill, he traversed the waiting line, foiled the maître d' and sidestepped two bustling waiters. He felt supremely confident that in this milieu he'd be able to take her by surprise.

"Unlike the fog, Cantrell, you do not walk on cat's feet." Nikki looked over her shoulder and smiled at his disgruntled expression. "Come on, sit down. You can eat Carlos' salad before the lettuce wilts."

"So, where is he?" Roman sniffed the air and whistled, "Cloying cologne."

"Matches his personality. Alvarez is what I call too-too. Too handsome, too suave, too attentive." She wrinkled her nose. "Just way too much of everything. Including an accented voice designed to induce orgasms."

Roman choked on a cucumber slice. "Did it?"

"Don't strain yourself, Cantrell." She handed him her glass of water "The mention of Rudy's name was quite castrating. Actually, the guy may turn out to be a great source. He's back at the lab checking out those stones." She smeared butter on another warm slice of bread. "What are you doing here?"

"I just happened to be in the area closing a deal on the golf course when hunger struck and I remembered you were lunching here and... All right, all right, can that look, Holden. I wasn't being convinced either."

"Jealousy makes you blush, Cantrell. What? No comeback?"

"I'm all out of words, but..." He reached under the table and squeezed her knee. "I'm getting a few ideas. Did I tell you how beautiful you look?"

"We can talk about what I look like later." Shifting her legs, she dislodged his groping hand. "Find out anything new on your hijacking?"

"Alex got a more complete autopsy on Glenn Ennis. Seems he was electrocuted, which induced a heart attack." Roman chewed reflectively. "Funny thing, though, there were no burn marks on the body."

He confiscated the last slice of bread from the basket. "I should be getting a preliminary report on Hartwell's Atlanta trips later tonight. Just got finished ordering secure voice/data telephones to be installed over there this afternoon. They can't be tapped or monitored."

"Another possible leak plugged." Nikki pushed aside her empty salad plate. "I wish Carlos would get the lead out."

"Maybe his analysis will match Alex's report of nice, clean, all-American tumbled stones."

"That's exactly what Alex should have reported, Cantrell."

He held up his palms in defense and changed the subject. "Weren't you supposed to talk to some special-effects people this morning?"

"Bright and early." She shuffled through her notes. "Crossed four off my list of five. Two are doing miniaturizations; another is working on animation; and the fourth's re-creating those clay models that are enjoying a revival in TV commercials.

"The last one is housed in the boonies of Lauderdale and no one seems to answer the phone. I thought I might drive over there tomorrow and see 'The Gadget Man.' At least that's what my movie source called Nathan Ives. He's been working with robotics and has supplied a half dozen of them to Hollywood. My informant also mentioned that Ives is eccentric as hell and has more than a few peculiarities. That last comment came in the company of a weird laugh."

Nikki made some squiggles in the page margin. "If Ives does prove interesting enough for a profile piece, I'll have Darnie start digging."

"Does this mean you're giving up the tabloid life?"

"In a heartbeat." Her lips curved upward. "I am going to try to keep the tabloid salary scale. Sometimes Matt Cortlund can be such a tightwad. You should see how he fine-combs expense accounts and — " Nikki inhaled. "Move over to the next chair Cantrell and don't say a word. The chemist is coming back to roost."

"Again you wound me, Nikki." Carlos inspected Roman before settling his dark gaze on her. "Am I so easy to replace?"

"You are an original, Carlos." She introduced the two men, amused when they acknowledged each other with polite nods. "Now, how did you do with the analysis?"

"He has eaten my salad."

"I'll order you another." She signaled for the waiter.

"No. Don't bother." He tried edging his shoulder higher than Roman's but failed. "Limp greenery cannot offer a man like me the sustenance with which to pursue life's pleasures. I need —"

"I know. I know. Rare meat." Nikki kicked Roman's ankle when she saw his mouth gape open. "This joint is packed, service is slow, but I'm sure your Kobe beef will be out soon." She tapped the table. "Now, about the stones, Rudy said you'd be able to find some answers."

The mention of Borgianno's name halted Carlos's guttural Spanish expletives. He pulled the samples from his pockets, took a deep breath and centered himself. When he spoke, he was all business. "First, let me ask you once again where you got these stones?"

"A sugarcane field in Belle Glade."

"Most unusual." He rubbed his jaw. "In fact, quite improbable. That's why I needed to be positive. I checked them with a variety of test equipment I have in the lab including a mass spectrometer, X-ray florescence and an electron microprobe, like the one used to analyze the moon rocks. They all showed something very strange. Frankly, these elements don't occur in nature in this concentrated form."

Nikki poked at the stones. "What are they?"

"The largest group, the white ones, are iridium; this blue-gray is osmium; and the silvery stone is rhodium. All but osmium are mixed with platinum. All have no business being in Florida. And all are in a very pure phase."

"Where are they found?"

"Canada, Alaska, Russia. Rhodium is a by-product of nickel manufacturing. Industry uses it as a coating to prevent wear and corrosion on scientific equipment and electrical parts. When mixed with platinum, the alloy is used in thermocouples and is not soluble in acid.

"Osmium has the greatest density of all known elements," he continued. "It is refined from the same ore as platinum and used in electric light filaments. What you have is very pure and can potentially be dangerous."

"This little rock? Dangerous?"

"Yes. Water boils at two hundred twelve degrees Fahrenheit and is harmless. When osmium is heated above three hundred ninety-two degrees, it gives off a vapor that can cause total blindness."

Her pen moved quickly across the notebook page. "Well, they did prove unique and how they strayed from their normal environment is a question in search of an answer. But," Nikki frowned. "They are of this earth."

"Iridium isn't."

"Isn't what?"

"Found in large quantities in the earth. In fact, it's quite rare and normally found..."

"Found where?"

"Perhaps I'm getting a little ahead of myself," Carlos explained. "Let me tell you about iridium. It is one of the hardest of all metals, melts at two thousand four hundred ten degrees Celsius and boils at four thousand five hundred twenty-seven degrees Celsius, and resists corrosion better than any known metal."

She considered all that. "What's it used for?"

"Its chief use is to harden platinum. It's also being used as a catalyst in hydro formylation." He grinned at her questioning expression. "Simply put, hydro formylation is an industrial process involving a chemical change where a small molecule can be added to a larger molecule to form an aldehyde. To answer your next question, aldehydes are volatile, reactive compounds that are very important to industry for a variety of products."

"That still sounds innocuous enough," she said. "I don't suppose iridium has any other interesting secrets?"

"It's also quite possibly what killed the dinosaurs."

"Dinosaurs?" Nikki stared at him. "How in hell did we drag dinosaurs into this?"

"Well, several years ago scientists discovered underground concentrations of iridium between sediments deposited at the end of the Cretaceous Period, when extinction of the dinosaurs occurred, and the Tertiary Period."

"You mean they ate it and died?"

"Not exactly, and let me add that this is just one of the many controversial contenders in the 'what killed the dinosaurs' debate. Some scientists believe that sixty-five million years ago a giant meteorite or asteroid collided with the earth and that the iridium was the residue of that collision. "

Nikki scratched her head with her pen. "You've lost me, Carlos. What has iridium to do with asteroids?"

"Oh, did I forget to mention that? While iridium is quite rare on earth, it is plentiful in meteorites and asteroids."

"Plentiful in meteorites and asteroids," she repeated, staring from Carlos to Roman, who, with a smile, pointed skyward with his index finger. Nikki tried to shake off the UFO implications but couldn't, at least not fully.

Checking back through her notes, she asked, "About these aldehydes. You said they're used in various industrial processes and are quite volatile. Like...like..." She swallowed. "Could they be used as fuel?"

Carlos was thoughtful for a long moment. "Fuel? Mmm...aldehydes are like alcohol in some ways, and that is used as fuel. But, no, Nikki, the heat content in an aldehyde is much less, so its fuel value is not great. Of course, one day someone might create something that could react with an aldehyde and generate power."

"Iridium is the catalyst in creating the aldehydes?"

He nodded. "All three of these elements are technically demanding substances used only by technologically advanced countries." Carlos focused on the stones. "They are very rare, very expensive and available in extremely limited quantities." He leaned forward, his voice low. "What you've got here is worth a fortune, Nikki."

"I'm not interested in money, Carlos. Just the who, what, how and why." When the waiter appeared with their entrees, Nikki quickly confiscated the stones and shoved them into her purse.

Now she knew what they were.

How they could be used.

But who in hell was using them?

According to Alvarez, it would have to be a technologically advanced civilization.

Higher than ours?

How were these elements being used?

"Maybe as fuel." she murmured. "Fuel used to power objects that fly. Christ, I must be crazy. Asteroids and meteorites and things that go bump in the night..."

Roman's voice invaded her musings. "Huh? What?"

"I wondered what you were—"

"Going to do with my steak sandwich? It's all yours, Cantrell." She pushed the plate toward him. "Eat hearty, boys. Carlos," Nikki stood up and extended her hand, "Rudy was right. You are a great chemist."

"Then you will tell Tío Rudy that I did not disappoint you?"

"Absolutely. Enjoy your lunch, boys, have the fried Oreos for dessert. I'll pay the tab on the way out."

"Nikki..." Roman struggled to rise but failed to get leverage. "Where the hell are you going?"

"The Air Force." She issued him a salute and blew him a kiss.

Chapter 26

While the maître d' was tracking down the bill, Nikki slid into a quiet corner, pulled out her sat phone and punched in a direct number to Homestead Air Force Base. A very nasal masculine voice droned, "Colonel Meyers's office."

"General Holden calling the colonel."

"General...uh...who?"

"Holden," her voice was sharp. "And the general does not like to be kept waiting."

"Yes, ma'am!"

She didn't have time to pop a dinner mint into her mouth before a familiar voice chuckled in her ear. "General, huh? Last time you called me, Nikki, you were only a major."

"'I gave myself a promotion. How are you, Ned?"

"Fine. Even better hearing that sexy voice of yours."

"How'd you like to take the voice and the rest of me to lunch? Someplace nice and private off base."

"Nik...are you... Hell, are you here in—"

"Miami."

"Well, hell's bells, girl, get on over here. I'll meet you at the...I know, the Cambridge House. It's Florida's version of New England. That's a mix of rustic charm and ceiling fans," he added with a laugh. "There's a billboard for it on US1. Just follow the directions and...Whoa, wait a minute. Is this a free meal?"

"I'm picking up the tab, Ned." She smiled at the maître d' and scribbled her name on the credit voucher, adding a liberal tip that would require a lot of explaining to Matt. "All you have to do is bring yourself and..."

"Uh-oh...what?"

"All the information you have on unidentified flying objects. See you in a bit."

Chapter 27

"You've got two of the most lascivious blue eyes I've ever seen, Colonel."

"All the better to eat you with, my dear. These baby blues and three divorces are why I'll never make general!" Ned Myers held both her hands. "Look who's talking about eyes." He winked extravagantly. "You get more beautiful every time I see you. Which isn't often enough. How're Matt and Becky? I expect to get up to Saratoga the end of next month to watch their horses run. Right now I'm up to my ears in—"

"Paperwork," she finished for him. "They're fine. You look great. Military trim."

"I'm thinking of writing *The Barracks Food Diet*."

She laughed at his grimace. "Look at all these medals! I can barely see your uniform." She tapped his chest. "They don't give those out for paperwork."

"No, just for breathing the right way on a particular day." Sliding an arm around her bare shoulders, he guided her to a corner table in the quiet, nearly empty restaurant. "I'm going to be sixty-two in four months, Nikki. I'm ready to retire. Ready to spend my days fishing and eating fattening food and sleeping. God help anyone who dares blow a bugle in my ear at five-thirty in the A.M.—" His finger sliced across his throat.

She settled in a chair, watching him pull out the one next to hers. "I was sorry to hear from Matt that you got divorced again. I rather liked Cheryl. We all had a good time when you visited Chicago last year."

"Yeah, I liked Cheryl, too." He ran a hand through his short cropped gray hair. "Unfortunately, she began not liking me liking Milly."

"Milly?"

"'That's who I'm dating now."

Nikki clicked her tongue against the roof of her mouth. "Ned sounds to me like you were dating Milly then, too."

His grin was irreverent. "Charm. I just can't seem to turn it off." He winked at the teenage waitress, who blushed. "Are we eating or is this just a pumping mission?"

"We are definitely eating. Make mine a cheeseburger with everything and a double order of fries."

"Make it for two." Ned waited for the waitress to depart. "Now, what's with this call about UFO information? This isn't your usual beat, Nik."

"Matt's idea, he just bought *Scuttlebutt*," At his snicker, Nikki took a deep breath. "I'll tell you something Ned it's getting curiouser and curiouser." She pulled out her notebook. "I've got two hundred sightings logged in the last three weeks. Two hundred. Something must have showed up on your radar."

"'Lots of things show up on our radar, kid." He opened his briefcase and extracted a thick file. "All are easily explained. These are probably what your people saw."

Ned slapped down a black-and-white photograph. "First off, you got your Willie Fudds. Translated, that's a radar plane. You can see that from certain angles this oval-topped design might easily be mistaken for a flying saucer."

Nikki studied the picture for a moment. "Yes, it certainly could. Especially at night, in a hazy sky and...radar planes, they fly low, don't they?"

"Altitudes vary. We assign high and low. They do, however, fly in a figure-eight formation with their radar tracking two hundred miles in every direction. They are out there workin' their wings off, Nikki, nailing drug smugglers. Who are also operating low-flying aircraft."

He added another photo. "This, believe it or not, isn't even an aircraft. It's a contrail. Condensation," he clarified, "the water vapor that forms in the wake of a plane. Short cons reflect a lot of light, atmospheric winds twist them into shapes, their dissipation is very slow and sometimes, the rotating beam behind the plane's cockpit can create interesting optical illusions." Ned moved the file aside so the waitress could serve lunch. "There are a few things I don't have pictures of, Nikki."

"Like what?" She liberally painted the fries and burger with ketchup.

"Well, about six months ago we had a rash of phone calls on a UFO night sighting. Turned out to be a Japanese rocket that was launched to deploy two satellites. The rocket was on its third orbit, on a northeast track that brought it across the Gulf of Mexico, Florida and northward over the Atlantic. As I recall"—he crunched into a pickle—"that rocket was observed in Michigan, Ohio and as far north as Maine."

Nikki swallowed a mouthful of burger. "Are you saying the Japanese launched another rocket about three weeks ago?" His enigmatic smile made her glower. "Come on, Ned."

"Let's just say I didn't say they didn't. Honey, everyone's launching everything these days and mostly from the Cape." He speared into the stack of fries. "Then again, there's always a meteor running amok. Over a thousand people were injured in Russia when a ten ton meteor hit a few years ago. One hit Ontario this past spring. Some poor farmer in India was personally slammed. It's the end of July and we get jammed up when the *Delta Aquarid* meteor shower hits, August for the *Perseid* and then in November the *Leonid* meteor shower rains down. That one is particularly brilliant."

"Don't meteor showers give the shooting-star effect?" She shucked through her notebook. "The reports I've got all say the same thing: object resembles the planet Saturn, glows red, dances across the sky and disappears. Somebody mentioned a cloaking device."

Ned hooted. "Notice how these UFOs never land at a military base so we're able to check out these cloaking devices. I think the Syfy channel just ran the *Philadelphia Experiment* again."

"I know all about the cigar-shaped UFOs that turn out to be blimps." Nikki's finger tapped down a list. "The weather balloons, hot air balloons and drones."

Ned groaned. "Damn drones. There are over fifteen hundred different drone models out there, too many with lasers that are bothering pilots. One model now has vertical flame throwers."

He rubbed his forehead. "In your time-frame we also had a paraglider in that area who had decorated his chute with rainbow LED lights. Along with a couple guys in those flying wing suits that were trying to set a new record for some magazine. They were doing early morning flights carrying a variety of colored smoke flares.

"Don't forget all the worn-out satellites that keep falling?" Ned added, picking up the litany. "We've gotten airline pilot reports of burning space debris. There's a lot of that up there, Nik. As it falls through the atmosphere, burning and disintegrating, people do see weird visual effects."

Ned scanned the dining room, making sure no one was in hearing range. "Because I know how trustworthy you are, Colonel Holden"—his hand slipped inside the briefcase—"I'm going to show you a few things that officially don't exist. What's this look like to you?"

Her eyes widened. "Except for the wheels, it's a flying saucer!"

"It's a prototype of an experimental fighter. This is what happens when the British Osprey has a baby with a Marine Harrier," he laid a second photo down. A third glossy was added. "We've got three hundred and fifty-five of these babies in service already," he reported proudly. "You can see the saucer's got a much shorter wing span and a more oval shape. On takeoffs and landings, the wings rotate horizontally while the plane moves vertically. Add to that, it has the standard red lights and is much quieter than normal aircraft."

"That certainly sounds like a good match to the UFO sightings," Nikki agreed. "Have you been testing this around here? Oh...damn...not another of your 'maybe yes, maybe no' smiles, Ned." She pushed her hands through her hair. "Listen, I'm not in the military secrets market and you damn well know I'm not going to publish any of this. I really do need the facts, sir."

"Even I'm not sure of all the facts, ma'am," Ned admitted. He returned the photos to the safety of his briefcase. "I do know that a top-secret missile was launched in the past three weeks and it carried an unarmed re-entry vehicle that *could* have produced some sightings.

"We've also had some fun visitors here at the base," he pulled out a couple more photos. "These are going to be press releases shortly. The SAAB 37 Viggen, the French Dassault Rafale and the new Swedish JAS 39 Gripen all flew in during your time period. As you can see depending on the view, they all look slightly UFO-like.

"My new favorite is this," Ned slapped another photo on the table. "Meet the Airlander 10 airship. It's a hybrid of a blimp, a helicopter and an airplane. Its nickname is the 'flying bum'" he winked, "because of the rounded end."

"Hmmm...that does look like that cigar-shaped craft a few people mentioned."

"Of course, there is this." He rummaged through the file folder.

"I don't think I like the satanic grin that's spread across your face, Colonel. Hey, that is a flying saucer!" Nikki pulled the photo closer.

"Sure is. Fifty feet in diameter. More blinking lights than a Christmas tree."

"I get the feeling there's a punch line to this story." She pushed the photo back at him.

"Absolutely." He tapped the saucer. "Man-made. As a matter of fact, this is just one of...oh, I'd say a good baker's dozen of homemade UFO's we've encountered. Let me tell you, they appear very real on film but up close and personal..." He shook his head.

"Hell," he continued, "we've even got recorded interviews from people insisting they've had a close encounter, been examined and probed by aliens. Some even gave themselves burn marks or bizarre tattoos just to make the story convincing. There's one guy who says he mated with a lady from Saturn."

Nikki nodded. "Yeah, I met a woman who swears she's carrying an alien baby. I guess everyone wants their fifteen minutes of fame."

"You got it pegged, kid. So, what d 'ya think? Did I provide any answers?"

"Just gave me a few more questions." She twirled a French fry in a puddle of ketchup. "I'll tell you, Ned, I've got one hundred and ninety-seven people who've witnessed the red, glowing UFO and I've got a gut feeling it's a scam of some sort. The three other reports are alike but different." She told him about the boomerang-shaped object before pulling out the baggies of stones and the sugarcane leaves.

"Belle Glade area? Hmmm. Wait a sec, I've got a computer log someplace." He thumbed through the print outs. "Belle Glade...a week ago, you said? Not there, not there... Well!"

"Well what?"

"This is sensitive."

"Colonel, remember you are briefing a general. Come on, Ned, what's so sensitive?"

"We had a radar plane in that area that did report a return on their scope but no visual sightings. That could have been something."

"Something? You mean like space debris, contrails, or, and I quote, 'a misinterpretation of various conventional astronomical and aerial objects seen under unusual circumstances?"

"Now, don't sound like that, Nikki. What the hell did you expect the boys to report? We saw the *Starship Enterprise*?"

Her hand settled on his shoulder. "Sorry, sorry. I'm just so confused. I'll tell you, Ned, I like dealing with things that are concrete not these con trails."

"I know you do, kid. That's why I've never minded being one of your sources. You're thorough, you're fair and you're honest." Ned was thoughtful for a long moment. "You know what, Nik? You really need a crash course in science."

Noting her approving expression, he continued. "Come back to the base with me. I'll phone a few trusted friends, pave a path and you can add new names to your source file." His silver eyebrows wiggled. "I think the University of Tennessee's Space Institute is a quick trip you should make. They'll be able to give you some concrete technology that just may answer your questions."

"Sounds good. Let's go."

"Sit down, General Holden. I haven't had any dessert. After that, we'll head to the base and get you outta those clothes."

Chapter 28

The late news flashed on the silent bedroom flat screen at the same instant Roman heard water running in the kitchen. Nikki! He stopped pacing, yanked off his clothes, kicked them under the bed and dived between the sheets.

Breathe deep and relax. Give no hint that you've been sweating bullets all evening wondering where the hell she was. After all, weren't you the big shot who promised never to clock her comings and goings and interfere with her career?

No nagging. No why didn't you call. Keep the talk light and easy. Let her take the lead. Besides, he grinned, *she has come home.*

"Hi...oh, sorry." Nikki grimaced. "Did I wake you?'

"Nope, just catching up with current events." He aimed the remote control and snapped off the set.

Her low-heeled sandals sailed through space. "I didn't realize I was going to be this late."

"I thought you'd gone and enlisted. I see you've lost your clothes and are wearing a green flight suit."

"Me? In a regimented environment? We're talking court-martial in two minutes. I got the deluxe grand tour of Homestead Air Force Base and was taken for a Top Gun-style ride in a jet." Settling on the edge of the bed, she massaged her feet. "I did start to call but...well I need to program your private cell and the house phone into the sat phone. Thanks for leaving the gate open. I need the code for that, too."

"Here, let me do that." He grabbed her ankles and swung her legs around, resting her bare feet on his naked chest. "So...did the Air Force give you anything?" He kneaded the hot, calloused sole on her right foot.

"Just a headache. More and more questions. Fewer and fewer answers. Ned Meyers, he's my source, doesn't supply me with government rhetoric. Mmm...that feels good."

Nikki collapsed backward on the mattress. "By the way, I'll be heading for the Space Institute in Tennessee on Wednesday. Just for the day. Ned suggested a crash course in science and I think he might be right."

She shared her information with Roman. "I don't know what to believe, Cantrell. Flying saucers here, there and everywhere. Rare elements in a sugarcane field. Plus there was a true unidentified blip on a radar screen in the Belle Glade area. I sent a text to Darnie to check and see what DARPA is doing." Rising up on her elbows, Nikki winked. "Your tank hijacking sounds more and more plausible by the minute. What's new on that front?"

"Alex went through the mélange of tire tracks and footprints made in the cane field. Zilch. That area was in constant use plus there's an automatic irrigation system."

"No impressions of any kind where the hijacking happened?"

"If you mean caterpillar tracks? Nothing. No footprints either. Yes, I know, it's weird."

"Weirdness seems to be the byword these days." Her toes tickled amid the dark hairs that matted his chest. "Did you get a report on Hartwell?"

"Only partial."

"That heavy sigh tells me you didn't like what you got."

"I think I've got a man leading two lives."

Nikki wiggled her feet free and sat up. "How so?"

"While he has a standing reservation at the Hyatt two weekends a month, his room is never occupied." At her raised eyebrow, Roman explained. "Ed always books the twentieth floor. He tips the maid heavily for services not rendered. She knows what beds and towels are used. He doesn't use either." His hand rubbed his jaw. "However, he drops in daily to pick up his messages and he does conduct business in the restaurants. He just doesn't sleep there."

"He is sleeping somewhere," Nikki pointed out. "Perhaps with someone?"

"I've got an operative working on that end and another checking out the Atlanta banks. Hartwell's local personal and business accounts don't show any transactions from Georgia, nor do his credit card vouchers pick up anything but the Hyatt invoices."

"Are his business charges legit?"

Roman nodded. "Seem to be. I'll tell you something, Nik, his business is not increasing in proportion to the time and money these Atlanta weekends are costing. That includes his charity obligations, as well."

"Double lives can cost big bucks, Cantrell."

"Five million?"

"Depends on how long this has been going on. Did you check with Rudy?"

"Yes, his fences report no contacts. He's putting the word out outside of Florida, too." His dark head inclined against the stack of pillows. "All that gold and silver is just sitting someplace..."

"Waiting for a good detective to find it." She slid off the bed. "Well, I think I'll go find a hot bath." Nikki went to work on all the Nomex flight suit's zippers and tabs, tossed it on Roman's wooden valet and watched as it slid off something gray, landing on the carpet. "Hey, what's occupying my spot? Cantrell, this is..." She turned around. "This is a Hartwell Armored Services uniform."

"Yes and in..." he glanced at the digital clock, "...four hours, Alex and I will be driving a Hartwell Armored Car. Ed's got a small but valuable shipment going out and we thought we'd see if anyone wants to hijack this cargo."

The look of concern on her face made Roman smile. "It's perfectly safe, Nik. We're even getting a chopper escort. The route is short. Hell, I should be back in time to cook you breakfast."

"I'll hold you to that, Cantrell. You know how nasty I get when I miss a meal."

Chapter 29

He thought for sure she'd kiss him good-bye.

Nikki kept sleeping.

Soundly.

Despite the deliberate commotion he was making.

Roman was half out the bedroom door when the sound of her voice and her words rearranged his lips into a smile. "Hey, Cantrell, I already know you're a tough guy. You don't have to keep proving it. So, if a tank does show up, make sure you protect your cute ass and don't let that tat get scratched up."

An hour later, Nikki stopped pretending she was asleep. Stopped pretending she was detached about Roman's undercover assignment. Rolling over, she settled comfortably on his side of the mattress. Living with Roman Cantrell was changing her. Not only had she given herself physically now she'd become emotionally intimate as well.

That made her—angry!

Her fingertips rubbed the sudden tightness from her forehead. Angry because all this caring and sharing was making her vulnerable.

Angry because now she was thinking about someone besides herself.

She didn't like that either.

Nikki sat up. "Am I angry enough to pack up and leave?"

Her question echoed around the room.

Searching for an answer.

Finding only silence.

Until, from a dark corner deep inside, a tiny, seldom heard voice forcefully responded, *No. Risk more. Attain more.*

"Attain what? Love? Shit, having a conscience is going to be a fucking pain." She walked into the kitchen and made coffee.

Chapter 30

Her radar clicked in before the security panel showed the gate was opening. "Seven A.M. and all's well." Nikki allowed only the bathroom mirror to witness her smile.

When Alex and Roman walked into the kitchen, they found her seated at the island reading the comics. "Hi, guys, your coffees are getting cold." She glanced over the newspaper at them. "Hey, why the long faces? Jeez!" The paper fell as she jumped up. "Cantrell, you...you weren't..."

"Hijacked?" Roman shook his head and reached for the steaming mug. "Nothing. Nada. The most goddamn boring drive I've ever taken."

Alex settled on the stool. "We set a beauty of a trap and didn't catch a thing."

"Well, maybe five million was all they needed."

Both men grunted.

"I made breakfast."

They grunted again.

"Hey, I do know how to cook."

"Burritos for breakfast are not—"

"Cantrell, I never *make* burritos. I buy them. I did make ..." With a flourish, Nikki opened the microwave oven door and pulled out a steaming platter. "Ham and cheese omelets."

He sniffed. "Say, these look and smell like the real thing."

"They are the real thing." She added two large glasses of orange juice to the counter.

"From scratch?"

"Hey I can make more than ice from scratch." Nikki placed the carafe next to the oval serving platter between their two place settings. "Eat hearty, I'm off."

Roman stopped chewing long enough to notice her white pencil skirt and flowing white and navy trimmed blouse. "You're all dressed. Makeup, too."

She ruffled his hair. "What a detective. I'm off to track down...Uhh...say Alex I wouldn't look at the headlines until after you finish eating."

"Why not...oh, fuck!" Alex tossed the paper at Roman. "Somebody leaked to the Herald about the hijacking. I'd better call in." He scraped his bar stool back, grabbing his cell and headed for a quiet area in the living room.

Roman's arm captured Nikki around the waist. "Isn't it a little early for you to be off and running?"

"It's the early reporter that catches the worm. I found your note this morning. Thanks again for adding all the phone numbers to the sat phone, leaving me a front door key and the gate code.

"Oh one more thing, Duncan and Edgar will be stopping by with paint samples, office furniture choices and to measure for the solar shades. I told them that Manuela and Santi will be here until eleven to let them in." Her index finger flowed along the strong line of his cheekbone, followed the curve of his jaw and outlined his lips. "Get some sleep. I'm off in search of The Gadget Man. Nathan Ives. Maybe I'll bring you home a robot."

He kissed her palm. "I prefer just you."

Chapter 31

Apparently land developers had yet to discover this odd little corner of Fort Lauderdale. "That is if I'm still in Broward County." Adjusting her sunglasses, Nikki peered through all the Blazer's windows and frowned. No condos or country estates. No commercial buildings or warehouses. No swampy farmlands or migrant camp grounds. Nothing save wispy Australian pines, thick-trunked palms, mango groves and lush tropical vegetation. Scenery reminiscent of an African rain forest.

The mailing address for The Gadget Man was a post office box. There was no web page that she was able to find. Despite repeated tries at different hours of the day, the phone at Ives Incorporated failed to be answered. *Google Maps* turned out to be useless.

Using the rough directions from her Hollywood contact and stopping twice for help at a gas station and a live bait stand that also made tacos, which were pretty damn tasty, she was finally able to locate the blind drive that led to Nathan Ives' three acre research facility.

Shifting into four-wheel drive, Nikki focused on navigating the rutted stretch, fighting the steering with each twist and turn. Her concentration was so intent that when a building unexpectedly blocked her path, she slammed on the brakes. The car came to a neck-snapping halt inches away from concrete steps.

"Just think what would have happened if you were doing five miles an hour," she murmured, massaging the back of her neck. Nikki expected someone to come out of the building.

No one did.

Getting out of the car, she sighted five huge warehouse-style buildings that were devoid of visible activity. Was Ives Incorporated still in business?

An elaborate gold-and-black OFFICE was stenciled on the opaque window of the door. Below it hung a white eyelet triangle, whose blue embroidered words proclaimed: ATTACK CAT ON DUTY.

The attack cat was the first to acknowledge Nikki Holden when she walked inside.

She gratefully inhaled the air-conditioned coolness while she tracked down the source of the welcoming purr. The cat wasn't difficult to find. He lay comfortably ensconced on a huge red silk pillow that occupied the room's only chair.

Nikki didn't know much about cats, however she didn't think this little creature qualified for such a mature title. He couldn't have weighed more than three pounds. When her finger gently stroked a beige stripe, the jug-eared kitten curled into a tight furry ball. She failed to coax him out of his protective position. "Some attack cat you are."

She explored the room. The walls were nothing more than cheap paneling and the floor's original color had long been obscured by dirt. Beyond the four-foot-high counter that belted the room were two peeling metal desks and two equally worn wooden typing chairs. Both desks appeared to have been ransacked. Papers, catalogues and stationery were scattered across the top, spilling into open drawers and onto the floor.

No activity.

No personnel.

No sounds of any kind.

Nikki would have guessed Ives Incorporated had been abandoned. Except –

There was the kitten.

The air-conditioning.

The familiar prickling of hairs on the back of her neck.

Her radar never failed.

Someone was watching.

How long before they'd make a move?

Chapter 32

Nikki decided to provoke some action and wandered back to the kitten on the elegant cushion. Clearly the tiny feline was held in high esteem. Perhaps relocating the silken bed onto the filthy floor would initiate a response.

She had lifted it only a few inches when the front door swung open.

"Ahhh, a visitor. Sorry you weren't properly greeted."

"Your attack cat...or should I say kitten, did quite well."

"His mother does a much better job of when someone arrives."

"You're Nathan Ives?"

"Of course. You are?"

"Nikki Holden." She extended her hand. He ignored the greeting, letting the pockets of his white lab coat consume his small hands.

Small was the operative word. Nikki towered over Nathan Ives' pear-shaped body, the top of his head barely reaching her shoulder. His hair was so white and so oddly styled she was positive it was a cheap toupee.

His darkly tanned face also demanded attention. Deep lines ran alongside his mouth straight down his jaw, making his face look puppet-like. But the man was no dummy.

While his physical features appeared comical and his voice came out a slow drawl, Nikki saw the power and control radiating in his eyes.

Weren't eyes the mirrors of the soul?

He walked around her, muttering her name. "Holden...Holden. Nathan doesn't place you. Are you a salesman?"

Nikki felt as if she was being circled by a vulture. "No. Paul Warner -" she saw his black eyebrows lift in recognition, "suggested I visit The Gadget Man."

"Very good. Another movie. What studio do you represent?"

"None. I'm a reporter for the Cortlund Publishing Syndicate." That stopped his circling. She handed him a business card. "I'm looking into special effects and Paul told me about your robots."

"Nathan doesn't do special effects." He dropped the card on the floor. "Nathan's robots are quite real. Nathan is a scientist."

There was no missing the arrogance of Nathan Ives. He even spoke of himself in the third person. Nikki played to the man's ego. "That's exactly why I'm here, Mr. Ives. You're more than a scientist. You're a genius. Your genius needs to be celebrated."

She watched him grow two inches, in all directions. "What better way to celebrate your scientific achievements than in print? Cortlund Publishing owns the number one magazine in science today—"

"Are you speaking of *Science Realm*?" At her affirmative nod, Ives looked thoughtful. "That magazine has yet to seriously disappoint Nathan. Although Nathan's achievements have always frustrated others who were less intellectual."

Nikki counted to ten before speaking, her tone like treacle. "You and your work should be acclaimed. No, no...*need* to be. Goodness, Mr. Ives." This time, when her hand settled on his arm, he didn't pull away. "You must get the recognition your brilliance so richly deserves."

"Why don't you call me Nathan?"

"I'd be honored." Her lashes lowered demurely. "I realize that my visit is unscheduled, I have been calling."

"Nathan only answers a phone when it pleases him."

"Absolutely, why allow a mechanical instrument to interrupt your work. Nathan, I am on a deadline and you are just too important to reschedule. Besides, the October issue, the one your interview would be in, is always our biggest seller."

He studied her for a long moment, his brown eyes closely inspecting her features. Nikki felt like a lab specimen being readied for a microscope. It was a struggle to keep her expression happily vacuous. The only way she could stop her eyes from changing into icy white chips was to think about Roman Cantrell.

"What do you know about science, Miss Holden?"

"Frankly, what *I* know isn't important. You, Nathan, will do all the speaking and I'll just be your writing tool." Pulling a reporter's notebook and pen from her correspondent's bag, Nikki casually clipped a mini voice recorder that also doubled as a video camera on the shoulder strap. "Only you can tell the Nathan Ives story."

"Only Nathan should." He checked his wrist watch. "Nathan's time is valuable. Nathan will say something once and only once and..." His exaggerated sigh, echoed around the nearly empty office. "Nathan will have to simplify all statements for you and the rest of the scientific community. For their sakes, Nathan will make the effort. Come along, wasting time costs Nathan ideas."

She followed him outside and into the huge blue painted warehouse on the left. Nathan Ives started talking about himself the minute they entered. "People snickered at robotics when Nathan touted it on the automotive assembly lines. Now of course, industry has finally caught up. However, as usual, Nathan surpassed them.

"I'm sure you recognize these robots. This little droid spider bot," he patted the rainbow colored head, "will be featured in an upcoming kids movie. These two titanium and graphite bots with their jaws-of-life style arms have been in many action movies." He gestured toward cyborg-style robots Nikki definitely had seen in the movies. "No actors were needed. They were programmed to handle exactly what the director requested. That included running, driving, climbing, both are strong enough to pick up cars and trucks and throw them. These are the ultimate in autonomous machines with artificial intelligence."

"Isn't that the name given to making computers think?"

"Very good, Miss Holden."

When she saw his eyes narrow, Nikki cursed herself for slipping. "*Science Realm* did a story on that last month," she added smoothly.

"Yes...yes, they did. Some foolish statements were printed. Nathan has a staff of five who have created an android that has a twenty-thousand-word vocabulary. The *Ives 5000* also does routine household chores like dusting, vacuuming and serving food. It can act as a burglar alarm and even play hide-and-seek, using wave forms to search. Meet Calliope, she has the most beautiful voice." When Ives snapped his fingers, a fourth android moved out of the dark corner. "Request something, Miss Holden."

Staring at the five-foot-tall very feminine machine, Nikki kept blinking in Calliope's every attribute. Her face and figure were so real it sent a chill down Nikki's spine. "I'd like a glass of water." Her ears registered a very faint whirling sound then she watched a series of facial muscles contort the flesh-like features into a smile. Seconds later, the Ives 5000 smoothly walked across the floor to the water fountain, retrieved a paper cup from the wall-mounted container, filled and carried the cup to her in its delicately-shaped hand. "Very impressive. Not a drop spilled."

"Of course not." Ives snapped his fingers again and the robot turned off. "This model is going into production to aid the handicapped. It will do elementary tasks, such as feed people, retrieve objects, turn pages of a book and dispense medicine. This android will be the ultimate companion. Nathan has equipped it with stereo, radio, miniature TV and a complete memory bank of games. Plus Calliope is anatomically correct in every orifice to comply with all needs."

Android sex, who but Nathan Ives would think of that? Due to years of practice, Nikki was able to keep her face void of any expression and continued with the pandering. "A very noble undertaking, Nathan. How about the price?"

"Nathan is able to keep the *5000* affordable."

"Your developmental costs must be astronomical." She noted the work stations overflowing with equipment. "How do you get your funding? Grants?"

"Grants!"

From the rage on his face and in his voice, Nikki knew she'd hit a raw nerve.

"Do you know what it's like filling out endless forms in quadruplicate when you should be creating and discovering? Do you know what it's like to live from grant-to-grant? Waiting for your intellectual inferior to decide whether you get more money? Do you know what it's like trying to explain your achievements to people who aren't capable of understanding even basic scientific principles?"

When his fingers lanced through his hair, Nikki was positive the plastic looking toupee would slide off his head and shatter on the concrete floor. "Miss Holden, do you realize that more people trust in lucky numbers than understand science. Only one in fourteen Americans knows the fundamental laws of gravity, friction, heat, electricity..." Ives gestured wildly. "Less than one third know how a telephone works and only nineteen percent know anything about radiation.

"The American public is spoiled and lazy. They turn a switch, push a knob, punch a button or aim a remote. That is all the science they know." His lips twisted in a sneer. "That is all the science they are capable of understanding. Those are the people who control the grants. Nathan no longer has to waste time dealing with them."

"Yes, Nathan, I can see how annoying it must have been for you," her tone soothed. "Have you turned to private backers?"

"Nathan. Answers. To. No. One. Ives Incorporated is a privately held corporation and Nathan is the only shareholder." He was silent for a moment before adding, "The movie industry has been quite generous." A rear door opened. "Ahh, here come two of Nathan's staff. This is Charles Reese and Doug Phillips."

Nikki nodded a greeting. Both men were in their late thirties, clad in lab coats and carrying clipboards thick with papers. Reese was nearly bald, his "hello" vague and his expression serious behind heavy, black-rimmed glasses. Phillips was attractive, with curly blond hair and an easy grin.

"They're working on another medical advancement." Ives motioned to her. "These are myoelectric limbs." He held up a prosthetic arm. "Quite state-of-the-art. They are personalized in weight and size for each patient. Totally natural looking. While others are fooling around with plastic 3-D printed prosthetic appliances and implants, Nathan has created the real thing. These are constructed with electrodes that pick up and augment the weaker signals when a patient contracts or relaxes his residual muscles. Now, that in itself is not new. However, shake this hand, Miss Holden." He watched her actions approvingly. "How does it feel?"

Nikki swallowed. "Like my own. The skin, the warmth, the look...This is amazing."

Ives nodded. "Nathan has done the same with legs and feet. Previous myoelectric limbs have had their limitations. These don't. Price won't be a factor either." He sniffed and hitched up his pants. "Nathan has also perfected implantable computer chips that will help restore nervous system function lost to crushed or severed nerves.

"Phillips, show Miss Holden your hand. Now flex the fingers. Individually. Together. Would you believe this hand had been crushed underneath a car?"

She shook her head.

"There's just a small scar on the thumb that Nathan reattached," Doug Phillips pointed out. "I'm even playing the piano."

"How about picking up tiny objects?" Nikki pointed at some small nuts and bolts on the workbench.

"No problem." Effortlessly, Phillips relocated them from the table to her palm. "The hand is sensitive to pain, cold, heat and the finer things." He reached over and let his fingers sift through her copper hair. "Just as I suspected. Silk." His knuckle flowed along her jaw. "Very...very soft."

Nikki returned his smile. "You're lucky Nathan was able to help."

"Help! Nathan gave him back his life," Ives corrected her. "Come, come. Nathan has much more going on here that needs to be included in the article." He hesitated a moment. "Phillips, tidy up in the green building."

"Right away."

The smile Ives focused on her was enigmatic. Nikki knew he was playing with her. For what purpose? His ego, probably. He was definitely a man who had to be in control.

"Miss Holden, Nathan will show you the work with superconductors."

Nikki blinked at the sun's brightness as they went from one building to the other. She checked the recorder as Nathan Ives continued his litany on superconductors.

"Ceramic conductors, when cooled to very low temperatures, offer no resistance to the flow of electricity. They waste no energy. Nathan hates waste," he added brusquely. "Right now the National Academy of Sciences is looking into the commercial possibilities."

Ives shooed two of his other assistants away from a work table. "Here's the standard parlor trick. Nathan places this piece of superconducting material in a petri dish. On top, is this magnet. Now comes liquid nitrogen. It cools the material. When it becomes cold enough..."

"The magnet is rising. Floating in the air and..." Nikki leaned closer, "...spinning."

"That's right. An invisible magnetic cushion has been formed. This magnetic levitation is a power that can be applied to factories and assembly lines, making it no problem to lift heavy objects." Ives leaned against the table. "There are so many applications using superconductors."

"Like?" Her pen was poised over the notebook.

"Detecting the heat of missiles in outer space. Everything done with electricity needs to be reexamined. Medicine is using them in MRI machines. The list is endless."

"How are you using them, Nathan?"

"Mmmm...Nathan won't give any details but quote me as saying soon Nathan Ives will show the scientists of the world and industry as well as the Japanese and Chinese, who the leader in research really is."

This time Nikki witnessed a most unctuous smile and a pompous sweeping of his hand. She cleared her throat. "Robotics, prosthetic appliances, superconductors...My goodness, Nathan, I'm going to insist *Science Realm* devote the entire October issue to you. Can there be any more?"

"Of course. This is just a beginning." He checked his watch. "Too much time...too much time. Quickly. Quickly. Outside to the green building."

They bypassed two large, black warehouses. When Nikki questioned their function, Ives dismissed them with a careless wave. "Storage. Equipment. Parts." He trotted across the compound. "Come. Come. Hurry. This must be the last."

His sudden laugh surprised her. As he held open the metal door, a red-and-black danger sticker captured her attention. "Lasers?"

"Fiber optics and optoelectronics. Nathan is using optical pattern recognition in our robotics and mosaic sensor technology." Ives quickly pointed out and named the various instruments in the lab. "It would be a waste of time to present the linear, nonlinear and space-variant operations that can be achieved on optical processors. Nathan will provide a detailed report for you to include in *Science Realm*."

"That would be appreciated." Nikki noticed that all five of Ives' associates had assembled in the fiber-optic lab and were preoccupied at various equipment stations. "I'm curious about the lasers." The instant she said that, Nikki found herself the object of everyone's attention.

"Ahhh...lasers."

Again, she heard Ives' amusement.

"A very useful, unique instrument. Did you know they could be used as weapons, Miss Holden?"

"Yes. Yes, I did. They're also being used in a variety of surgeries."

"Very good." Ives' dark eyebrows arched. "Very good, indeed. Nathan uses laser diodes. In all cases, multiclass three-D distortion-invariant object identification is Nathan's main issue." Another smug smile was delivered.

"I'd appreciate a detailed report on that, too, if you wouldn't mind, Nathan."

"Of course. Nathan wants this article to be perfect. Since Nathan is the subject everything must be accurate." He waved her toward another door. "Nathan's office."

A dozen steps later had Nikki back inside the attack cat's domain where the kitten was still curled asleep on the silk pillow. She scratched the animal's head. "Odd little round ears on your pet."

"Nathan crossbreeds cats," Nathan explained, rummaging through the open drawers on the desk. "If there was more time, you could meet his parent. Ahh, here they are." He handed her two folders. "These are two texts Nathan authored for the National Academy of Sciences. Use them in the article and that way, there will be no errors or—"

Chapter 33

The office door swung open, interrupting Ives and catching Nikki off guard. The woman who entered shocked her. Nikki blinked at the walking centerfold. A sizzling, smoldering sex object packaged in sheer halter-topped tunic of taupe silk that barely covered voluptuous breasts, an exaggerated ass and long legs housed in black leather stiletto heeled thigh-high boots. A large diamond pierced her naval.

Her face looked as if it had been airbrushed to perfection, framed by a mass of waist-length black hair and highlighted by a pair of huge, frosted pink lips that appeared permanently pursed. When she licked them, Nikki saw two rounded gold studs on her tongue. A leather dog collar, with a leash-ready ring, served as a diamond-studded choker around her slim neck. When she spoke, Nikki heard a little-girl's lisp.

"Darling—"

"Nathan didn't send for you." Ives looked her up and down. "You're off leash."

"No...no...it's right here." She pulled a thin black leather tether from under her thick hair. "I need some money for shopping."

"You always need money."

She slithered tight against him, her palm curving around his burgeoning crotch. "I want to get that third tongue piercing. Remember? You wanted three round studs running up and down Little Nathan and I aim to please my master."

"Damn right." He unbuttoned his lab coat and searched his trouser pockets. "Take Nathan's credit card. You know your limit, now get out."

"Aren't you going to introduce me?"

"There's no point."

"Nathan!"

He inhaled deeply, wheezing slightly. "Deena is Nathan's current wife. This is Miss Holden from *Science Realm Magazine*."

"Are you going to be taking any pictures?" She fluffed out her hair.

"Pictures? Why, yes." Nikki nodded, then turned a beaming smile on Ives. "We will be needing a cover photo of you, Nathan, and of course whatever shots of your lab you think would be important."

"Today?"

His frown put Nikki on alert. "No, certainly not. You have my number. I'll leave the time and place entirely to you."

"What about pictures of me?" Deena persisted. "Our house? The decorator just finished all the changes I wanted. It's only on the other side of the compound and I think-"

"It's Nathan's house. Nathan will tell you what to think." Ives' reminder was brusque. "Since this will be in the October issue, a photo of you would be totally irrelevant."

"Oohhh...wait...what does that mean?"

"That you'd better go shopping." Yanking on the leash, he pulled Deena to the front door and pushed her outside. "She makes the perfect pet. She does everything Nathan tells her. But she's getting too old."

"Old?" Nikki swallowed down the bile that burned up her throat. "She can't be over twenty-two."

"She'll be twenty-three next month. Deena doesn't satisfy Nathan anymore. Women never do when they get old. Divorce is quite routine."

Nikki repeatedly tightened and relaxed her jaw. She would not allow Ives to take over her mind and make her feel powerless. "Nathan, how many women have disappointed you?" She was pleased that her tone reflected none of her rage.

"Deena's the seventh. Nathan never leaves a woman disappointed." Hitching up his trousers, he pulled them tight against his groin and stroked the burgeoning crotch. "Whenever Nathan has to start hurting them it's over. Young women are of particular interest. They look their best naked."

His liver-spotted fingers traced the V-neckline on her white blouse, over the top of her breasts, before traveling down the inside of her left arm. "You look like you have tasty secrets inside. Nathan enjoys new temptations."

Nikki found herself coming under his scrutiny. She watched his beady brown eyes rudely focus on her face, her breasts, her pelvis and her legs.

She felt raped.

Again.

Once had been enough.

Jaw set. Eyes narrowed. Nikki stopped playing nice. "I'm way over your age limit, Mr. Ives. Besides a collar and leash is not a good look on me."

"Nathan has never had a redhead before. It is real, isn't it?"

Before she could answer or even guess his intentions, Ives pulled a hair from her temple. Nikki let her eyes do the talking. When he stepped back, she knew they had turned into icy daggers. "Don't do anything I'll make you sorry for, Mr. Ives."

"It's all in the name of science, my dear Miss Holden. You could be Nathan's crowning achievement."

He was laughing at her.

Again.

Nikki stored her anger. "Since you're so concerned with time, don't let me waste any more of yours."

Ives shrugged. "Don't forget these." He handed her the folders. "Nathan will call you about the photos." His shoe kicked her business card across the floor.

Chapter 34

Roman and Alex were outside talking when the Blazer sped up the driveway. Both men sprinted for the safety of the front lawn.

Brakes squealed. The car lurched. A door slammed. Seeing the expression on her face, neither man doubted that Nikki Holden was in a rage.

"Hey, Nik, hold on." Roman reached to grab her swinging left arm as she stalked past them.

"Don't touch it!"

He pulled his hand back.

"This arm needs to be sanitized." She gestured wildly. "I need to be scrubbed."

Confused, Roman stared from her to Alex and back to Nikki again. "You look fine."

"And clean," Alex added.

"I'm filthy." She shuddered. "Dirty. Disgusting."

"I thought you went out on an interview."

"I did. Nathan Ives." She shuddered again. "Alex. Put that self-serving, despicable bastard on your list."

"What list?"

"The ten most wanted."

"What for?"

"What for?" she repeated loudly. "I'll tell you what for. For...for being a short egomaniac." Her finger jabbed Alex's jacket lapel. "No, no...he's a megalomaniac with a Napoleonic complex and loves to hear the sound of his own voice. Ives -" she jabbed "-is a legend"— jab, jab—"in his own"—jab—"fucking mind! You have my permission to torture the little monkey with a dummy's face, plastic hair and a pencil dick."

Alex stepped back, massaging his chest. "Okay, got it...torture is on the table."

Roman grinned. "That's what I love about you, Nik. You never have trouble finding people to get mad at."

"Mad? I've gone beyond mad, Cantrell. Nathan Ives is my target and I'm going to take aim. That's what the investigative reporting business is all about."

That unholy light in her eyes was back. "Nik, some targets fire back," he cautioned.

"Fine. Let him. I think the bastard was counting on me being frightened off. But his little mind game didn't work. Ives doesn't value people. Especially women. You should have heard the little twerp. 'I never leave a woman hungry,'" she mimicked. "He left me nauseous. He probably couldn't find his dick with a magnifying glass. He talks about himself in the third person. Ives expected me to kiss his feet and his cock!"

Roman opened his mouth, then closed it. He inhaled deeply. "Can you rewind a bit? Exactly what the hell happened? What did he do?"

"Besides making the insinuating statement that the only way a woman looks good is when she's naked and wearing a collar and leash, the little weasel undressed me with his eyes. He ran his finger down my arm; had the gall to pull a hair from my head to see if the color was real; and...and...he touched my blouse." She shuddered again. Abruptly, Nikki yanked the white shirt free and tossed it backward.

The garment landed on Alex's head.

"I can't stand it anymore. I'm going to Lysol my body. Burn that blouse." She stalked into the house.

Alex wiped the blouse off his face and handed it to Roman. "I pity Nathan Ives. Talk to you later."

Chapter 35

Roman tripped over Nikki's low-heeled sandals in the foyer, picked up her skirt in the hallway and scooped her bra and briefs off the bedroom carpet. Steam had already fogged the entire bathroom and was billowing into the bedroom.

"Nik, are you all right?" Hearing an unintelligible response, he pulled the shower door open. She was brushing her teeth under a torrent of hot water that was attacking her body from the pulsating jets. The icy glare she sent his way made him hastily snap the door closed.

Thirty minutes later, wrapped in a giant white towel, Nikki stumbled to the center of the bed. Roman frowned at her deep pink skin. "You've scrubbed yourself raw."

"And I still don't feel clean." Breathing heavily, she pushed at the wet hair coiled on top of her head. "Every once in a while, Roman, I meet a bastard like Ives who brings the memory of being raped by one of my mother's johns out of a dark corner."

Sitting next to her, Roman let his fingers interlace with hers. "You should have turned Ives into a soprano."

"I was going to. I could have easily picked up the little bastard and thrown him across the room. Until I realized the son of a bitch was playing head games with me. Laughing at me." She turned toward him. "But not at the beginning."

"Tell me."

"Well, the man is crazy, colorful and performance-oriented. He answers to no one except maybe the IRS and I doubt that. I'm betting Ives Incorporated is buried in a paperwork trail all the way to the Grand Caymans." she added thoughtfully.

"The thing that really blisters me is that Nathan Ives is a true genius. You should see the work he's done in robotics, with prosthetic appliances and in implanting computer chips to restore normal functions to damaged limbs. He's harnessed superconductors and he's working with fiber optics, lasers...Hell, who knows what else.

"I've got to admit I was damn impressed. Not with the human stain of a man. Just his accomplishments. At first I played and pandered to his monstrous ego. I was curious. This guy was going to be either a genius or a blowhard."

Roman chuckled. "Sounds like he's both."

"Too true. He is brilliant. Even I began to make excuses for tolerating and encouraging his conceit. Ives is doing extraordinary work that will aid the handicapped. I figured I could stomach his pride and vanity and even write a damn good article on his scientific prowess. Ives, himself, overshadowed all his achievements."

Her fingers combed through her damp copper curls that tumbled to her shoulders, her forehead puckered in concentration. "I'm trying to remember. Seems to me things started changing in the fiber-optics lab. I questioned the laser sign. That amused him. Ives started to taunt me about using lasers as weapons. He spouted enough polysyllabic terms to give Einstein a headache. He was laughing at me, Roman, because I didn't understand a damn word he was saying. I just can't figure the joke." She tilted her head. "Do you know how a telephone works?"

"Do I know what?" Roman's eyes widened.

"How a telephone works, other than pushing the buttons? How about radiation? Or the basic scientific principles of gravity? Heat? Electricity?" She patted his knee. "Don't worry, you're part of an enormous club. According to Nathan Ives only one in fourteen is able to communicate and understand basic science. The rest of us are lazy, stupid...hell...fill in the blanks."

"Everyone is ignorant about something."

"Not Nathan Ives."

"How about his views on women? I recall you raging about being nauseous."

"I'll say. He likes them young. They disappoint him when they get old. Old, Roman, is twenty-three. Hell, Ives is no movie star. Wait, wait, I take that back. He'd qualify as a combination eighth Disney dwarf and a puppet. If his hair is not a toupee, he should sue somebody. He kept hitching up his pants to show off his crown jewel." All of a sudden, Nikki started laughing. "I just pictured him naked!"

She sniffed and leaned her head on Roman's shoulder. "The weird thing is he's on his seventh wife. Or, more correctly, he's getting ready to dump Deena. Too old. What a bimbo."

"Bimbo?" He slid an arm around her.

"She's beyond anything reality TV has to offer. She's a staple-in-the-navel walking parody of sex, with a huge mouth and duck-bill lips. No telling where they've been. Plus she was heading out to shop wearing a dog collar, harness and a leash. What kind of a woman does that?"

"For some it's bedroom material or..." He grimaced at her expression. "That was rhetorical right?"

"I know all about S&M...geeze...save it for the privacy of your own home unless she wanted someone to walk her." Nikki straightened up. "That's another thing that teed me off. I hate a woman who views herself solely as a sex object and here was a living, breathing specimen. She was wearing this thin silk...I guess it was a dress...that was no bigger than four handkerchiefs...the cheeks of her ass, the diamond in her navel and most of her breasts in full view.

"She was going shopping like that. Out in public and... Do you know what she was going shopping for? She was going to get a third stud in her tongue because it would sexually pleasure Little Nathan better. Seriously? Is that what you men want?"

"Personally I think you do just fine with that little curl your tongue does...damn...rhetorical again." Roman's chin hit his chest.

Nikki inhaled a controlling breath. "Being one of the first women sports reporters I've had my share of sexual harassment. That was nothing compared to his mind games. After she left the office, Ives turned and did this little number on me. My first reaction was what was he seeing in me that made him think I could be like her? That I could be turned into a submissive leashed pet. That I looked like a whore, too."

"Never. Nikki! No rhetoric this time." He gave her a shake. "Hell, that son-of-a-bitch totally played you."

"I flubbed. I took the bait. Shit. I should have kicked Little Nathan and no amount of mouth-to-prick would have resuscitated his pencil dick."

"I'll do it."

"My hero." She tousled his black hair. "No Cantrell, I'll stick to the old adage that the pen is still the mightiest of all tools." One eye lowered in an outrageous wink. "Besides, you'd never find him. Ives' research facility is almost in Palm Beach County." She told him the directions.

"Hmmm...why does that sound familiar?" He snapped his fingers. "That was the armored car route Alex and I drove." Roman watched her yawn and nod as he mentioned the route number. "Have you had lunch? Anything to drink?"

"Nope."

"I'll fix you something."

"Okay, that might help."

"Say, Nik?" When she looked over at him, he grinned, "Did you ever picture me naked?"

He ducked when a throw pillow was aimed at him. Ten minutes later, when Roman returned with a bed tray, he found Nikki fast asleep.

Chapter 36

Nikki yawned and stretched. The most wonderful aroma kept tantalizing her nose. She exchanged her bath towel for a sleeveless sweatshirt dress and padded out to the kitchen. "Mmm...Cantrell, you have been busy cooking. Gosh is that a strawberry trifle? Lunch smells great." She watched him ministering to a pan in the oven.

"Indoor barbecue chicken. It's raining again. Rudy sent the trifle via Duncan who brought over more design ideas for my home office. By the way, this happens to be dinner." Roman shucked off his protective mitts.

"Dinner! Why didn't you wake me?"

His hands framed her sleep-flushed face. "Because you obviously needed to rest." He kissed her nose.

"I need to call Darnie." Wriggling free, Nikki ran for her office and seconds later she was smiling at hearing a familiar voice. "Hey, girlfriend, are you up for more research?"

"Absolutely, what do you need, my sister."

Nikki easily visualized the very petite Darnie flexing her skilled fingers over the computer keyboard. "Nathan Ives. Ives Incorporated. Right now his home base is a research facility in Fort Lauderdale. He's a scientist working in robotics, computers, fiber optics and lasers." She kneaded the back of her neck. "I'll email you detailed notes of my interview with him today. Funny thing, though. He didn't have any framed degrees in his office. He did mention something about working on auto assembly lines."

"Give me a description, Nik, just in case I run into more than one."

Nikki's laugh was harsh. "He's an original. Napoleon size. White hair that looks like a plastic helmet...you know like a Lego's figure. Sharp...very sharp brown eyes. I'm very interested in his finances. He's into some heavy R&D work and claims he funds it all on his own. No grants. No collaborations. When do you think you'll have something?"

"I'll start working on it right now, Nik. I can check with DARPA to see if he's involved in any of their projects. I have a friend who's a genius at getting into financial institutions but you didn't hear that from me. I've got a tropical storm hitting in the next hour which should put out the newest string of wild fires but it might also make my on-line connections iffy. I'll get back to you tomorrow. What's your new cell number?"

"I'll call you tomorrow. I'm heading for the University of Tennessee's Space Institute. Say, maybe someone there might know Nathan Ives."

Hanging up the receiver, Nikki yelled for Roman. "How long before dinner?"

"Another half hour."

Nikki smiled when his face appeared in the doorway. "I want to type up the notes I made at Ives' research lab today and send them off to Darnie. Maybe *Google* can figure out what the hell multi-class three-D distortion-invariant object identification is." She was pulling out her notebook when the house phone rang. "For you, Cantrell."

"'Tell them to hold on. I'll take it in my office so you can keep working."

She'd finished her third page of typed notes before Roman returned. "From the expression on your face, that was not good news."

Chapter 37

Roman settled on the edge of her desk. "That was my operative in Atlanta."

"About Ed Hartwell?"

"Yeah, finally found out where he's been sleeping." Roman stared at the ceiling. "Seems Ed's got more than another woman. He also has a seven-year-old daughter and an entirely separate life going on in Georgia."

Nikki whistled. "What are you going to do?"

"Tell him what I know. See what he says." His hand massaged his jaw. "Five million dollars buys a lot of freedom, Nik."

"Anybody try to fence any of the cargo yet?"

"Not according to Rudy. He calls me four times a day." Roman grinned at her. "I think he's enjoying his private investigating stint." He picked up the printed copy of the notes she'd typed and whistled. "Nathan Ives is a busy boy. Where's he getting his funding? Grants?"

"That's another word that turned him into a raging volcano. Nathan does not fill out forms in quadruplicate to be read by his intellectual inferiors." Her fingernails drummed across the desk top. "Ives said that the movie industry has been very generous. Somehow I doubt Hollywood's been forking over enough bucks to pay his five assistants and keep his warehouses filled with equipment."

"Who are these two guys? Reese and Phillips? Maybe they're all doing something for the private sector?"

"Those are two of his five minions." Nikki made an exaggerated shudder. "Why do I feel I'm insulting the little cartoon characters? Darnie is checking on all of them. I'll know all about the birth, life and finances of Nathan Ives by tomorrow. I might just get lucky at the Space Institute and someone might know him."

Roman's eyes widened. "I forgot about your trip. Any idea what time you'll be back?" He tried to sound casual.

"I have to fly out of Miami. I'm booked on..." She punched an app on the sat phone. "Flight twenty-three arriving Miami at seven-twenty. Okay I think I just texted a copy of my ticket to you at any rate it's pegged to the bulletin board. Hmmmm, I'll only miss the first couple hands of the poker game tomorrow night." Nikki laughed at his expression. "You forgot that, too. You're the host, Cantrell."

He pulled a Post-it note from her desktop. "I've got to get in drinks and food and - Oh, hell, there goes the oven timer."

"I'll write you a list."

Pausing at the door to ask her a question, Roman found Nikki staring into space. "Since when does ordering food cause you this much concentration?"

"Not the food. Nathan Ives. Too bad his ego and conceit ruins all his good work."

"Yeah, and Ed Hartwell's charitable front covers a multitude of sins."

Chapter 38

Nikki's Blazer stopped alongside Roman's Jaguar as she headed out the front gate. "I thought you were grilling Ed Hartwell this morning?"

Roman got out of his car and leaned into her open window. "The bastard skipped out on our meeting. According to his office, he's heading for Atlanta. I've got operatives waiting to nab him at the airport or his love nest."

"Did you tell Alex?"

Roman nodded. "But, Nik, if extramarital affairs were illegal, the jails would be overflowing."

"Maybe Hartwell does more than screw around up there."

"Meaning, if he engineered the hijacking and is running scared, he'll try to fence the cargo." His expression was thoughtful. "Think Borgianno's got connections in Atlanta?"

Nikki grinned. "Rudy's got connections everywhere. I'm waiting for you to say 'I told you so' about your pal, Tony Mackey. He still being a good boy?"

"'The goodest. Although Alex is dogging his every move. I just wish something would break soon. While the newspaper article was sketchy, the reporters are busy burrowing."

"They'd love to get their hands on Mackey's tank-and-commando story."

He rolled his eyes. "Even I dread seeing that in print. You all set to tackle science?"

"I'm loaded with questions. I just hope they have some answers." She patted her bag. "I'm bringing the rock samples from Belle Glade for a second opinion. I talked with Teresa Hutton this morning and agreed to write an informative article on UFOs for *Scuttlebutt* as long as I didn't have to use the words 'bizarre' or 'mind-boggling.'"

"Now, what time did you say your flight comes in tonight?"

"The plane will land during your third hand of poker. I'll be relieving all of you from your money a half hour later." She winked.

Roman tugged her braid. "You look like a sexy college co-ed."

"Grey jeans were among my purchases and I had a Tennessee orange T-shirt. Cantrell, don't tell me that's another one of your fantasies?" Her eyes widened. "I didn't think you could blush that much."

A nerve twitched in his cheek. "We'll just see who blushes later tonight."

When he started to pull away from the window, Nikki's hand against the side of his face drew him back. "What?"

"Ever think I might have a few fantasies?" She pressed a hard kiss against his lips.

Chapter 39

Nikki realized the biggest mistake she had ever made was telling Professor Jack Charlton that she wanted to be turned into a scientist.

"I agree," he nodded. "Everybody should attain some level of scientific literacy. Ned Meyers instructed me to give you the grand tour and answer all your questions without adding any of my own. So, let's go."

The boyish glint in Charlton's blue eyes should have registered a warning with Nikki. She tempered his zealous enthusiasm with a mental notation of his age. How much energy could a man of seventy have?

Too much.

Too. Damn. Much!

The Space Institute was part of the Graduate School of the University of Tennessee, Knoxville and had been established over twenty years earlier to provide academic resources for the Air Force's nearby Arnold Engineering Development Center. Nikki was positive Professor Charlton showed her every inch of the 365-acre campus and, in a separate tract, the Coal-Fired Flow Facility.

She gave up taking notes, mostly because she couldn't spell ninety percent of the words he kept tossing at her. Magneto hydrodynamics, heterogeneous condensation, centrifugal compressor flow-induced vibration problems and the ever-popular atomic absorption spectrophotometer made Nikki tuck her pen and notebook away.

"Jack, you have given me four years of college science in five hours, my sneakers have holes in them and my brain is begging for a time out."

They retired for an early dinner in the Andy Holt Center. "Well, how am I doing?" Jack settled his rangy form in a dining chair.

"You are doing swell." Nikki grinned at him. "I keep wondering what the hell I'm doing here and why I thought I could ever understand science."

Laughing, he adjusted his bifocals tighter on the bridge of his nose. "You probably know more about science than you realize. Let me demonstrate. What's this?"

"I don't suppose a falling napkin is what you're after."

"Nikki..."

"Okay, okay. Do it again." Elbows on the table, chin balanced in her hand, she watched a wadded napkin get thrown in the air and bounce on the table.

Seeing her frown, he prompted, "What goes up...must come down..."

"Gravity!"

"Very good. And for right now, the correct answer."

"Why just right now?"

"Because a group of scientists are seeking evidence of a new fundamental force in the universe. A fifth force that counteracts the effects of gravity."

"Antigravity? Do you think it exists?"

Jack ran a hand through the thin, gray-brown hair that thatched his scalp. "I don't know. There are four basic forces that govern all matter. Gravity. Electromagnetism. A so-called 'weak' force which causes some radioactivity. And a 'strong' force that holds together the nuclei of atoms.

"Gravity is the weakest of known forces, so if antigravity is out there, it's thought to be only one hundredth of the strength of gravity and its effects infinitesimal. That's the wonderful thing about scientists. We're always looking for something new."

Nikki shook her head. "Yeah, just when you think it's safe to sit under an apple tree."

"Why another frown?" He cut into his chicken fried steak.

"Because the only scientific principle I know is probably going to end up being outdated."

"You know more than gravity." Jack reached for her unused spoon, huffed on the bowl, then pressed it against her nose. "Voila." The spoon shimmied but didn't fall.

Her eyes crossed. "This is science?"

"Certainly. Don't wiggle your nose. Think about what's going on between that metallic spoon and your face."

"I think it's causing everyone in this dining room to stare at me."

Jack aimed his fork at her. "Then think faster."

"Okay, okay. The metal utensil is sticking to my skin."

"Sound like a scientist," he ordered, buttering a yeast roll.

She was quiet for a moment. "The spoon is...adhering. Adhesion."

"In physics class terminology, adhesion is the force that holds together the molecules of unlike substances whose surfaces are in contact." He retrieved the spoon. "In this case, the condensation that formed when I blew on it acted like glue. Here's another one."

He placed an empty bread dish on an open napkin. "This one works better with a tablecloth but—" Yanking sharply, he removed the napkin while the plate stayed on the table. "Sometimes the dishes go flying. Now, what did you see?"

"Resistance to motion..."

"Of two moving objects," he continued, "or friction. I love seeing knowledge dawn on faces when science is put in easy-to-understand actions. Most people when confronted with physics feel stupid and the math is so overpowering, many just give up."

She smiled. "Well, you've made my day exhausting and informative."

"Most of which you didn't understand. That's because I was trying to impress you with our research facilities and laboratories." Jack cleared his throat. "I was showing us off."

Nikki swallowed a mouthful of mashed potatoes and reached for her notebook. "Except for those polysyllabic words you science-types like to throw around, I was able to keep up with most of the tour. Let's see. Physics, atmospheric sciences, computers, fluid dynamics, energy conversion, propulsion and combustion, remote sensing.

"I really appreciated the extra time and all the questions you answered when we were in flight testing and space systems. Ned showed me some photos of prototype planes, satellites and missiles at Homestead. Viewing them up close...well, I can understand how they could be mistaken for UFOs."

"Especially when you add unusual atmospheric conditions," the professor continued. "I must admit, UFOs have always fascinated me. Did you know that the term 'flying saucer' was coined in 1947 when a pilot sighted nine crescent-shaped, tailless objects flying well over thirteen hundred miles per hour? A year after the sighting, Air Force investigators concluded that the saucers were of interplanetary origin?"

She jotted this in her notebook. "I wasn't aware of that. Ned reluctantly admitted that when he first joined the Air Force he was told never to ask questions about flying saucers. He does, however, have a file filled with civilians who do ask questions. Now he's got me."

Jack nudged her for the sugar caddy. "You still feel the majority of the sightings were caused by some fake effect or optical illusion?"

"I really do. Something Ned said actually reinforced that feeling." Nikki leaned forward. "The damn thing made itself visible to nearly two hundred people, Jack. So why didn't it show itself off to NASA at the Cape? Or Patrick Air Force Base? Or Homestead?"

"Did my pal the colonel really expect aliens to request a runway?"

Nikki held up one hand. "All right, maybe Ned and I are too logical. What about physical evidence? Nothing."

"When a jet flies overhead does it leave any ground evidence?" He ducked when she threw her wadded napkin at him. "Sorry, sorry. As you can see, for every point there is a counterpoint." Jack sipped his coffee. "Although, I've got to admit your Belle Glade UFO landing impressed me. Especially your little rock collection."

"Thanks again for your analysis."

Jack flashed a wolfish smile. "If you really want to thank me, leave them with me. Finding iridium, rhodium and osmium in a sugarcane field in Florida is a bigger discovery than antigravity." He checked his watch. "Well, we've got ninety minutes before I run you back to the airport. What else can I show you?"

She groaned. "You mean I have to move? Oh, wait a minute, maybe you can give me the joke to this punch line." She sifted back through her notes. "Here it is. Multiclass three-D distortion-invariant object identification. I *Googled* it and just came up with more polysyllabic words."

"Is that supposed to be funny?"

"Nathan Ives seemed to think so."

His brow furrowed. "Nathan who? Today?"

"Yesterday." Nikki told Jack about her visit to Ives Incorporated. "With all the wonderful work Ives is doing, I could suffer his ego, gladly. I still can't figure out what was so damn funny in the fiber-optics lab. Bringing me in there amused him and so did showing off all the unpronounceable equipment and my noting the lasers."

Jack scratched his cheek. "I can't figure it. We do optical pattern recognition in our fiber-optic labs and we use laser diodes and holographic optics to reduce the size and weight of the systems."

"'What are diodes?"

"High vacuum electron tubes used as—" Her upraised palm silenced him. "Want me to try explaining holograms?"

"I know them." She reached into her purse and pulled out her VISA card. "The little three-dimensional eagle protects the card from being counterfeited. I've also seen them on book covers, greeting cards. Fun stuff."

"Fun stuff?" Jack chuckled as he refilled their coffee cups. "The optical elements don't recreate images, they just bend light. In fact, they are cheap, easily shaped and lighter than glass lenses and mirrors. They can combine laser light of varied wavelengths for simultaneous transmission of telephone calls on one optical fiber.

"The fun stuff as you put it comes from people seeing what they think are true holograms in movies and on TV. Those are just special effects and in many cases 3-D glasses are needed. Holograms are now being used in forensics, especially virtual autopsies."

Jack pushed aside his dish. "Overall, holography's potentials are stunning. Besides the few commercial applications and art showcasing, holograms are already being used to control light in greenhouses, in medical research, architecture, computer graphics and even textbooks that contain a three-dimensional object on a two-dimensional page. Listen, let's head over to the research lab and I can show off what we're doing."

Driving across the causeway over the AEDC Wood's Reservoir, Jack answered Nikki's many questions as simply as possible. "A hologram is produced by splitting one laser beam into two beams. Basically, this is what happens: one part of the split laser beam is diffused by a lens and hits the film. The other, also diffused by a lens, bounces off an object and then hits the film. The resulting three-dimensional image, the hologram, is the photograph of the intersection of the two beams."

"How is that used in a greenhouse?"

"Sheets of holograms are placed in the windows to channel sunlight throughout a dark building. As the light passes through the holograms, the rays are bent and redirected to brighten any part of a room. Certain plants, such as...well, a very good example is seaweed. The Japanese are major users of seaweed in their diet. Seaweed is harmed by certain wavelengths of light and holograms can be constructed to exclude those dangerous wavelengths." He edged his Toyota into a parking space.

"Holograms aren't new, Nikki. Nobel laureate Dennis Gabor developed holography in 1947 to improve the electron microscope. His techniques were rather crude and his experiments went largely ignored for close to fifteen years until the construction of the laser."

She stepped inside the fiber-optics lab. "1947 was a big year, Jack, first flying saucers now holograms. Perhaps both are just optical illusions."

"Come on, I'll treat you to some optical illusions, Miss Holden." Jack introduced her to the three research scientists still working in the lab. "Here's a computer-generated three-dimensional color hologram of the human brain."

At first, Nikki found herself leaning away from the vivid image. "I feel as though I can reach out and touch those...those... Jack, what are those?"

"Nerve endings." He gave further instructions to the computer terminal operator. "We can rotate the image, highlight certain parts - there's the frontal lobe. Now we can add overlays. That shows you the brain's blood supply. Medical researchers are also experimenting with techniques using acoustical holograms. They'll use a sonic probe and three-dimensional imaging to examine the human body without surgery."

Jack pressed in another programming function. "Here's an architectural hologram, showing a complete view of a pyramid. This hologram is aiding automotive design engineers." He checked over his shoulder. "They're finished setting up another holographic display. Take a look at this, Nikki."

"A bowl of fruit?"

"Try a piece."

Her hand reached for an orange but found— "Nothing!" She tried again. "I can see them but I can't feel them. Hmmm...yet..." She squatted down, inspecting the bowl from all sides. "No matter where or how you look, the fruit has depth, color and I could almost swear, smell."

He was startled. "The last is your imagination. The rest is pure holography. No batteries, lights, knobs, or dials and it's silent."

With difficulty, Nikki stopped trying to pick up an apple and turned her attention to the laser setup. "It's that simple to project, Jack? Just aim the laser at the film plate?"

"More or less. Now, over here -" he guided her to a work station "we've got the laser, the beam splitter, two mirrors set up with lenses and our object. In this case...put your purse down."

Jack handed her a pair of protective eye goggles and showed her where to safely stand. "The laser beam is split. Remember your lesson on how this works?"

Nikki nodded.

Jack turned off the laser. "Now, you've got ten seconds to ask questions while this develops, then it's off to the airport."

"Did you destroy my purse?"

Jack laughed. "No. It may glow in the dark...Hey, just joking."

"How long will the image last?"

"Indefinitely. In fact, once the constraints of materials are worked out, holographic-style data storage would outstrip all current methods. Now, it's time for me to show off. This new automatic system requires almost no training. All you do is press the button and—"

"My purse!" Again, she wasn't able to feel what her eyes could see. "Amazing."

Nikki was still asking questions when Jack Charlton ordered her out of the car and into the airport. "Come back anytime, Nikki. I...Say, what's this?"

"Iridium, rhodium and osmium pellets, Professor." She placed them in his palm and closed his fingers around them. "Thank you." She laughed at his wide-eyed expression.

"You are very, very, very welcome."

Chapter 40

In the twenty minutes she had before boarding her flight, Nikki made two phone calls. The first was to Roman's cell. No answer. The second was to Darnie. "Come up with anything on Nathan Ives?"

"Hold on, let me pull him up. Ives, Nathan. Sixty-two years old. Boy wonder. Graduated high school at thirteen, whipped through eight years of college in less than three. At sixteen, he was quickly snapped up by private industry but kept being dismissed. Age could have been a factor."

"More likely it was his charming personality," Nikki muttered. "Where was he working?"

"You were right about his working in the automotive industry in the late sixties when robots were streamlining the factories. Detroit had him a good dozen years. Ives shifted from one automaker to another ending up at Chrysler. I'm not exactly sure what he worked on at Chrysler. He's presented quite a few papers, one on re-designing the battlefield for the twenty-first century using android robot soldiers and—"

"Yeah, Darnie," she interrupted. "Nathan Ives made his accomplishments well known. Listen, they're calling my flight. Thanks."

"Okay, I'll call you back when I get the rest of the Chrysler story."

Two items kept gnawing at Nikki on the return trip to Miami. The first was the familiarity of the holographic laser setup at the Science Institute and the second was Chrysler. If she could just think...just think..."Nathan Ives!"

"I beg your pardon?"

"Sorry." She smiled an apology to her seatmate and pulled out her notebook. So that was the big joke about the multiclass 3D distortion-invariant object identification. It was a holographic laser setup.

Why the secrecy? Why didn't Nathan Ives want to show off his genius with holograms?

Nikki was still wondering about Ives and holograms when she started her car and Chrysler popped back in her mind. "I don't even own their product." She patted the Chevy Blazer's steering wheel.

Snapping on the radio, she hoped the nine o'clock news would refocus her attention. It probably would have, if Nikki hadn't caught the end of the commercial: "Be Army strong."

"Tanks!" Nikki's eyes widened in remembrance. "General Dynamics[1] acquired the battle tank division of Chrysler and received a contract to build the U.S. Army's M-1 tank the same time Nathan Ives worked there." Pulling out her cell to contact Roman, she found the battery nearly drained and her car charger didn't match the sat phone's plug. She sent a text and hoped it would make it

Nikki wasn't quite sure exactly why she missed the turn-off to Fort Lauderdale or how it happened that half an hour later the Blazer was left on the highway shoulder so her legs could navigate the rock-strewn blind drive that led to Ives Incorporated.

---

1.   http://www.crocodyl.org/wiki/general_dynamics

Chapter 41

"Nothing like the host being late for his own party," Alex called as Roman sprinted up the front steps of the house. "Where've you been?"

"Downtown Miami giving a deposition on the Freemont case. It went on too long."

"Hell, that was, what? Eighteen months ago?"

"The wheels of justice, pal. What's with the box?"

"Oh, ran into UPS when we drove up." He handed over a large square carton. "It's for Nikki from Matt Cortlund."

Roman frowned at the package, then, with a shrug, tucked it under his arm. "Too small for clothes. Okay, guys, step aside so I can open up." He smiled greetings to the three poker regulars: Bob Marks of the DEA, Tito Rojas from ATF and John Ames of the CIA.

"That reminds me." Alex tapped the lock. "You'd better make Nikki a key. She cracked this with her lockpick the other day."

"Already done." Roman grinned at him. "Knowing Nik, she'd prefer to keep using that pick. Old habits." Tossing his navy sports jacket and striped tie on the sofa, he released the top two buttons on his shirt and rolled up the sleeves.

"Say, where is Nikki?" Marks followed Roman into the quiet house. "I'm into her..." when he saw Cantrell's arched brow, he grinned, "let me rephrase that...I owe her seventy bucks but plan to recoup my losses."

"I'll join his club," Rojas added. "She pocketed fifty off of me. You never mentioned the lady was a card shark, Roman."

"Who knew? Nikki never fails to surprise me. She's in Tennessee." He jerked his thumb toward the bar in the game room off the kitchen. "Console yourselves while I put out the food. Manuela made salads, an antipasto and I picked up some lean corned beef and

224

rare roast beef. We're deli tonight. Hey, don't look so glum, John. Nikki promised to be here for the third hand."

Chapter 42

Where was the moon when you needed it? Frowning at the heavy cloud cover, Nikki reached into the pocket of her gray jeans for a penlight. She had carefully checked the perimeter of Ives Incorporated and hadn't noticed security measures of any kind, save for another hokey 'attack cat' sign.

Her movements were sure and quick despite the dark surroundings. Her every step was accompanied by loud, shrill sounds from the vibrating male cicadas and a deep chorus of tree frogs.

The office and warehouses loomed dark.

Gloomy.

Quiet.

And, she hoped, empty.

Nikki ignored the buildings she'd already visited, concentrating her efforts on the pair of long, black-sided warehouses.

She slipped in and out of the shadowed corridors at the rear of the buildings until she located the first door. Holding the tiny flashlight in her mouth, she deftly worked the lock with a pick. A smile lit her eyes when she heard the snap.

But her initial success proved short-lived.

"Damn!" she muttered. "I expected a tank."

The storeroom was filled with equipment, tables, file cabinets, boxes, supplies. Anything and everything but an M1A1 Abrams Combat Tank.

Arms folded, Nikki leaned against a wall. Maybe there was no tank. Maybe the fact that Nathan Ives had worked in the military division of Chrysler was just a coincidence. Maybe her idea that he had somehow stolen a tank was as...was as... "Crazy as Ives is!" Her hand slapped her cheek.

After relocking the door, she stared at the last warehouse. Then, with a shrug, she murmured, "As long as I'm here."

The last warehouse was larger than all the others and constructed with a massive set of overhead doors. Carefully searching, Nikki finally found a normal entry door. Again, the tumblers smoothly responded to her lockpick. She eased into the dark interior.

All was not quiet.

Nikki flattened against the inner wall, struggling to control her erratic breathing while straining to recognize the odd noises.

Everything thing seemed magnified. Gradually, she began to identify the sounds.

Scratching.

Shuffling.

Her tension eased.

Rats?

Raccoon?

Maybe a night-hunting armadillo?

Her anxieties subsided completely when she heard the throaty purr and hungry mewing's of Nathan Ives' attack cat. Apparently the jug-eared kitten made its bed inside this building.

The striped tabby was not on Nikki's agenda. Aiming the flashlight's tiny beam out of the entry bay, she cautiously walked into the main room. Her eyes widened at her discovery.

No tank.

Just—

"Bloody hell it's Hartwell's armored tractor-trailer!" Nikki's eyes widened in astonishment. She stared at the truck for a long time. No wonder Nathan Ives wasn't worried about filling out grant forms. Five million dollars in precious metals would fund a lot of research.

"Damn if it isn't needed research," she murmured.

Suddenly, the vision of Glenn Ennis's corpse loomed vivid.

Was five million dollars the current value of a human life?

Quickly, silently, she exited the warehouse and retraced her shadowy path around the buildings.

Nothing had changed outside.

The cicadas and frogs were still harmonizing.

In the distance, she heard the honking bellows of the swamp gators.

She was halfway around the yellow storehouse when her radar kicked in.

The hairs on her nape prickled a warning.

She slid for cover along the side wall, edging ever so slightly around the corner for a guarded look-see.

The moon proved an ally this time. The path from the office to the rutted drive that led to the highway was clear. Still...she couldn't shake off the feeling that something or someone was out there.

Waiting.

Watching.

For her.

She changed direction and began to run charting a zigzag course away from the buildings and into the jungle-like underbrush that surrounded Ives Incorporated. Her breathing came in jerky gasps. Her lungs tried to suck oxygen past a heart that kept growing –

Larger.

Noisier.

Faster.

Straight ahead was the blind drive.

One hundred yards beyond was her car.

And safety.

Nikki plunged forward, moving more swiftly than the terrain would allow.

She pushed aside the palm fronds that slapped her body.

Lashed back at the short pine branches that needled her face and snagged her hair.

Tangled vines twisted around her shoes and clutched her ankles.

Finally, they succeeded in tumbling her to the ground.

Nikki took advantage of the forced rest to gain strength and search for a measure of composure.

What or who had she been running from?

She glanced over her shoulder, peering into the night.

Nothing.

She listened for signs of an enemy.

Silence.

Taking a deep, calming breath, she pushed herself up on her knees.

Then she saw the eyes.

Amber eyes.

Glowing in the moonlight.

Fifteen feet away.

Blocking her path to freedom.

Dumbstruck, Nikki discovered the owner of those eyes.

Nathan Ives' warning sign wasn't as hokey as she'd believed.

There was an attack cat on guard duty.

A four-hundred-pound, eight-foot —

"Tiger."

Nikki stared at the waiting beast.

The tiger stared back.

She waited for it to attack.

It didn't.

Her gaze narrowed.

In fact, the animal didn't move a muscle.

Nor an ear.

Nor its tail.

And especially not its massive tooth-filled jaw.

Odd.

Wasn't she downwind of the tiger?

Wasn't she supposed to be dinner?

Wasn't a tiger a night prowler in search of food?

Of course, this tiger could be satiated.

And as tame as...as the kitten. Ives had made a crack about meeting the mother.

But were wild beasts ever really tame?

Nikki didn't want her sudden movements to upset the tiger.

Then she remembered the punch line to Ives' lab joke. Maybe she couldn't provoke this tiger no matter what she did.

Because it wasn't real.

Because it was only a hologram.

Then again –

She could be wrong.

After all, to create a holographic tiger, you needed an original to work from.

And there was that tiny cub.

Plus the Nathan Ives factor.

Which animal would he choose to protect his property?

Real?

Or illusionary?

Ives was just crazy enough to use the former.

With her gaze fixed on the tiger, Nikki cautiously arranged her body into a crouched running position. The animal still didn't react.

So she did.

Fast!

She hadn't run more than a few yards when she felt a sharp stinging in the back of her neck.

Her entire body began to shake.

Her fingers and toes curled inward.

Drool ran down the sides of her mouth.

Her legs were unable to hold her weight.

Nikki Holden was unconscious before she hit the ground.

Chapter 43

Bob Marks dealt the third hand of poker between bites off a stick of pepperoni. Roman Cantrell picked at his sandwich and folded with a pair of jacks in the hole. Tito Rojas won the fourth and fifth hands. John Ames bemoaned the small pot he gained in the sixth. Alex Lazarus never bothered to collect the few dollars from the seventh. By the eighth deal, Cantrell was pacing rather than playing.

Fifteen minutes later, so was everyone else.

Chapter 44

"Her pulse and blood pressure are returning to normal. We were damn lucky with her. I keep remembering that armored truck guard."

"His death was his own fault. That man's veins were clogged with cholesterol. Obviously, his heart was an inferior organ. Nathan has told you before. Nathan refuses to take responsibility for other men's weaknesses."

"Weaknesses! Dammit, Nathan, your laser stun gun is still much too powerful for humans. Why won't you listen to me?"

"Don't preach. When this becomes a democracy, Douglas, Nathan will let you know."

Doug Phillips' gaze faltered. He lifted a shaking hand to his face only to have Ives grab hold of his real fingers.

"Never forget Nathan gave you back your life." Ives' smile grew broader as he squeezed his chief assistant's hand. "No one tells Nathan what to do or how to do it. Understand?"

Phillips's head bobbed. "Yes. Yes. Nathan, I was just..." His words died as the pain kept increasing. "I am sorry," came his strangled whisper.

Ives' chest expanded. "You're a good boy, Douglas." He slapped him on the back. "Nathan thinks of you as the son those barren wives have failed to produce. One of these days—" Nikki's moan redirected his attention. "Ahh...Miss Holden appears to be rejoining us. Her color's coming back."

Nathan sighed. "Douglas, from the first Nathan had a feeling she was going to be a bit of an annoyance. Rather like a pesky mosquito that needs to be swatted." His voice was hard. "Shame really. She's quite attractive, except for that broken nose." Ives bent down for a closer examination. "Hmmm, doesn't appear that there'd be a problem with the cartilage. Might prove interesting." Abruptly, he smiled. "Yes, yes. Nathan will do it...Nathan will reconstruct her nose. The surgery certainly won't be a challenge by any means. But it'll be an amusing change of pace."

"'Am I supposed to be impressed or frightened by your offer?"

"Miss Holden speaks."

"Miss Holden will be doing much more than that if you touch her nose," Nikki warned. She struggled to find the energy to sit up on the pile of straw that served as a bed. She was in a cage...the floor strewn with straw.

Nathan Ives observed her feeble attempts with undisguised interest. "You are quite an engaging specimen, my dear. Capable. Quick. Adept. Curious. Much too curious," he added harshly. "Although Nathan did find your actions tonight quite fascinating viewing."

Breathing hard from exertions that had gotten her nowhere, Nikki gave up and relaxed back onto the straw. "Really, Nathan, you overreacted. If you'll remember, I did tell you I'd be back to take pictures." Her tongue mopped an excess of saliva from her lips.

"Pictures? Nathan never knew this -" he held up her lockpick "-could be used as a camera. You did, however, use it with amazing agility on Nathan's warehouse doors." Noting her expression, Ives smiled. "Nathan was watching your every move, my dear. The compound is equipped with motion and noise detectors as well as heat-sensing cameras and biometric sensor alarms."

"Let's not forget the attack cat," Nikki added. "Well, Nathan, enlighten me, was the tiger real or a hologram?"

He failed to shield his surprise. "You are quite bright, Miss Holden. So you know about holograms, do you?"

She nodded. "That was the punch line to your joke in the fiber-optics lab. You were showing off a holographic laser setup and laughing at my ignorance."

"Ignorance is a much healthier state in this case than knowledge, my dear." His hand cupped her chin. "Someone should have taught you to curb your curiosity. Remember the old adage about it killing the cat."

Her eyes were expressive weapons as she freed herself from his touch. "Did you kill the cat, Nathan? Was your tiger real or—"

"Alas, you encountered one of Nathan's early, crude holograms, Miss Holden. As for the cat." He gestured with a flourish. "She's right behind you." He watched Nikki's slow painful maneuverings. "Sheba is content right now because she's nursing her cub. But she can be a most formidable enemy with a vicious temper."

Ives walked across the cage Nikki was in, reached through and knuckled the bars on the tiger's cage. "Sheba!" The sound of his voice sent the tiger into a growling, snarling frenzy. An icy shiver washed over Nikki as Nathan Ives laughed. "She despises Nathan. Nathan's been experimenting on her with artificial insemination. Sheba gave birth to twin 'liger' cubs. Half lion, half tiger. One cub was weak and died during an examination. This one is strong. But Sheba hates the way Nathan keeps taking him. Science, however, must prevail."

Nikki decided not to pursue what type of experimentation Ives was doing on the tiny cub. She tried sitting up again, noticing her muscles seemed more responsive. Her fingers and hands, toes and legs were tingling with life. Even her brain was more alert, more...inquiring. She was damn interested in learning more about this mad scientist. "You know, Nathan, I really didn't find your tiger hologram all that crude."

He pivoted on his heel. "Yet you ran from it. Which meant you didn't fear an attack."

She fluttered her lashes slyly. "Frankly, that's only because I had just come from another holographic display. Although, it was nothing compared to your life-size tiger. I saw a very small bowl of fruit."

"A bowl of fruit, you say?" Ives crossed the large cage with short quick strides. "Fruit, really? My God, how utterly infantile. How tragically useless. The scientific community never fails to entertain Nathan with their lack of imagination. A bowl of fruit!"

His sudden, violent burst of laughter made the white hair that helmeted his head jiggle up and down. It also sent the tiger into another tail-thrashing rage, but Sheba still refused to abandon her greedily nursing cub. Ives wiped the moist amusement from his eyes and called, "Did you all hear Miss Holden? A holographic bowl of fruit!"

Twisting around, Nikki saw Doug Phillips along with three other assistants busily working at one of the many lab tables that ringed the rear of the tractor-trailer.

Ives settled his stubby form on a stool. "Nathan wouldn't waste time even admitting to creating such a foolish hologram. In fact, those dilettantes shouldn't be bragging about any of the holographic uses they've developed.

"Holograms today are more novelties than science. Trinkets, toys, produced by amateurs for entertainment and the most minuscule of scientific applications. Even the small freestanding hologram that MIT did is nursery school compared to what Nathan has done, Miss Holden."

The power in his eyes and the growing forcefulness of his voice made Nikki inch farther away on the straw. There was no doubt in her mind that Nathan Ives had crossed the line of sanity. When she spoke, she made sure her voice was gentle and soothing. Her words pandered to his ego. "Nathan, you've positively entranced me. Exactly what have you done?"

"Nathan has done what Nathan always does, my dear. Take that extra step. To create reality from illusion." He leaned forward. "Nathan has advanced science beyond the twenty-first century into another millennium. Nathan has created holograms that are so real, so solid, so life-size, so—so—" His abrupt laugh showed all thirty-two teeth. "So heart-stopping they...they ..." He jumped off the stool. "Well, see for yourself, my dear. Nathan's hologram hijacked that armored tractor-trailer filled with a five-million-dollar cargo."

Nikki contemplated Ives. Hands clasped behind him, he was parading back and forth in front of her like Napoleon or Hitler reviewing the troops.

"Nathan did that. Nathan created the ultimate weapon. Nathan has an army that is indestructible, unbeatable, easily duplicated and uniquely portable and compact. A military force of sixty armed commandos carrying bazookas, grenade launchers, missiles and -" he paused in his pacing..."- a tank. An M1A1 tank."

Ives rose up and down on his toes. "Nathan was the design engineer on that tank over thirty years ago. Nathan created a computer guidance system far superior to anything they have even today. But was anyone interested? Not then. They will be now. Now, Nathan will make them honor genius. No...bow to genius."

She let him march back and forth two times before pandering to his ever expanding ego. "Nathan, I'm totally fascinated. How were you able to conceive your holographic army? I mean...the weapons? The tank?"

"Oh, the weapons were easy enough to come by." He perched on the stool again. "Expensive, though. Nathan had to deal with a rather unsavory element. The military outfits were readily purchased. The six of us were the army. Nathan just kept duplicating until there were sixty commandos in various positions, holding a variety of firepower."

"And the tank?"

"Ahh, the tank. My dear Miss Holden, the M1A1 is the crowning glory of Nathan's holographic army. Been fascinated with holograms since learning about them. Nathan has been experimenting, refining, perfecting them for years. Nathan made holographic plates of the tank and a few other military vehicles while working for Chrysler. Now, Nathan is able to call them up in three-dimensional splendor whenever the mood strikes." He grinned and elevated a black eyebrow. "The mood strikes Nathan tonight."

"Tonight?"

"Yes, yes." He strutted across the floor. "That five-million-dollar cargo is giving us a bit of a problem. Reese is off to meet with a...a..." Ives paused, "a fence? So, in the meantime, Nathan needs capital. Quick, ready cash. Tonight, Wells Fargo is coming to Nathan's aid. They are shipping a million dollars in U.S. currency to a Palm Beach bank." He checked the pocket watch housed in the pocket of his white lab coat. "Hmmm, as a matter of fact, in about three hours they are going to make a very generous donation to the Ives Foundation."

Pushing a swath of tumbled curls off her forehead, Nikki relaxed a bit noting her coordination had returned to normal. "Nathan, how are you able to find out about the routes and cargo? Do you have inside help?"

When Ives shook his head, the toupee slipped sideways on his scalp but he didn't seem to notice. "Nathan relies only on Nathan, Miss Holden and, to varying degrees, on Phillips, Reese, and Nathan's other three assistants. As for knowing the routes and transactions? Quite a simple maneuver. Nathan invaded their computer systems. Nothing is impossible. Take Hartwell Armored Services for example.

"Nathan encountered no difficulties at all with hacking into their system. Nathan easily tuned into the electromagnetic energy radiating from Hartwell's cables and equipment and generated a live copy of the data that was moving through the system.

"While their own drivers didn't know the cargo or the computer-created route, Nathan did. The lasers and the holographic army effectively stopped the armored tractor-trailer. The commando group easily disarmed the two guards using Nathan's laser stun gun."

"One of those guards died."

Ives gestured aside Nikki's remark. "His own fault. The man was weak. Inferior. Nathan refuses to be accountable for others." He inhaled expansively before refocusing on her. "Frankly, my dear, Nathan wishes we didn't have to pack up the main laser and plates so you can see how solid, how real Nathan's holographic army appears."

Reaching out, he fingered her hair. "Oh, well, Nathan will be able to show you all that later. After all, you won't be leaving." His thumb and forefinger sculpted her nose. "Hmmm, Nathan will make a holographic image of you, my dear. Before and after."

Nikki hid her revulsion behind a syrupy smile and a studiously relaxed manner. "Nathan," she cooed, "your genius is quite irresistible. I'm very anxious to learn about all your experiments." She regarded his preening with enigmatic eyes. "Now...is your holographic army your only creation?"

"Certainly not!"

She winced inwardly. *Be careful not to insult the man.* "How silly of me," she said apologetically. "Your abilities are unlimited."

"Unlimited...yes, yes!" Ives rubbed his small, liver-spotted hands together with enthusiasm. "Nathan likes that word, Miss Holden. Nathan's abilities and power are unlimited. And with tonight's Wells Fargo hijacking coupled with the Hartwell cargo, Nathan will also have unlimited funding."

"What will you be doing with all of that money?"

"Oh, so many things, my dear. So very many things in the areas of robotics, superconductors, prosthetic appliances, lasers, fiber optics. Nathan's genius will be endless. One day, one day very soon. Nathan Ives will be known not as The Gadget Man but as the Miracle Man. No, no." He drew himself up to his full height. "No, Nathan will be revered like a god. Yes, Miss Holden, a god. Nathan is already rewriting the laws of science. Nathan will bring life back to the dying and the disabled." He thrust his tiny balled fist under her nose. "Power so great that the entire world will kneel at Nathan's feet."

Nikki watched his satisfied smile turn into a grin. The grin emitted a chuckle. And the chuckle broadened into laughter that brought Sheba to all fours. Heedless of the cage, the tiger lunged at Ives. Her enormous paws slashed between the steel bars, shaking the entire structure. When that proved futile, Sheba clamped her powerful jaws on the metal and tried to wrestle apart the cage.

Nikki wasn't sure who she should fear the most—Ives or the tiger. Each was propelled by madness. She observed Ives' odd reaction to Sheba. Instead of moving away and quieting down, he deliberately leaned into the bars of Sheba's cage. Baiting. Taunting. Teasing. Then, from his pocket, he withdrew a tiny silver gadget, aimed it at the roaring tiger and snickered as Sheba collapsed with a whimper.

"Nathan's enemies will also fall that quietly," he promised. "That swiftly. That easily."

"Is...is Sheba dead?"

He swiveled around. "Goodness, no. She's just temporarily disabled. Much like you were, my dear." Ives held out his hand so Nikki could see the object he held. "Nathan's super stun gun. It emits a laser barb that immobilizes by reducing muscle control and balance. Sheba will be unconscious for...oh, maybe fifteen minutes. But," he cautioned, "she'll be in a rage when she awakens. So stay away from this side of your cage."

Ives glanced at his busy assistants, then checked his watch and frowned. "Hurry, Phillips, time is passing quickly." He sauntered back to Nikki and stared at her for a long moment. "You know, my dear, Nathan Ives is so much more than just physical accomplishments. Nathan is not all work and no play."

"No one could ever accuse you of being dull."

He laughed again. "Oh, Miss Holden...Nikki. You have no idea just how true your statement is." His entire face became animated as he settled once more on the stool. "Nathan prides himself on being a true Renaissance man. One skilled in more than the sciences. One who enjoys life to the fullest. That's why Nathan has been having the most wonderful time playing a game with the entire state of Florida, perhaps the nation." He leaned forward. "Nathan created yet another ingenious hologram. A flying saucer"

Ives' hair bobbed up and down as Nikki's eyes widened. "Yes, yes, my dear, what fun Nathan is having! First there was a miniature spacecraft, circular in design, painted silver with red blinking lights. Then, using a holographic process Nathan developed, the saucer was enlarged to over fifty feet. Nathan has been making it transverse the night sky with charming regularity. It dazzles everyone who sees it."

He chuckled. "Nathan must admit to loving the scattered newspaper accounts of the sightings: 'Air Force Baffled,' 'Observatories at a Loss,' 'UFO Claims the Sky.' One evening, Nathan teased an AWACS plane." He grinned. "Oh, Nathan would love to see the report that pilot filed."

Before she was able to garner any more information, Doug Phillips intruded. "Nathan, we're ready for you to supervise the loading."

"Excellent, excellent." He rubbed his hands together. "Regretfully, Miss Holden, Nathan must leave. But never fear, my dear, we'll all return in about three hours. Please, remember...heed the warnings and stay quiet. Do not disturb the volatile Sheba. When she awakens, keep away from that side of the cage."

Ives loomed over Nikki and, abruptly, his finger traced the crook in her nose. "Yes, when Nathan returns, Nathan will fix this for you. A few preliminary surgical sketches tonight and operate in the morning." He examined her features closely. "Straightening your nose will make you a near-perfect beauty, my dear. It's really a shame that you're so old. Then again, Nathan just might decide to enjoy an older woman. Sex with Nathan will make you weep with ecstasy. No one else will be able to satisfy you. No one except Nathan Ives."

"I'd be insulted if I didn't get your full personal attention." Nikki gifted Ives with her best "fuck you" smile. She watched his departure with relief, staying motionless on the straw until he and the others were gone.

It proved a struggle to stand. Her legs were rubbery and she teetered until her equilibrium returned. Gradually, she regained full control. Her strength grew with every breath; her muscles functioned normally. When she moved to study the lock on the circus-style cage door, she discovered she wasn't alone.

"Hey! You!" she called to Ives' assistant. "What would it take to get you to let me out?"

He shook his head and lifted the last carton. "Nathan would kill me."

"He's crazy. Bonkers. Nutso. A real Dr. Dementia."

"Yeah, but he pays well." The lab man saluted the tractor-trailer and slammed the door shut behind him.

Sheba began to growl and snuffle into what Nikki could only imagine was going to be a very rude awakening. "At least he left the lights on." Tiptoeing past the now snorting tiger, Nikki viewed the outer room from every corner of her enclosure. While the lab tables were loaded with assorted equipment, all was at least fifteen feet out of reach.

Nikki prowled around her own cage. The sturdy steel bars were wide but not wide enough for even the slimmest body to wriggle through. Sheba's cage was much larger and pushed against the back wall of the warehouse. When Nikki stood in the front corner of her cage, she could see the lock on Sheba's.

Apparently Nathan Ives' scientific abilities hadn't run into creating some sort of laser-biometric lock. He had used a rather glamorous heart-shaped antique padlock. Nikki felt around the front of her cage door. "Yes!" She had a duplicate.

It would be a snap to open.

If she had a lockpick.

Or a hairpin.

Or a nail file.

Or even a paperclip.

But she didn't.

Still...

The tiger's loud, guttural yawns and moving front paws made Nikki think faster as she rebraided her hair. "Sheba...calm down, we girls have to work together." She stopped pacing and smiled. "Well girlfriend," Nikki winked at the tiger, "I didn't binge watch all those episodes of *MacGyver* for nothing."

Chapter 45

"Nikki's plane was delayed two hours on the runway in Nashville." Roman reported to the others as he cradled the receiver.

Alex checked his watch. "That still leaves ninety minutes unaccounted for."

"Are you sure she made the plane?" Tito Rojas swirled the ice cubes in his glass of bourbon.

"The airline clerk said her ticket was used." Roman hunched his shoulders, his large hand rubbing the back of his neck. "I know Nikki isn't one to punch a clock, but she was very definite about being here for the game."

"Eager to stiff us again?" Bob Marks joked, but his laugh was forced. "How about luggage?"

Roman shook his head. "No it was just a day trip."

"Car trouble?"

"She'd have called," Rojas added.

Alex grimaced. "She didn't have your cell or home phone number the other day."

"I programmed both of them into her sat phone. Fuck, fuck., fuck...I had my cell off for the deposition and..." Roman pulled his phone from his trouser pocket waiting for it to power up. "Okay...looks like she did call but no message...the time was right around when she was supposed to board the flight. Hmmm...then there's two letters of a text: h...e..." He frowned and looked from one man to another. "H...e... maybe help?"

"Enough speculation." Bob Marks pushed himself off the sofa arm. "Let me call a friend of mine on airport security. I'll have him check out the parking lot and see if her car's still there." At Roman's nod, he hit an app on his cell. "Description?"

"Midnight blue, twenty-two year old Chevy Blazer, luggage rack, Illinois plates."

Marks repeated the information to his contact. "Martin's sending three of his men to the short-term parking lot. He'll report back in five minutes or so."

Cantrell nodded his thanks as his right fist repeatedly hit into his left palm. "You know, Nikki went hunting for information in Tennessee on her UFO story. Just maybe that information led her back to her source at Homestead Air Force Base. If I could just think of that major's name. Or was he a colonel?" His fist hit harder and faster while his companions offered "did it sound like" suggestions.

"How about I get that Roladex off her desk," Lazarus headed for the hallway. "You could plow through that and see if anything jogs."

"Good idea," Cantrell agreed. "Teresa Hutton's number is in there and—" The shrill ringing of the phone at his elbow made him jump, then smile. "Probably her right now." He scooped up the receiver. "Hello."

"Ahh, Roman, Rudy Borgianno here."

Cantrell frowned and shook his head at four expectant faces. "Yes, Rudy, what can I do for you?"

"It's more what I can do for you, my friend. Someone tried to dispose of that precious metal cargo tonight."

"I'll be damned. Hold on a sec I'm putting you on speaker, Alex Lazarus is here. They tried to fence the hijacked cargo tonight. Okay, Rudy, what went down and where?"

"An associate of mine just happened to be doing some...exchange business in the right place at the right time. We were all lucky because the dealer is out of state."

"Where?"

"Atlanta, Roman."

"Damn." Cantrell rubbed his face.

"Ed Hartwell's there."

Lazarus had put into words what Cantrell had been thinking. "I've got men on him. They'd have called if he'd made any kind of move. Unless he was able to ditch them and they don't know—"

Borgianno interrupted. "Hartwell? That's not who my friends have in custody."

"Who the hell do they have?"

"Reese. Charles Albert Reese. Bald, fortyish, glasses, a cerebral type." Borgianno's deep chuckle filled the wires. "Very out of his league when it came to making a deal. He embarrassed the other patrons."

"Charles Reese? Never heard of him. Roman?"

"Got me. What's Reese saying, Rudy?"

"Nothing but his name. The only thing in his wallet was a driver's license and a couple of gas credit cards. He's from Miami." Borgianno gave them Reese's address. "So far my associates are making his detention quite pleasant. If you'd like, Charles Albert Reese will confess to just about...everything."

"No!" Lazarus broke in. "No, no, thank you. The FBI certainly appreciates your offer but we do have laws that must be followed."

Rudy sighed. "A very limiting and restrictive policy." His voice became jubilant. "This calls for a celebration. Roman, why don't you and Nikki come round for a midnight buffet? Alex, you're also invited."

"Thank you, Rudy, but Nikki's not here." Roman hesitated a moment. "She went to the University of Tennessee for that UFO assignment. Don't know when to expect her. You know Nik."

"Yes, I do. Well, when she gets in, give her my love. Alex?"

"Very kind, but..."

"I understand perfectly. Your superiors, et cetera." Borgianno's voice was smooth. "Let me tell you where Mr. Reese is being...entertained in Atlanta."

Lazarus scribbled down the address and politely said thank you before hanging up. "I'm going to call the bureau's Atlanta office," he pulled out his cell, "What a break!"

"Yeah, now if I can just get lucky and find Nikki." Exhaling sharply, Cantrell massaged his face and tried to rub away the weary confusion that veiled his mind.

Tracking. Hunting. Locating. Finding. That was his stock-in-trade. His forte. And he was damn good at his job. Yet, right now, when it was of vital importance, he found himself totally impotent. Any coherent thoughts became tangled with the recent memory of Nikki hooked up to tubes and wires in the hospital.

"I got her phone file." Rojas set the oversized Rolodex on the kitchen island. "John and Bob are sifting through her desk. I'm halfway through B and haven't found a military notation yet. She's got one helluva who's who in here."

"And one helluva code system," Marks added as he returned from her office. "John and I are both cipher experts and we'll be damned if we can figure out her mixture of hieroglyphics, shorthand, numbers and -" he held up three sheets of paper "- what appears to be..."

"Morse code," Ames finished for him, snapping his finger against the raised pages. "Or more correctly, Holden code."

Lazarus rejoined them. "The Atlanta machinery should be there in ten minutes. This Reese is a wild card, Roman. He's not a name from any research I've got on either Tony Mackey or Ed Hartwell. But even if he does bring in a hotshot lawyer to cut a deal, we'll still get to the mastermind behind the hijacking." Tito's mutterings as he flipped through Nikki's index interrupted him. "Anything yet?"

Cantrell shook his head. "I was thinking about calling Borgianno back. Maybe he —

The telephone bleated. "Probably Martin at the airport." Marks said as he grabbed the receiver. "Yeah? Oh...Who? What...uhhh, wait a sec." He turned to Cantrell. "For Nikki. Someone named Darnie?"

"Yes..." He took the receiver. "Roman here, Darnie, Nikki's not here right now, can I help you?"

"Oh. Well, she wanted me to get back to her tonight and — "

"You've spoken to her?"

"Sure, she called me from the Nashville airport. I thought she'd be back by now."

"So did I."

"How's that?"

"'Nothing." Cantrell cleared his throat, "What did she have you working on?"

"I've been putting together some information on Nathan Ives."

"Ives? Right, right, her new target." He puzzled for a moment. "Nikki called you about Ives from the airport?"

"Yes. She was very anxious to see what I could get on his Detroit career."

"Anxious, huh?" The fog lifted in Cantrell's brain. "Okay, Darnie, why don't you tell me what you told Nikki and then I'll take down the new information?"

"Fine. Let me scroll this data back a bit...There we go. Nathan Ives—boy genius. Graduated high school at thirteen, completed eight years of college in three. Age and ego were his biggest problems. He headed to Detroit and began pushing robotics, much to the dismay of the United Auto Workers."

Cantrell frowned. "Robotics was his big thing?"

"Not really. Ives' push was too early and too fast. He shuffled around and finally was smart enough to turn his genius to computers. He settled at Chrysler and stayed there for five years working in their military division.

"Now here's the new information Nikki was waiting for. Ives designed a computer guidance system for their weapons division. Unfortunately, his superiors weren't as supportive of his endeavors as he felt they should be. They came to a parting of the ways."

Darnie gave a lyrical chuckle. "Maybe they should have listened to Ives. Chrysler was plagued with defects and costly modifications on the vehicle he'd been working on to the extent that it wasn't acceptable even for training. As a matter of fact, the tank –"

"Tank?" The receiver nearly slid off his ear. "Did you say tank?"

"That's right. Ives was working on the M1A1 Abrams Tank. Say, you sound like you know this tank, Roman."

"Let's just say it's become a major part of my vocabulary these days." He rubbed the stubble on his jaw. "You supplied some missing puzzle pieces, Darnie. Although I've got the feeling Nikki connected them earlier. Thanks." Turning to Lazarus, Cantrell reported the gist of the conversation. "I guess Nik was right when she told you to put Nathan Ives on your wanted list."

Lazarus was doubtful. "Just because Ives worked on the tank doesn't mean he owns one. You can't go to...to...*Tank-M*ax and buy an M1A1, Roman."

"I admit I haven't got all the pieces, pal. But it's damn coincidental and...and..." He snapped his fingers, "fuck...I filed that name away... The guy who tried to fence the gold...Reese? Hell, he's one of Ives' minions." Roman had to laugh at the assorted facial expressions that stared at him.

"I'm betting Nikki put this whole thing together too. In fact, knowing her penchant for getting all the answers, she's probably investigating his place right now." Cantrell's face grew darker, harsher. "Just maybe she's in trouble. Damn...that woman can get me so discombobulated that I can't think straight."

Roman again ignored his friends' expressions. "Hell...I put a GPS tracker in that sat phone. I probably should have put one on her ass." He pressed an app on his phone "Let's see if it can locate the Blazer. If there's an ounce of battery juice left..."

"Okay, okay." Lazarus retrieved his cell. "Let me call and get a warrant—"

"By that time, I'll be introducing myself to Nathan Ives." He strode over to the fireplace wall and hit a concealed button. "Borgianno was right when he said your rules are limiting and restrictive."

Cantrell pressed in a code that unlocked a panel. He withdrew a stainless steel, double-action Smith & Wesson .45 caliber semiautomatic. "'I'm a pre-Miranda type of guy."

He slapped in a full magazine and retracted one bullet into the chamber. "No rules, just a good old-fashioned dose of brutality." He pocketed two extra nine-round clips in his black slacks. "This"—he held up the massive gun—"will get answers from Nathan Ives."

"That piece is a great intimidator," Lazarus agreed, angling his body to block Cantrell's path. "But I don't think it'll stop an M1A1 tank. Or that it will cause even one of those sixty commandos to blink."

"I've known worse odds. So have you."

Tito Rojas stepped between them. "I think we can up the odds a bit. ATF is always interested in large stockpiles of illegal weapons."

"And the CIA," John Ames added, "would love to find out if this Ives character plans to use his commandos to overthrow the United States Government."

"The DEA can always find probable cause," Bob Marks chimed in. "Plus, I've got a new Range Rover outside that I want to test the struts on."

Grinning, Cantrell jerked his thumb toward the gun cases. "Five against sixty? I pity them." While the others were getting ready, he checked the tracking software that triangulated the location of Nikki's car. "Well look at this. Ives' facility is right in that area. That's the armored-car route we took, Alex. I remember Nikki saying there was a blind drive. Her Blazer should mark the spot. Let's go."

Chapter 46

Nikki's Blazer didn't mark the spot.

Cantrell cursed the dozen extra minutes wasted searching for the driveway.

When they found it, Marks' parked the Range Rover on the shoulder. "Good thing you brought that Mag-Lite, Roman or we'd have been hunting 'til the sun came up."

Cantrell adjusted his light from flood to spot and aimed it on the soft ground. "The Blazer was here all right. She's got a blemish on the right front tire." The toe of his shoe nudged the tread depression. "See that pyramid design?" He snapped off the light and clipped it to the lanyard on his belt. "Nikki's in there."

"Let's go get her." Rojas adjusted his shoulder holster. "We've enough probable cause—from kidnapping to illegal weapons, to national security, to—"

"Checking the suspicious sugar they sprinkle in their coffee," Marks finished. "How do you want to play this, Roman?"

"Building-by-building search," he cautioned, "remember, Nathan Ives is called The Gadget Man. This place could be wired for anything."

They moved with the precision of a well-choreographed assault team. Cantrell scanned the area with a mini night-scope. The image-intensifying lens turned dark into light as it sliced through the shadows, seeking shapes, silhouettes, movement or shine.

He saw nothing.

Again, he swept the compound, this time sliding an infrared filter over the lens. Crisscrossed crimson alarm beams shot into view. Cantrell sent the scope down the line of men. "'Nikki probably tripped one of those," he whispered to Lazarus. "Other than that, there doesn't appear to be any visual threats.'"

They hit the main office first.

Empty.

They dashed in and out of the shadows, keeping their bodies as low as possible. Cantrell's careful strategy and succinct directives kept them from breaking any of the signal beams.

The blue warehouse fell.

And then the yellow.

Nothing.

No one.

They regrouped on the blind side of the first black warehouse.

Lazarus blinked the burning sweat from his eyes. "No tank, no weapons, no cargo, no—"

"No Nikki." Cantrell breathed heavily. "Shit, maybe I was wrong. Maybe all that info on Nathan Ives was just coincidental. Hell, she could be back at the house right now wondering where we are."

"I don't think so," Ames murmured, returning to the group with the night-scope. "I just caught the shine of a car bumper around the side of this building. And the alarm beams are doubled."

Their advance was slow.

Careful.

Cautious.

Stay alert.

Stay alive.

The war chant pumped through Cantrell's brain. His reflexes were sharp. His body tense. He kept waiting for the moment of confrontation.

The bumper belonged to Nikki's Blazer. "It's clean," Rojas reported, handing Roman the Mag-Lite.

"That's something." He remembered the last time the Blazer had been found. Spattered with blood. Nikki's badly beaten body stuffed in the rear.

Cantrell shook his head to clear away the grisly memories. "So far so good. We haven't tripped any alarms. At least any we've spotted.

But Ives and company could be watching and waiting for us in either of these last two buildings."

"Which one do you want to hit first?" Marks wiped his face on his shirt sleeve.

"Let's try the big one. It's large enough to hold a tank."

"Or an armored tractor-trailer," Lazarus nodded.

"And Nikki," Cantrell added hopefully.

Cantrell's watch ticked off ten minutes.

An eternity.

But prudent restraint was needed to navigate through the intricate infrared alarm beams that protected the massive warehouse. The simple cylindrical lock fell to his pick. He led the way inside.

The five well-armed men filed soundlessly into the entry bay. Their eyes strained to make sense of the shapes and shadow. Their ears were tuned to every sound.

Roman's raised hand stalled further movement. Cocking his head, he listened to the odd noises. Scratching and a steady guttural huffing.

"What is that?" Lazarus hissed in his ear.

"Sounds like an animal." He sniffed. "Smells like one, too. Damn, maybe the only thing we've got in here is Ives' research lab."

Cantrell directed Lazarus and Ames to circle right, Rojas and Marks to flank left, then indicated that he'd zigzag down the center. One by one, they slipped out of the alcove and shielded themselves in dark corners.

Cantrell became a nebulous specter that secured one shadow after another.

Listening.

Waiting.

Moving.

Each step measured.

Methodical.

Precise.

He was primed for a battle that kept slipping away.

Lazarus broke the silence. "Jesus H. Christ! Roman, turn on the Mag-Lite and aim straight ahead."

When he snapped on the flashlight, Hartwell's armored tractor-trailer was illuminated. "My hunch proved right." Cantrell played the beam around. "Any sign of Nikki?"

"Hey, Roman, over here."

As he ran around the truck, the flood light bounced off boxes, tables, and equipment until it finally pooled Marks and Rojas. "Where is—"

"Shhh..." Rojas held up a warning finger. "Aim that over there and see if you see what we think we see."

"What in hell—"

"Shhh..."

Reluctantly, Cantrell did what he was told. "Shit! That's a...that's a..."

"Tiger?"

"Tiger."

Sheba's rapid pacing and huffing turned into a more volatile greeting. With a snarling growl, the big cat threw her weight against the cage. Her massive paws slashed between the bars, clawing the air.

"Very much that's a tiger," Marks repeated.

"Nikki's not...She can't be..."

"Calm down, this is as far as we got." Rojas took control of the shaking Mag-Lite and trained it around. "Wait a sec...Look, there's a second cage."

They edged around the angry tiger whose glowing yellow eyes focused on their every move. "Here she is! Nikki!" Cantrell yelled to the figure curled in a fetal position on a pile of straw. "Nikki!"

When he rattled the cage, the tiger snarled and growled louder. "Ives must have drugged her. Here, angle the light on the door."

Cantrell fumbled in his pocket for the lockpick, deftly opened the antique padlock and sprinted into the cage. "Nikki!" His hand hovered above her shoulder. "Nikki ..."

Suddenly the entire warehouse was flooded with light.

Chapter 47

For a split second, the five men were blinded and frozen in the brilliance. Then they scattered for cover, weapons ready for action.

"Guys, guys, I am really disappointed. Especially in you, Cantrell."

Hearing Nikki's voice, Cantrell scrambled up from the cage floor and blinked until the straw bed came into focus.

She was still there.

Same position.

Hadn't moved.

He hesitated a moment, holstered his gun, then walked over and put his hand on her arm. "Nikki?"

His fingers embraced nothing but air.

Then the figure vanished.

Cantrell backed away.

"Here's the real thing."

He turned and found her standing in the doorway of the cage. "Nikki?" When he saw the unholy light gleaming in her eyes, he knew she was the real thing, "Nikki."

She laughed at the positive note in his voice. "Absolutely!"

"Then what...who -" he jerked his thumb back. "was that? Mirrors? Magic tricks?"

"Much more than that." Nikki saw the concern in his eyes and slid her hand into his. "I'm perfectly fine. Were you worried?"

"Would you like to count the gray hairs?"

"Later." She gave him a lewd wink, then smiled at the others who were assembling in the cage. "Hi, guys. I hope you didn't eat all the poker food, 'cause I'm starving."

When they all started questioning her at once, Nikki held up her hands. "Take it easy, you're upsetting Sheba and her cub." She pulled a giant dog biscuit from her jean pocket and tossed it into the tiger's cage. "There you go, sweetie."

"Sweetie?" Roman shuddered. "I'd thought you'd been her dinner."

"Not a chance. We became great friends while I was breaking out of this cage. She's even nicer since I found a box of biscuits for her." Nikki made an exaggerated kissing sound at Sheba, who had settled quietly in a far corner sheltering her tiny cub. "Besides, the only person she'd like to sink her teeth into is Nathan Ives."

Roman folded his arms across his chest. "What about Ives? I guessed that you put two and two together with the information Darnie gave you. She called." He rocked back and forth on his heels. "I'd like to know what in hell that...that...whatever, that duplicate of you was? And—"

"Where is Ives?" Lazarus interrupted.

"And his commando unit?" Ames added.

"What about the tank?" Rojas put in.

"I'd just like to know what in hell's going on," Marks rubbed his forehead.

"It's not all that complicated," Nikki explained. "Everything revolves around Nathan Ives. The man is a genius and his developments in robotics, prosthetic appliances, fiber optics, semiconductors...I mean, name it and he's made the better mousetrap." She shook her head. "It's a damn shame he's crazy."

Roman wrapped an arm around her waist. "You sound almost sorry for Ives."

"In a way I am. He is brilliant and he'll be the first one to tell you," she added wryly. "But that doesn't alter the fact that he killed Glenn Ennis when he hijacked Hartwell's truck."

She looked from Roman to Alex. "He's got a super laser stun gun. A little thing that fits right into the palm of his hand. He zapped me with it -" she felt Roman's arm tighten around her waist "and Mackey and Ennis. Apparently Ennis had a weak heart and the power was enough to kill him."

"Are you sure you're okay?"

"I'm fine now," she told Roman. "That damn gun turns a body into quivering Jell-O in a matter of seconds and it takes quite a while before your brain, muscles and nerves get back in sync. It's strong enough to knock out Sheba."

Alex leaned against the cage wall. "Do you know how he managed the hijacking, Nik? Does he have a tank and an army?"

"Yes, yes and yes, but not exactly." She pointed out the door. "Come on, I'll show you how it all works. Oh, by the way, Alex, Ives and his merry men are, even as we speak, hijacking a Wells Fargo bank truck."

"What!"

"Not to worry, he'll be back here with the troops and the haul in about an hour. He's planning to operate on my nose."

"How's that?" Roman turned her to face him.

She nodded. "He's into perfection and he's planning on getting into me."

"Fuck him."

"What a horrible thought!" Nikki grimaced. "One I refuse to entertain. As a matter of fact Cantrell, I was just getting ready to blow this joint. I'd finished hot-wiring the tractor-trailer..." she laughed at their expressions, "hey, a girl has to keep her hand in the game. With all the equipment around here, it wasn't that complicated. Then you and the *A-Team* showed up on the monitors."

"Monitors?" Roman's brow furrowed. "What monitors? How did you get out of the cage? With a lockpick?"

"Nope. Ives found the pick. I used this." She handed him a curved piece of flat steel with pointed tips.

His dark eyes narrowed. "What the hell is that?"

"I told you. Never underestimate the power of cleavage. It's the underwire from my bra." She grinned. "Worked like a charm on that padlock, of course I'm out a thirty-eight dollar bra."

"You're having a good time with this, aren't you?" Roman accused.

"The best." She rubbed her palms together. "And it gets even better. Well, guys, it's time to introduce you to the wacky world of Nathan Ives."

With a flourish, she gestured at four large levers centered on a paneled wall. "The first works the lights, the second those overhead doors, the third I haven't quite figured out yet." She frowned, then smiled. "The last is my favorite."

As she pulled down the lever, the wall slid open, revealing six video monitors. "You were all very good about not tripping any of the infrared beams, which is what did me in." She hit her knuckle against a screen. "I'm afraid the motion and noise detectors registered your maneuvers, plus..." She pressed a few buttons. "Ahh...here you all are. I took the liberty of recording this for you. These five rainbow blurs are your body heat that was sensed by Ives' hidden cameras."

Marks stepped closer to investigate. "Christ, this state-of-the-art security system looks like it came out of a science fiction novel." He exhaled sharply and faced the others. "If Ives had been here, we would have come face to face with his sixty-man commando unit."

"There isn't any commando unit," Nikki informed them. "Well, at least not sixty of them. Exactly. There's six but only five tonight because they sent Reese — "

"Reese!" Alex interrupted. "Charles Albert Reese?"

She nodded. "Why?"

"Borgianno called," Roman explained. "Reese got caught trying to fence part of the Hartwell haul in Atlanta a few hours ago."

"They were having trouble liquidating the precious-metal cargo," Nikki explained. "That's why Ives went after Wells Fargo's ready cash tonight. Follow me and I'll show you how six can turn into sixty and the mystery behind the M1A1 tank."

She led them to a lab table. "This is the punch line to that joke in the fiber-optics lab. Ives told me I was looking at a multiclass three-D distortion-invariant object identification, but it's not."

Roman shook his head. "It's not what?"

"A multiclass three-D — " His glare stopped her. She laughed and patted the equipment. "This, gentlemen, is Nathan Ives' tank, his army, his little UFO spoof on the state of Florida and the Nikki Holden you were trying to shake in the cage. All you do is press the button and —

"Nikki!" Roman did a double take when her life-size curled image appeared on the lab table. He reached out, but again was unable to touch what his eyes told him was solid. "What the hell is it?"

"A hologram."

"Hologram? They're those little three-dimensional stickers on charge cards."

"I told you Ives builds better mousetraps. He has created full-size color holograms. He's been playing around with them for thirty years. Before he left Chrysler he made holographic plates of the tank and other military vehicles."

She settled on the edge of the table, watching while they stared at the hologram. "I made this simple one of myself. Ives' equipment is almost a duplicate in operation to the one I saw at the Space Institute. It works a lot like a camera. I just snapped in a plate, set the timer and got into position. The lasers do all the work and ten seconds later an image is developed. A startling true-to-life image."

Rojas whistled. "You can say that again. So you're telling us is that Nathan Ives created a holographic army."

"Right. Like he said it's completely portable, very compact, yet has the same shock and persuasion value as the real thing. He does have a few real weapons, though," she cautioned, "but not sixty and not a tank."

"What the hell is his purpose?"

"Therein lies the rub, Cantrell." She slid off the lab table. "Ives got tired of the scientific community laughing at his suggestions. He was tired of filling out grant forms, tired of doing paperwork instead of research. Using his computer and electronic genius, he was able to tap into both Hartwell's and the Wells Fargo security systems, to get the manifest information and the routes.

"His holographic army was visually powerful enough to stop the armored trucks, the laser stun gun knocked out the guards and he and his men took the cargo. Ives figured three or four million would fund a lot of research." Nikki exhaled forcefully. "A lot of needed research."

Roman's hands settled on her shoulders. "He could have done it legally."

"I know."

"And without killing Glenn Ennis."

"I know that, too." She stared at him. "Hey, I'm not excusing the guy. It's just a damn shame his genius had to be warped."

Roman changed the subject. "Didn't you say something about UFOs?"

She laughed. "Another holographic scam of Nathan's. He created a miniature alien spacecraft with red blinking lights. Then, using another holographic technique, he increased it in size to over fifty feet. He was getting his jollies reading about all the UFO sightings."

"Hey, why the sudden frown?" Tilting her chin up, Roman smiled into her eyes. "This proves your theory that all those UFO stories were a hoax. Not exactly the story that *Scuttlebutt* was hoping for but you did find the truth."

"Partial truth. I never got the chance to ask Nathan if he was behind the Belle Glade UFO. If he was the one who left the assortment of out-of-this-world pebbles. If he...Whoa, look at the clock, Ives and company are due back here any time."

"We'll be ready for him," Roman said evenly. "You said there were five of them?"

"Yes and they do have legit weapons, plus that damn stun gun."

"Okay, no problem." He massaged his jaw. "Bob, you'd better stash your Range Rover out of sight. Nikki, reset the hologram you made so they'll think you're still caged. And, we'll just -" he drew his gun from the shoulder holster, "ambush them when they return."

"Try not to shoot anybody, Cantrell," she cautioned. "I know how you and Alex hate all that paperwork."

Chapter 48

"Nathan loves perfection, Douglas," Ives stepped inside the dark warehouse. "Tonight was letter-perfect."

"I'm just grateful the stun gun didn't cause another death."

"Douglas!"

"Sorry, Nathan. I'll get the lights." Hastily, Phillips moved across the room and pulled the first lever. "Shall we bring the truck in here?"

"Not yet. Just have the others unload the laser and plates for right now." Ives set the stun gun and an Uzi on an empty lab table and began shedding his camouflage suit. "Nathan needs to check on our guest. Miss Holden seems rather quiet."

"Sheba's certainly not." Phillips left to give Ives' instructions to the other men, then returned carrying a bazooka. "Can't you give that cat something, Nathan? Her growling drives me up the wall."

"Why so nervous tonight? Everything went perfectly."

"I know, I know." He ran a hand through his close-cropped curls. "I just wished Charlie had called before we left. He's really out of his element, Nathan."

"Nonsense, Reese is fine. Nathan will check the computer to see his report and—" A crash interrupted him. "Damn it! Watch those fools! What did they break?"

"Nothing. Just dropped one of the helmets. Okay, we've got everything inside. No, no, Richards, put that box on the table. This one over there." Phillips winced as Sheba's snarling increased. "Christ, Nathan, that cat goes crazy the instant she gets your scent."

Ives laughed loudly, then laughed again at the tigers growing anger. "Nathan will first quiet Sheba down with another shot from the stun gun then deliver a milder dose to Miss Holden." His fingertips had barely touched the metal stun gun when a voice rang out.

"Hold it right there, Ives," Roman Cantrell ordered, stepping out from behind the tractor-trailer. "Put your hands up."

Ives turned his head sharply, but his toupee failed to follow. "Who in hell are you?"

"FBI," Lazarus said from the left. "Lay down your weapons!"

"ATF." Rojas confiscated a Mac-10 from a startled assistant. "I hope you have the paperwork for this."

"DEA." Marks stated, blocking the open door.

"CIA," added Ames.

"OB/GYN," Nikki finished. "And when we say spread 'em, Nathan, we mean business." She threw a grin at Cantrell. "I just love initials. Ah-ah, Nathan," her hand pushed the stun gun away, "I think you've played with this toy enough." She watched his puppet-drawn mouth open and close in silence.

"Over here, Ives." Lazarus ordered, pushing the short inventor against the wall next to Phillips. "I want you all to listen carefully while I read you your rights."

"The Wells Fargo truck is out there all right." Marks reported, securing the entry door. "Hey Tito, there's a brand new Stinger missile launcher over here."

Rojas chuckled. "Now, I know they don't have paperwork on that. Nice operation, fellows. I don't know when—"

Suddenly the lights went out.

"Nobody move!" Lazarus ordered. He searched the wall above Phillips's head and pushed up the lever. "That was real stupid." He turned Phillips around. "What the— where in hell did Ives go?"

Quickly, Cantrell checked the tractor-trailer cab but found it empty. "Bob?"

"He didn't come this way."

"Or over here," Ames called.

Cantrell moved on Phillips, picking him up and slamming him against the wall. "There must be an escape hatch. How's it work?"

He backhanded him hard across the face. "I don't have to play by the rules," he warned, and flung Phillips spread-eagle against the wall.

When Phillips tried groping for the lights again, Cantrell elbowed him in the spine. Phillips's hand slipped and hit the third lever instead. "Oh, God...Nathan..." he groaned, crumbling to the floor, "I'm sorry."

Sheba's growling and snarling took on angrier proportions.

"Christ, you don't think that lever lets the tiger out?" Alex shouted.

"Nikki, get in the cab!" Cantrell's warning vibrated in the unexpected silence. "What...what happened? Wait, Nikki, don't—" But she'd already disappeared. Roman sprinted after her.

"A door in the back of Sheba's cage opened and she took off," Nikki turned to him. "I guess—"

They heard a scream...a terrifying, shrill, piercing scream that sent goosebumps up Nikki's arms. She leaned against Roman. "I guess Sheba didn't believe in that old adage, never bite the hand that feeds you."

Chapter 49

"I'm so glad that Doug Phillips was able to help animal control get Sheba safely into her cage. I have a feeling she would have come back on her own, she wants to be with her cub." Nikki stopped walking and turned to Cantrell. "She is an endangered species and a nursing mother and she didn't eat *that* much of Nathan."

Roman kissed her nose. "So you've bonded with the tiger?" At her grin, he continued. "I think both Sheba and her unique cub will find a good home at the zoo. I mean a liger...when he's fully grown...well, they can be upwards of nine hundred pounds."

Nikki started to laugh. "I think the animal control officer was more fascinated by the Widow Ives. Can you believe she showed up in that fishnet and black leather corset and G-string?"

"Don't forget the dog collar and leash," Roman added. "I'm not sure bimbo is an endangered species and she seemed quite willing to be walked by him."

"I don't think she's going to be the merry widow for too long. Ives said he was divorcing her so I'm betting he had quite the prenup, considering she was wife number seven." She cast a sidelong glance at Roman. "What did you think of the merry widow?"

"Didn't waste a gray cell, she's definitely not my type."

"You have a type?"

"Fearless redheads with a stubborn streak and the world's hardest ass." He gave her a playful slap on said ass. "You've got quite the story to report."

Nikki sighed. "On so many levels. Both Matt and Teresa won't be happy knowing that *Scuttlebutt's* UFO headlines were based on a hologram. It will be interesting to see that alien baby Muriel Feinburg claims she's pregnant with."

Her second sigh was heavier. "Then there's Nathan Ives. I will give him the obituary in *Science Realm* he deserves. His achievements are beyond impressive and so very needed. Maybe if Doug Phillips and the others get a good attorney they can work out a deal with the government to continue working on many of those ideas."

"So what are you going to do with your reward money?"

"What reward money, Cantrell?"

Roman held open the door of her Blazer. "For finding Hartwell's truck and then there's the Wells Fargo truck. On Hartwell's alone...two percent of five million."

"I think that's a nice sum to donate to the handicapped. The Wells Fargo reward will go to the veterans." Leaning against the top of the car, Nikki stared up at the star-bright sky. "I'd still like to know if Ives created more than one UFO hologram. I still have that boomerang-shaped object that left the iridium deposits in Belle Glade to explain."

"Phillips says no. He's singing like a bird in there to Alex and company." Roman gave her a push inside. "Come on, let's get home as I recall we have a few fantasies to engage in. Oh, Matt sent you a package. Too small for clothes."

"Damn...it's my August surprise." She wrinkled her nose. "Nope not thinking about it...fantasies you said?" She rubbed her hands together. "Now you're talking! Hey, what's the matter?"

"I just thought I saw..."

"Saw what, Roman?"

"Nikki didn't you say that other UFO had amber and green lights? And an odd shape? And..."

***

Thank you for taking the time to read Dark Corners. I hope you enjoyed it enough to post a short review and mention it to a friend. Word of mouth is an author's best friend and much appreciated. Thank you. Elaine Raco Chase.

What happens when Truth becomes Stranger than Fiction - Again?

As an author, it's so much fun to write a book and then have your fictional premise begin to take on the truth. All of the UFO material in **Dark Corners** is actually fact! I know I was stunned as well. Feel free to *Google* it all and be amazed except of course for Muriel Feinburg, to the best of my knowledge she never did have that alien baby.

All of the hologram, robotics and prosthetic appliance information are true as well. So is the plastic food – well not so plastic just made off a 3-D printer with edible pastes, sauces, herbs and spices.

There was an armored car hijacking of similar material, although no one mentioned a tank and armed commando unit and blessedly, there were no fatalities.

I had my first experience with holograms in 1970, doing a tech paper at KAPL – Knolls Atomic Power Lab in Schenectady, NY. That's where I met Dr. Penny and he showed me my first hologram. I stored away all that information, as well as a hologram of the planet Saturn, just because I felt it could be useful for a later story. And it was!

The University of Tennessee Space Institute did issue the following **Special Report** when Dark Corners was first published by Bantam Paperbacks in 1988.

Special Report

Space Institute Plays Role in Mystery Novel
By Gary Smith
UTSInformation 8/8/1988

More than 200 UFO sightings are reported in Central Florida during a five week period. A well-known national tabloid assigns a top investigative journalist to develop a very big – and very human story. The reporter soon realizes that she needs a crash course in science to fully understand the facts she has uncovered. Where should she go for this brief encounter with the world of high technology? The University of Tennessee Space Institute, of course!

Sound like fiction? Well, it is, to a degree. Actually, it is the story line for a new mystery novel recently released by Bantam Books titled '**Dark Corners**.' And the Space Institute is featured in Dark Corners as a primary source of the scientific information for the main character.

Author Elaine Raco Chase has blended fact with fiction to produce an adventure that contains a wealth of detail on state-of-the-art technology to support her fictional characters in pursuit of alien invaders.

One of the most intriguing aspects of Chase's novel is her formulation of a fictional research project at the Space Institute that closely parallels a current UTSI research program with surprising accuracy! The fictional research on medical imaging holography being conducted by Chase's character at the Space Institute is a fairly accurate representation of actual medical imaging research being conduction by Dr. Al Pujol.

Pujol's project has received wide-spread attention recently because of support from entertainer Ben Vereen which resulted in the donation of computer equipment by Sun Microsystems, Inc. Vereen visited the campus of the Space Institute recently to review the work being done in medical imaging research by Pujol and his staff.

And while Chase did research on the Space Institute prior to featuring it in her novel, her characters and projects were developed well in advance of the initiation of Pujol's program.

"That's amazing," said Pujol after learning about Chase's book. "She has described the research program we are currently conduction, and I am certain there is absolutely no way she could have known about our particular program prior to her publication date."

Chase received much of her information on the Space Institute from literature provided by the UTSI public relations office. However, she was concerned with attention to detail in describing the Space Institute and her fictional professor. In fact, on one occasion her concern extended to the point of calling the cafeteria at UTSI to obtain a description of the dining area layout and information on the menu items offered.

Chase said that she 'made up the professor and the research work, although the research project is based on solid technical facts. "I still get chills when I think that my professor and your professor were working on the same holographic project."

Chase said that she 'enjoys doing a blend of what she calls 'faction,' a mixture of fact and fiction." She spent a full year researching and writing Dark Corners.

Current research on fiber optics was obtained from NASA's Johnson Space Center. Robotics details came from Purdue University, Chemistry background was provided by the University of Houston. UFO information was provided by the US Air Force. New advances in holograms came from UTSI.

Meet Elaine Raco Chase

If you like sassy, laugh out loud, contemporary romances - some more explicit than others - you have found the right author!

Reviewers have called them: "cat & mouse" - "slow burn" - "hot and steamy" - "highly addicting" - "solid characters & lots of humor" - "amazing reads!"

I call them fun! My heroines are NOT: thin, petite, clueless or submissive. They are strong women who aren't looking for a man - until the right one comes along!

And those men! Tough-guy, alpha males who don't know what hit them! But do know they want MORE!

I also write explicit mystery/thriller's featuring Roman Cantrell and Nikki Holden. Plus Agatha Christie nominated non-fiction "How to write the Amateur Detective Novel" which is in the FBI Forensic Library at Quantico.

You can find me:

www.elaineracochase.com[1]

@ElaineRaco on twitter;

https://www.facebook.com/elaine.r.chase

https://www.facebook.com/elaineracochase

What's really fun – visit my Pinterest page and *see* Roman, Nikki, Alex, Darnie, Rudy, Duncan, Edgar and all the other characters! Plus places, food, clothes – everything!

http://pinterest.com/elaineracochase/

---

1.   http://www.elaineracochase.com

Roman Cantrell/Nikki Holden Mystery Series:

Nikki and Roman – reporter and detective. If they don't kill each other, they might solve a few murders. *"A star-crossed duo we are rooting for." Booklist*

Dangerous Places – South Florida ignites with death, destruction and sex! Now available in audio!

Dark Corners – A plot that is stranger than science fiction but as real as death! Now available in audio!

Rough Edges – Strange bedfellows, reluctant lovers, and an unbeatable team get back together to catch a killer.

Dead Heat – They're off...to the races at Saratoga and more than hay is being fed to the horses.

Killer Cuisine – Rudy's new restaurant opens in South Beach but there's more than food on the menu!

If you'd like to try some romantic spice:
What the reviewers are saying about Elaine Raco Chase –

"Just reading the summary of this book makes you really want to read it. I love that. I was hooked from the synopsis. I've read a couple books by Elaine Raco Chase and they were just as amazing as this one. She is a very talented author. This book is very well written and I love the details. This story is hilarious in some parts. Well written and clever." (**Caught in a Trap - Now part of Library Journal's SELF-e collection: featured selection #1 erotic romantic comedy**)

"It's not often I find a story with characters that are well rounded and realistic. I can recommend this story as one of the better written Indy books I've come across." (**Double Occupancy – on FB's Top 50 books to read after FSOG for over 3 years!**)

"Wow! Just absolutely Wow! I read this book in one night, I was so taken by the characters. This book was beautifully written, and the characters are so easy to fall in love with. My heart melted in an instant and I giggled so much through this book. Amazing read!" (**Rules of the Game – Voted #1 Erotic Romance by Turning Pages**)

"One of my must have's in any book is a plot - preferably one that has sharp-witted characters who are smart, independent and feel real. Elaine Raco Chase did not disappoint in creating the characters to exist within the world of design, architecture and luxury developments.

While there are two billion how-to articles on creating dialog that is both paced properly and sounds believable, Elaine has a book, full of dialog: fast paced, snarky, funny, businesslike, casual, even sexy. And it ALL sounds like a conversation you could overhear at any time, in many situations. That technique alone makes the book a worthwhile read - that it is combined and integrated into a tightly written, fast paced and sexy story makes this worth every one of the 5 stars." (**Designing Woman**)

"I must admit that I hated Noah for the first part of the book. What he did was beyond rotten and I cried. Then I caught a "clue" that later turned into fact. I now love Noah and I loved him with Marlayna. Funny, sexy read and now I am spending all my money on more books by this author." (**Lady be Bad**)

"A MUST READ!! Beautiful story about a girl who has been broken inside...or so she believes. I'm so glad I read this book. It was so moving! As you read this book you will laugh maybe even cry a little but you will find yourself falling in love with all the characters in this book! You will be pulled into the story as it captures not only your attention but your heart!" (**One Way or Another is a Classic Retro-Read and not updated**)

"**No Easy Way Out**" is a true Cinderella story!! Virginia is a highly intellectual woman with her Ph.D. She buries herself in her work and has no fun life at all! Her friends talk her into attending a masquerade ball and she meets Prince Charming who is dressed like a bandit and she is dressed like a sexy bunny! Well they have a very hot time on the balcony and when the clock strikes midnight she runs off in true Cinderella fashion! When she returns to work, you guessed it ...the bandit turns out to be one of her co-workers!! What follows is loaded with fun, trickery, love and lots and lots of laughs!" (**No Easy Way Out is a Classic Retro-Read – not updated**)

"With a touch of sophistication, plenty of sizzling sex, and a liberal dose of humor, **Special Delivery** poses the age-old question: Is there such a thing as love at first sight? After reading Roxanne and Bram's story, I'm thinking there is."

"Again, Elaine Raco Chase creates dialogue that repeatedly reinforces my belief that hers is some of the best I have read (or heard). There is humor, snark and gorgeous descriptions that place you in the wilds of Montana, with the never fail to amuse stops in the action. There is steam, there is swearing, and most of all - this is a feel good book that will have you laughing and smiling throughout." (**Dare the Devil**)

"This book has a fantastic storyline about a strong business woman who is feeling unchallenged in her life choice. Her best friend wants to help in more ways than one! The author has an exceptional way with the written word and the characters are well described and very interesting. I enjoyed this book immensely and will read more by this author in the future." (**Best Laid Plans**)

"What a hoot this story is as our heroine leads Daniel on a merry chase of "is she or isn't she?" But, though our hero may be infatuated, his ability to see through Vixen/Victoria's façade is a little clearer than either of them anticipated. **Video Vixen** is a bird's-eye view of the workings behind the scenes of a daytime soap, and it has a very authentic feel, giving the whole story credibility. With a lot of humor and a touch of "food for thought," Elaine Raco Chase has created an excellent read, especially for those who love a good soap opera. And don't we all?" (**Video Vixen**)

"Many romances are based on: attraction/lust/something 'clicking' at first sight. And these two have it, in spades. Rob is very much like my teenager, instant 'love' of anyone and anything...be it the new girl in school or a Wii game. Fast, fractious, and then I'm hit with "who?" Loved the story, loved the well-defined characters, loved the teenager - it's such a dialogue heavy book it would make a great TV movie." (**Calculated Risk**)

Note: Unless marked as Retro-Reads....all eBooks have been updated! And all are available as audiobooks.